"You're giving your son away?"

"It's the best for him," Bryan said, ignoring Jacob's happy squeals.

Laura looked through the photo album.
"I realize that your family was broken up just when it was starting, but you and Jacob need each other more than ever."

Laura felt her words of comfort were hollow. How could she possibly help someone else deal with his grief when she had such difficulty herself?

"The three of us were never a family." Bryan grabbed the album and snapped it shut. Jacob wailed, frantically reaching for Laura. She swept him into her arms and bounced him until he'd calmed down.

"I'm just not cut out for fatherhood. You make parenting look so easy."

"Abandoned. Confused. Angry. Afraid." Laura's tone hardened. "Easy? I know what you're feeling because I was there."

Why was it that this man could infuriate her at the same time her heart swelled with feelings she couldn't understand?

Books by Carol Steward

Love Inspired

CAROL STEWARD

wrote daily to a pen pal for ten years, yet writing as a career didn't occur to her for another two decades. "My first key chain said, 'Bloom where you're planted.' I've tried to follow that advice ever since."

Carol, her husband and their three children have planted their roots in Greeley. Together, their family enjoys sports, camping and discovering Colorado's beauty. Carol has operated her own cake-decorating business, and she spent fifteen years providing full-time child care to more than one hundred children, before moving to the other end of the education field. She is now an admissions adviser at a state university.

As always, Carol loves to hear from her readers. You can contact her at P.O. Box 200269, Evans, CO 80620. She would also love you to visit her Web page at www.carolsteward.com.

There Comes a Season
Carol Steward

Steeple
Hill®

Published by Steeple Hill Books™

STEEPLE HILL BOOKS

Steeple Hill®

ISBN-13: 978-0-373-36097-0
ISBN-10:   0-373-36097-5

THERE COMES A SEASON

Copyright © 1998 by Carol Steward

www.SteepleHill.com

Printed in U.S.A.

To everything there is a season,
and a time to every purpose under heaven:...
A time to weep, and a time to laugh;
a time to mourn, and a time to dance;
—*Ecclesiastes* 3:1,4

To Dave, who's always my hero;
to Sarah, Matthew and Scott
for your encouragement and understanding;
to my mom and dad for a strong base to believe
in myself; to my family and special friends,
for inspiring me; to my critique group,
for your patience and perseverance;
to all of you, thanks for believing in me!

In loving memory of my brother-in-law, Dan.

Prologue

"He's coming back! I know he is. He promised me, Mommy. Daddy said he'd take me fishing today."

"No honey, he's not." The tears fell from Laura Bates's eyes as she held her six-year-old son. Chad had seen the paramedics work on his father in the middle of the night and screamed when they took him away. "Chad, Daddy died. He can't ever come home."

"Why didn't you stop him! You should have stopped him!"

She couldn't control his anger, or the sting as his words pierced her heart. Though Laura understood that Chad didn't know what he was saying and how badly it hurt her, it didn't stop the guilt from digging deeper into her soul. "I tried. Believe me, I tried."

"I want Daddy!"

"I know. I do, too." She gave Chad a kiss and looked at her older son, T.J., who stood silently looking out the window toward the tree house he and his father had built the previous month. "Come here T.J.," Laura said gently. T.J. obeyed, dragging his feet. There were no tears in her son's eyes, just a stoic expression on his face.

T.J. took a jagged breath, and finally a terrified grimace appeared. Laura gently drew his stocky body into her embrace. "It's okay to cry, T.J., don't stop the tears."

"Uncle Ian said boys shouldn't cry."

"Uncle Ian is wrong. It's going to hurt for a long time, and if you want to cry, it's okay." Laura touched her forehead to his and they rubbed noses. T.J. grinned.

Her daughter, Carrie began crying as she joined her mom and younger brothers. She had always been her daddy's girl. Laura brushed the tears from Carrie's face. "I love you, Carrie, and so did your dad. He loved you kids very much."

"Oh, Mom." She sobbed. "I'm going to miss him so much."

"I know, punkin. It's not going to be easy." They sat in Todd's stuffed chair comforting each other for a long while before the beams of sunlight came through the maple trees and lit the breakfast nook.

Laura rubbed the back of her neck and shoulders and moved her fingers up to her temples and pushed hard, trying to force away the recurring memory of waking with a chill in her spine.

Her best friend touched her shoulder. "Laura, why don't you go lie down for a while. You need some rest. Family will be here soon."

"Thanks for coming, Barb. Sorry I woke you."

"It's okay. Go to bed, honey."

As Laura walked into her bedroom, she realized she was exhausted. She stared at the walls of the room she and Todd had shared, looked out the window, tossed and turned, but rest eluded her. *How could you do this to us, Todd? You said you'd see us in the morning, you held me last night. How can I ever go on without you?* Laura cried, and yelled, and pounded her fists into the pillow, as if she were still trying to save Todd.

Weary, she lay down, listening to the silence. Hers was not a quiet house. Her children were never quiet, Todd wasn't quiet and the toddlers and preschoolers she watched certainly weren't quiet. The silence surrounding her now was proof that nothing would ever be the same. She wanted to hear the laughter again, to see Todd chasing the kids through the house. She wanted to yell at all of them to settle down. "Oh, God," she silently prayed, "please let me yell at Todd to grow up again. The big kid never got the chance," she whispered.

Laura heard the faint drumming of raindrops on the roof, fast, then slow, then the splash of water as cars drove by. "How appropriate that you should make this a dreary, wet, good for nothing but curling up in bed day, God. At least you didn't make it a beautiful, sunny, perfect fishing day. You explain to the kids why their father won't be here to take them fishing anymore! You tell them who will answer their tough questions! You tell them who is going help them grow up, because I have no idea how to do all of this without him!" She pounded the tearstained pillow and shoved it under her head.

A few days later, Chad asked his mother, "Who will my new daddy be?"

Laura froze. "What makes you ask that?"

She could see Chad was surprised by her response and possibly a little embarrassed at his own question. "We talked about it in Sunday school."

"They talked to you about finding a new daddy?" She felt a sudden chill.

"No, but 'Lizabeth's daddy is getting married, and I was just wondering if you would."

"Sometimes parents do meet another person, fall in love and get married."

"If you get married, will you still love us?"

"I won't ever stop loving you. Getting married doesn't

mean parents will love their children less. God helps us make more love.''

Once they were home, Laura took Chad into her arms. ''Chad, right now, I'm not ready to find you a new daddy. I have you three, and that's all I need. I loved your dad a lot, and I'm not sure I can ever love anyone that much again.''

''If we ask God to help you, you can. I'll help.''

How in the world could she deny a little boy's prayers? God's words of reassurance came to mind, ''I can do all things through Him that strengthens me.'' She sighed. ''Thank you, love. I know that God could help, but give us some time, okay?'' Laura hugged him gently—for his innocence, his honesty and his naive faith. Time would only prove Chad wrong. She loved her son dearly, and wished this was one lesson she didn't have to let him learn on his own.

Later that night, she couldn't help but wonder if there would ever be a man brave enough to accept her and her three children? Someone man enough to dim these memories of her past? A man strong enough to dare her to love again?

Chapter One

Laura Bates opened her front door. A tall man holding an adorable baby stood on her doorstep.

"Mrs. Bates? As in the child care provider, Mrs. Bates?"

She extended her hand to shake his, admiring the darkest brown eyes she'd ever seen. "Yes," she said, uncomfortable being introduced as a married woman, but uneasy sharing her circumstances with strangers. "All the parents call me Laura. This must be Jacob." She smiled, hoping to set the father at ease over his obvious surprise at her age. "Come in."

Laura realized she was staring at him, and that their hands were still clenched. *Todd's only been dead four months. What am I doing admiring this stranger?* She loosened her grip, shoving her hand into her pocket as she moved out of the doorway.

Bryan stepped into the living room. "I must admit, I didn't expect someone so…young, Laura. My secretary led me to believe…" Bryan's deep voice, which was shadowed with a Southern accent, trailed off.

"Vicky didn't inform either of us very well," Laura

quipped. "I thought both you and your wife would be coming."

Jacob squirmed in his father's arms. Laura watched Bryan handle his son, his large hands seeming incredibly uncomfortable with this minute task. She noted a tan line on his left hand where a ring had recently been removed. Her gaze roamed up his arm to his broad shoulders and then to his face. She could see Bryan was tense. *No wonder the baby's cranky. Relax.* She wasn't sure if he'd heard her or was ignoring her comment. She let it go unanswered.

Two heads peeked around the corner and caught Bryan's attention. "Are these your children?"

Laura pushed her curiosity aside and focused on the question. "Yes. Carrie is ten, and Chad is six. My eight-year-old son is playing with friends this evening. Please have a seat." Laura motioned toward an overstuffed chair.

Noticing his double-breasted suit, she wished that she had worn something nicer than blue jeans and a sweater. *What should you have worn? A dress and heels? Get real Laura, this is how you always dress.*

She watched Bryan scrutinize the room. He surely noticed the well-worn antiques, piles of children's art overflowing from the rolltop desk, and jackets tossed beneath the coatrack by hurried children. He studied the family portrait hanging on the wall. It was a recent enough picture that one would assume just by looking at it that the same contentment existed in their lives today.

Before Bryan asked about her husband, Laura proceeded. She didn't want to talk about that tonight. "We covered the basics over the phone, but I hope you've thought of more questions."

Laura set a manila envelope on the table next to her as she tried to take her eyes off this surprisingly handsome man with a stern look on his face. *Business, Laura. He's here on business. And even if he wasn't, Bryan is obviously nothing like Todd.*

"Right." Bryan shifted uncomfortably in the chair, switching the fussy two-month-old to the other leg. "How long have you been baby-sitting?"

"Mom doesn't baby-sit. She's a *child care provider,*" Chad exclaimed as he entered the room. He walked over and sat with his mother while Carrie stayed inconspicuously around the corner.

"Chad, I'll be glad to answer Mr. Beaumont's questions myself." She wrapped her arm around her son and kissed his forehead. "I've been a licensed child care provider for six years. And as you can see, I've had over ten years of mothering experience. I'll be glad to give you references, Mr. Beaumont."

"Please, call me Bryan." He lifted Jacob to his shoulder and thumped the baby's back. "Vicky's recommendation is enough." After Bryan tried unsuccessfully to quiet his son, Chad crawled over and made funny faces at the baby.

Bryan's dark brown hair was cut conservatively, short in the back and stylishly long on top. Guessing by his appearance, his career came first. It wasn't just the suit. The crisp white shirt, silk tie and fine leather loafers gave him a sophisticated appeal. Laura admired the shadow of his beard, and found herself wondering if he'd had a long day, or if he left it, enjoying the affect it had on women. Whichever the case, it worked.

"Maybe he has gas. How long ago did you feed him?" Chad said, offering his youthful expertise.

Bryan chuckled, and again, Laura found herself distracted by Jacob's father. Her son's forwardness was bound to get her into a fix if she didn't do something to intervene.

"Chad, I'm sure Mr., um, Bryan can handle it. Why don't you and Carrie go downstairs to play. We'll be down in a few minutes to show him the playroom."

One corner of Bryan's mouth turned up. He reached out a hand to the youth and grasped his hand in a respectful handshake. "Thanks for the suggestions, Chad. Looks like my son would be in good hands here.'' Laura watched her son beam with pride at Bryan's attention. Chad and his sister raced for the stairs. ''What kind of schedule will you put a baby on?''

''What? Oh, schedule. I believe in letting babies set their own, within reason.''

''*No* schedule? At all?''

Relieved to be discussing children again, Laura relaxed. ''Babies normally settle into their own routine within a few weeks. Then again, just as they do, they hit a growing spurt or teething, and it changes. Flexibility helps.''

''I guess I didn't do so bad this week after all, then. How many children do you watch?'' Bryan's tension escalated as Jacob grew more fussy.

''Six preschoolers and my own three when they aren't in school. It sounds like a lot, but the limits really are reasonable.'' The baby wailed, and Laura put her hands in front of her. ''Could I hold Jacob for you?''

''My pleasure. Since his mother died, I've had a lot to learn about babies. Talk about a cram course on parenting.''

She felt as if someone had just punched her in the stomach. That would explain why Vicky didn't say anything. She wanted them to find that common ground. ''I'm sorry. I didn't realize,'' she managed to reply.

His jaw worked back and forth. ''I thought Vicky would have explained that when she called. Work's piling up at the office, and Mr. Mom I'm not. The nanny and I didn't get along, so I let her go. I've gotten myself in quite a mess.''

''Excuse me, Bryan…''

''Jacob's constant screaming convinced me that I needed to make some changes. Even as inexperienced as I am, I know when a baby needs something. Problem is, at the rate I'm going, I'll figure out what it is by the time the kid can talk.''

* * *

Bryan regarded the gentle way she held Jacob. In a matter of minutes, she'd calmed him down. She rubbed the baby's back as Jacob's big brown eyes searched her face. Bryan looked to Laura's left hand for a wedding ring, chastising himself for his interest, and surprised by his disappointment when he saw one.

He could almost feel Jacob's small body go limp in her embrace, and wondered if the baby had ever been held with such tenderness by his own mother. He doubted it. Bryan couldn't believe how wonderful it felt watching this woman cuddle his son.

The son Andrea had kept from him.

"Bryan, I know what you're going through..." Laura said.

Startling Bryan out of a bitter recollection of his wife, Bryan felt the muscles in his entire body tense. "You couldn't begin to imagine..." He stopped, realizing he almost dumped his resentment on this woman who seemed nothing like a stranger.

He looked up at her, feeling an unexplainable peace for the first time in days.

There was no doubt that he liked her. But was it the confident way she presented herself, her gentleness or the crystal blue eyes that invited him to open his heart? He gazed at her wavy hair, wondering if it was as touchable as it appeared.

What am I thinking? She's happily married. Get your mind back on business, Beaumont! What's wrong with you? Reprimanding himself, Bryan blurted out the first thing that came to mind. "Can he start right away?"

Laura seemed startled, hesitating before she answered. "The opening is available as of Monday, however..."

"Have you interviewed a lot of families for this position? It seems infant openings are in great demand."

Laura lifted her gaze to his, irritated at this man's pre-

sumptuousness. "I haven't advertised the opening yet."
Truth be known, she'd been picking up the phone to do so
when he'd called.

She looked back at the baby in her arms. As much as
her heart ached for these two and the pain they were feeling, she couldn't do it.

Laura considered how to tell Bryan that she wasn't up
to taking on a child who would need an extra dose of mothering.

"Mr. Beaumont, I think you'd be better off looking for
another live-in nanny under the circumstances."

"I beg your pardon?"

"I didn't realize the situation. I think a nanny might fit
your needs better. I'm sorry I wasted your time."

"Just a minute, *Mrs. Bates*. I'm staying with a friend—
until my house sells. The last thing we need is some
woman... I mean, a nanny's not a possibility. You came
very highly recommended, and I need someone to care for
Jacob."

Laura looked into Bryan's eyes, then at his son. Questions raced through her mind. She heard a little voice reminding her of the pastor's sermon the previous week: "Let
each of you look not only to your own interests, but also
to the interests of others." *But God, I have my own pain
to deal with. I haven't the strength to help a single father
who obviously has no idea what to do with his baby.*

Her personal struggle with this was far from over. She
couldn't say yes to Bryan Beaumont. This time, God was
expecting too much. Meeting her own family's needs was
more than enough to handle.

Running her child care business, baking cakes, shuffling
children between school and extracurricular activities
would have been enough. But now Laura was responsible
for her own duties in addition to those Todd had handled
prior to his death. There simply was no extra time or energy
for counseling anyone, let alone a chauvinistic executive

who was willing to exchange his paternal duties for his own career.

Before her emotions took over, she backed away, using her firmest business voice. "Before either of us make any decision, I recommend you review this packet. I also require that one parent visit during business hours before enrolling your child so you can see firsthand how I run my business. This also allows you to meet the other children that I care for. Enclosed in the packet is a copy of my policies, a letter outlining my child care philosophy, as well as a sample contract. Please read everything thoroughly." Laura motioned to the manila envelope on the table next to him.

The very way he handled himself told her that he was a man accustomed to success. If she was right, once the virile Bryan Beaumont experienced six preschoolers in action, he'd be out of her house quicker than a firecracker on the Fourth of July.

Bryan picked up the envelope, stood and walked over to her. "Thanks for reconsidering, Laura. I'll see you in the morning." He took the baby, and walked to an expensive foreign-made car.

"I have *not* reconsidered," she muttered as the door closed behind him.

Chapter Two

Bryan pulled to a stop at the red light, then brushed Jacob's dark fuzzy hair to one side with his hand. "How can one baby turn a man's life upside down?"

Jacob pursed his lips and grasped the finger Bryan offered, holding it tight until Bryan pulled to a stop in front of Kevin's house. Bryan took Jacob from the car seat, then shouldered the strap of the diaper bag and grabbed his briefcase.

After changing clothes and feeding Jacob his bottle, Bryan turned to Kevin. "I could use a run. You mind watching Jacob for an hour?"

"Mind? The kid and I have some football plays to discuss."

"I have my pager, if you need anything."

"Get out of here. We'll be fine. It's you I'm worried about. Take it easy today, you're not as young as you used to be." Kevin picked up the baby, then tucked the diaper bag under his arm and pretended to be charging through the offensive line on his way out the door.

Not for the first time in the last week, Bryan watched Kevin with envy, wondering how a dedicated bachelor had developed such a way with babies. Kids had always intrigued Bryan, but when his bride had announced that a baby would ruin her petite figure and her career, he'd eventually given up trying to change her mind. He'd directed his energy into his career, setting aside all hopes of a family. It was evident now that he wasn't father material.

Torturing himself more, Bryan remembered how tenderly Laura had held Jacob. *How could a woman who didn't even know the child have such an effect on him? It seems like the first time Jacob has relaxed in a week. I've got to convince Laura to take care of him.*

Bryan ran down the stairs and out the door. He cleared the last steps in one leap, starting his run at a rapid pace. Despite Kevin's warning, today was a day to push himself…again.

As he ran, his lawyer's haunting voice returned…. ''Bryan, Andrea's lawyer called this morning…. She died in an automobile accident yesterday. That's not all. You'd better sit down…. You have a son.''

A son.

His son.

Two days later, Jacob had arrived in the arms of a nanny. Three days later, they were on their own….

Bryan pushed harder.

Faster.

After extending his regime of rigorous sprints up and down the hill, he walked to stretch his aching muscles, grateful for anything that would take his mind off the ache in his heart.

Distracted by a group of boys playing football on the practice field ahead of him, Bryan ignored everything except the one boy who'd captured his attention.

''What a throw.''

An intense pain suddenly gripped the back of Bryan's leg. He grabbed his calf muscle as his body hit the hard ground. Bryan groaned aloud, struggling to stretch his leg.

From across the field, he heard yelling. "Help! Call 911! Call 911!"

"What?" Bryan turned to see what the boys were screaming about, when the kid he'd been watching suddenly dropped beside him, a look of terror in his huge eyes.

"Mister! Are you alive!"

Bryan saw another boy running off as if his life depended on it, and realized that they were talking to him. "Me?"

Relief spread like melted honey across the freckled face as the boy watched Bryan's every move.

"I'll be fine. My leg cramped."

"I thought you were dying or something." The fear disappeared from the young boy's face.

"I'm okay."

"Joey, come back! He's not dying!"

Bryan gritted his teeth and straightened his leg, then sat upright. "You have quite a team here. I'm Bryan Beaumont," he extended one hand while the other held a tight grip on his leg. "Coach of the McKinley Mustangs." He'd looked forward to coaching the eight and nine-year-old boys' football team for months. Ever since his wife had left him, to be exact. "Any of you signed up?"

A few of them nodded, but not the one with real potential.

Beads of sweat dripped down Bryan's face. He swiped the perspiration with the back of his hand, then rested it on his knee. He looked at the freckle-faced boy.

"Aren't you going to play?"

"I dunno." The kid shrugged.

"Do you like the game?"

"Sure," he said, as if it were the stupidest question he'd ever heard.

"Would you like me to talk to your parents?"

"I only have a mom. My dad died of a heart attack."

Bryan froze. So that what why the kid had overreacted to his collapse. "I'm sorry about that. How old are you?"

"Eight."

"You live near here?"

"I won't take you there." The kid backed away.

"That's good. It's okay. I don't mean to frighten you. I was wondering if your mom might be able to come over to talk to me."

"She's real busy."

"No problem. You ask her about playing." He turned to all the boys and added, "I'd like to have all of you on the team. We practice at McKinley Elementary."

"That's the school just around the corner," another kid exclaimed.

"Sure is. Anyone have a pen? I want to give you my phone number in case your mom has any questions."

One of the boys ran to his backpack and pulled out a stubby pencil and a scrap of paper. Bryan scribbled his first name and phone number for the youngster, then struggled to his feet after the boys were gone.

Upon returning to Kevin's, he found Jacob settled in his new crib, sound asleep.

Bryan filled the ice bag, grabbed a bottle of spring water, and hobbled into the den, hoping to forget his troubles.

"You cramped up again, huh? When are you going to realize Andrea isn't worth this torture?"

"Even dead, she's still a pain in the... Never mind. One of these days...years...I'm going to forget."

"One day you're going to realize she did you a favor."

"Real favor. Poor kid. I don't know anything about being a father. It's not like Andrea gave me any clue she'd changed her mind about kids."

Kevin looked at him, then back to the blueprints on the drafting table in front of him. "Other than grueling, how was your run?"

Bryan forgot the injury as the anticipation of coaching returned. Before he realized what he was doing, he was reenacting the play he'd seen just before collapsing.

"The kid is a natural athlete, Kev. I wish I'd found out his name, but I didn't want to scare him any more than I already had."

"You don't actually think his mom will call, do you? You know what women think of football."

Again, the simple reminder of his wife was enough to set Bryan's enthusiasm back ten yards. "You're right, she probably doesn't even realize the talent the boy has."

"That's a safe bet."

Bryan leaned his head back on the chair, resting his bottled water on one knee. He recalled his own mother's hesitation to let him play, and his dad's convincing argument. Remembering his father's death, Bryan realized for the first time that his own son was destined to an equal if not worse fate. He'd never even know the rare beauty of a mother's protective love. It was obvious that Andrea didn't care enough to think of anyone but herself.

Interrupting his thoughts, Kevin grumbled. "Don't even think it, Bryan. There are too many kids with problems for you to solve."

"The boy needs a little encouragement, a big brother, so to speak. He's eight years old!"

"Okay, so he needs someone. If I remember correctly..."

"You're the one who got me into coaching at all. It wasn't my idea." Bryan pointed to his friend, knowing by heart the lecture that was coming.

Before Kevin had a chance to speak, he added, "Besides, this isn't at all the same as with Andrea."

"You'll never change."

Bryan walked to the window, setting his glass on the sill. "I thought I could make it work. She needed someone to love her. It was good for a while."

"What wasn't good then? You were the new executive at Computex, women at your door all hours of the day and night."

Bryan interrupted. "Those women were on your door-step, not mine, Buddy."

"Like I said, they were good times." Kevin laughed, but Bryan continued to stare out the window. "Andrea had you under her spell. She knew what she wanted, and you were her ticket."

"How can I go on without her?"

"She left you almost a year ago, Bryan! Forget her." Kevin took a long drink, finishing his tea in one swallow.

"If she would have seen the counselor with me, we could have worked everything out.... And a baby!" Bryan mumbled an expletive. "She didn't even tell me about my own son."

"You're a saint, man. She leaves you without so much as a word, doesn't tell you or her lawyer she's carrying your kid, and you think you could have saved a marriage she never cared about."

Bryan closed his eyes and shook his head. "You don't understand, Kev. There has to be more to it...."

"What I understand is, you're better off without her. Snap out of it! Andrea didn't deserve you. What you need is a..."

"The last thing I need is a woman complicating my life."

Hamburger sizzled in the cast-iron skillet. Laura massaged her temple, trying to ward off the tension headache looming beneath the surface.

The front door slammed just before T.J. ran into the kitchen. "Mom. Can I play football this year? The McKinley coach came by the park and he wants me to play."

Before the words were out of her mouth, her son rushed through an explanation of how he'd come to talk to the stranger. After having seen his own father at the hands of the paramedics, she didn't have the heart to lecture her son about trying to help a stranger who'd appeared to need medical help.

"I don't know how we could fit that in this year, honey."

"But Dad said when I turned eight I could play."

"T.J." Her mouth went dry. How could she explain? "Please, Mom."

"Wasn't the sign-up last week?"

The smile disappeared. It didn't take a psychologist to see that she'd just broken her son's heart. Didn't every boy dream of being an all-star quarterback at one time?

"Here's the coach's phone number. Can't you at least call him?" Then as if he knew exactly how to turn the knife, he added, "Dad wouldn't have forgotten to sign me up."

She took the tattered paper and stuffed it into her pocket. *That was when Todd was going to be the coach. Things changed.* "Go wash up. Supper's ready."

If you'd take this baby, you wouldn't have to worry about the money. The fact remained, though, that Bryan Beaumont knew nothing about raising a child, which meant she'd not only be caring for his son, but also trying to teach another workaholic father how to be a dad. To make matters worse, this father wasn't her husband. This one was single, incredibly handsome and obviously had the means to substitute his love and attention with any number of material toys.

Both hands full, Laura kicked the refrigerator door closed. She set the gallon of milk and the skillet of hamburger gravy on the table, then sat down and waited for the children to settle before offering thanks. Their routine had changed so little, it was as if her husband were at a board meeting and would return before the evening was over.

After supper, she finished the dishes and helped the kids get ready for bed, still agonizing over both problems. She thought of calling Bryan's secretary for more information, as Vicky had been a client once, but realized how unprofessional that would appear.

Then she wondered if she should call the football coach. Out of the question.

What could she say? Thanks for your encouragement, but I just can't afford it? Not a chance. The last thing she wanted was some do-gooder giving them charity. It wasn't that there really was no money to spare, but she was trying to keep within a budget, and after buying new tires and paying the plumbing bill, it would cut into the emergency fund. Not a good way to start the month.

She could always go into detail about how challenging it was to transport nine kids to practices. Or spew out her personal sob story and sound like a whiny, helpless woman. Forget it. They'd manage. There would always be next year, after life had settled into a dull and boring routine again.

Football taken care of, she set her mind to the problem of filling her opening, or more to the point, how to *not* fill the opening. At least, not with the adorable son of a potently handsome widower who twisted her words to suit his needs.

Sleep. That would clear her mind.

Wrong.

The quiet only filled her mind with more guilt. The furnace kicked on, squealing at first, then dissipating to a rhythmic drone. *Oh, the joys of a fixer-upper. Before winter's over, the furnace too, will most likely need to be replaced.*

She rolled onto her stomach and covered her head with a pillow as overgrown branches of the giant maple rubbed against the side of the house. Another chore Todd had meant to do this summer.

Before long, the mental list of possible repairs had tripled, and her headache was pounding. "Okay, I get the message, God. You've always provided for our needs, and now is no exception. But why through a single father with an attitude?"

Chapter Three

The next morning, Bryan parked his white sports car in front of Laura's house. He saw the freckle-faced kid deposit a sack of trash in a barrel, then grab a basketball and shoot three baskets—all net.

Tucking Jacob into the crook of his arm, Bryan hustled up the driveway. "Hi. I'm Bryan. We met yesterday."

The boy looked puzzled.

"You were playing football. I'm the coach."

"That was you?" The boy's sparkling eyes grew bigger.

Bryan nodded. His smile couldn't begin to express his joy at finding this kid again. "Are you Laura Bates's son?"

"Uh-huh. You know my mom?"

She's a widow, and never said a thing. And I told her she couldn't begin to imagine what it was like to lose a loved one. Great one, Beaumont. Open mouth, insert foot. "I talked with her last night about watching my son. What did she say about football?"

"She said it's too late to sign up," he complained.

"Oh yeah? Let's go talk to her. We'll see what we can do."

Bryan followed T.J. into the kitchen and watched silently as Laura flipped pancakes.

"Chad, you're going to be late for school. Will you please hurry?" She pivoted, jumping when she saw Bryan standing in the doorway.

"Your son and I met outside. He invited me in. Sorry I startled you."

T.J., obviously forgetting football at the sight of warm pancakes, walked between Bryan and Laura with a plate piled high. Not that he blamed the kid. They looked delicious.

"Good grief T.J., you'd think I never feed you." She took several pancakes off his plate and returned them to the platter. "You may have seconds after you've eaten those."

Laura glanced back at Bryan, her face full of strength, shining with a steadfast and serene peace. "I didn't expect you quite so early, but that's okay. Help yourself to breakfast if you'd like."

Her other son sauntered into the spacious kitchen.

"Chad! You've been up for an hour, why aren't you dressed?" She excused herself, then disappeared with her youngest son in tow. A few minutes later, both returned, and the doorbell rang. Laura's workday was beginning. Preschoolers and toddlers arrived every few minutes and she introduced Bryan to each of the parents.

"How do you stay so calm with this chaos?"

She laughed, seeming very pleased with something. "It grows on you."

While she was busy feeding the toddlers and helping her children prepare for school, he mentioned registering T.J. in football.

She stole a guilt-ridden glance at her son.

T.J. looked at Laura hopefully. "Can I, Mom? Please."

"I'll discuss that with Jacob's dad. You and I will talk tonight. Right now, it's time for you kids to walk to school.

Have a good day. Remember, I love you.'' She kissed each child's cheek as they left. ''And no talking to strangers.''

After her children were out the door, she faced Bryan, arms across her chest. ''So you're the coach he met last night, huh? How's the leg?''

''Fine. I'm sorry about the stranger thing. He was hesitant, if that matters.'' By the look on her face, it didn't. ''He's got talent.''

''Oh, he's a natural all right. Just like his dad.'' She smiled, but her eyes were looking far beyond anything visible. She shook her head, then looked back at him. It was as if he could look right into the raw sores of her aching heart. ''I'm not sure I'm ready for him to play full-contact sports.''

''Has he played soccer?''

Laura nodded.

''There's more protection playing football than soccer. I'm helping coach the team at McKinley. I'd love to have him play.''

She proceeded to cut another pancake for a towheaded boy without any indication she'd heard Bryan.

''It's not too late to register,'' he told her.

''I know. That's not it.'' Laura washed another toddler's fingers before getting him out of the high chair, then cleared the dishes from the table while children dug through the toy box.

''Did your husband play?'' Bryan persisted.

''Todd was an athlete. Anything with 'ball' attached, consumed him. If he wasn't playing, we watched on T.V.'' She looked as if she actually missed that. ''T.J.'s so young. There's plenty of time for sports later.''

''Sometimes kids need an outlet to deal with losing a dad. Especially an oldest son who feels an obligation to take care of his mother. That's a heavy load for a boy his age.'' Bryan tried to block out memories of his father's death, memories that were especially strong during football season. "You didn't tell me you were a widow," he said accusingly.

She replied right away, "You didn't give me a chance." Her cool blue eyes eluded his and she sidestepped the subject. "Did you play football?"

Bryan smiled, recalling his own experience with the sport. "Wide receiver for Colorado University."

"Ah. Serious obsession."

Even though her smile was genuine, Bryan sensed a turn in their conversation.

"Very."

"What about coaching? You obsessed there, too?"

He realized Laura was now a mother interviewing the coach. "At this age, teaching the boys the basics and to enjoy the game is more important than winning. Obsession comes on down the road. High school, junior year at the latest."

Laura chuckled and bit her lower lip almost nervously. "I'll think about it."

"I hope you will."

During his visit that morning, Laura briefly told him that her husband had died of a heart attack, and shared that it was a continuous challenge to raise children alone. Her courage and determination was like a cold deep river flowing through her.

In turn, he told her that Jacob's mother had died in an automobile accident. That was all she needed to know.

"Why do you coach?" Laura asked over a glass of juice as the kids watched their favorite preschool program.

"What kind of question is that?"

"Forgive me. That didn't come out right. You obviously enjoy football, but it sounds like you already keep long hours at work, and with expecting a new baby in your house, I can't help but wonder why you chose now to volunteer your time. Most men have difficulty making time to coach even their own son's team. This doesn't fit the image you portrayed yesterday.''

He remained quiet, assessing the fact that she'd examined his image. It pleased him, and it bothered him. He couldn't afford to be distracted by some woman's romantic notions.

''Being a weekend quarterback isn't enough. I miss playing. And I'd made the commitment before I found out about Jacob.''

Bryan consoled himself that it wasn't a lie, exactly. When he'd agreed to help coach the junior league team, he had no idea he was going to be a father. No one need know that at that time he'd desperately needed something to take his mind off his wife's walking away from their marriage.

''What's the most important aspect of football?''

''At this age, or professional?'' He grinned, attempting to lighten her shrewd onslaught of questions into his character.

She stared back, obviously unimpressed with his humor.

''Okay, okay. Teamwork. No one is an entity unto himself out on the football field.''

''Are they anywhere?''

He looked again into her undaunted blue eyes, realizing her wisdom. ''Touché. So how about if we try this out, Mrs. Bates. You raise my son, and I'll coach yours. It's as easy and uncomplicated as that.''

Three weeks later, the football season had started. During that time, Laura had cleared up the majority of Bryan's questions about his new son. While he admitted feeling he'd never get the knack of caring for a baby, he was comforted by the knowledge that Jacob at least had Laura to meet the majority of his needs.

Bryan was a bit surprised when she accepted his offer to transport T.J. to and from practices in return for watching Jacob after her usual business hours during practice. It had been the first glimmer of her relinquishing any sort of personal responsibility. The death of her husband had obviously been a devastating blow, and she seemed determined to handle life's punches alone.

In the three weeks that he'd known the family, he'd come to understand what had drawn him to Laura Bates. She showed no signs of weakness. There was a part of him that worried about her. Would she give and give until there was nothing left of her? Or would she someday allow herself to grow whole again?

He admired her. Almost too much. And at the same time, he longed for proof that she was human; that she, like he, had her inadequacies as well. This selfishness was a quick, disturbing thought as he struggled to put the woman out of his mind.

After the second football practice, Bryan walked into the living room and handed the game schedule to Laura. "I hope T.J. remembered to tell you he needs to get a cup."

"No, he didn't mention it, but it'll be no problem. I'll send him with one tomorrow. He has a water bottle that we take camping."

"What?" Bryan stopped and looked at her.

"You said a cup didn't you? He drinks a lot of water."

Clearing his throat, Bryan rubbed his forehead with his fingers, twisting his mouth in amusement. "I meant a jock cup. You know, an athletic supporter."

Laura's cheeks colored. "Oh… Why didn't you just say he needs a jockstrap?"

"I assumed…never mind. You do realize that a cup is not the same as a regular jock, don't you?"

Laura watched in embarrassment as he tried not to smile.

"It's so refreshing to see a grown woman blush." Bryan smiled in spite of the fact he wasn't sure he liked the affect she had on him. "Why don't I take care of this?"

"We can handle it." Her voice raised an octave. "I

hadn't thought of this part of being a single mother, to be honest. I told you I wasn't ready for him to be in sports.''

"Let me pick him up after school tomorrow and take him shopping before practice. Taking all the little ones shopping must be a disaster. The store closes at five.''

"If you're sure you wouldn't mind," Laura said, absently stacking some scattered papers on the leather-top table. "I'll owe you one.''

"I'll hold you to that."

Chapter Four

Laura watched her three children climb into the tree house Todd and the kids had finished building only weeks before his heart attack. She wondered how their lives would be altered by his absence.

Would her sons grow up knowing how to treat their wives and children? How could she begin to answer the boys' questions about puberty? Her own brother was nearly ten years her senior. She knew nothing of what changes her sons would experience.

Would Carrie learn how to relate to men? She seemed so lost without her daddy. One minute she would be a happy little girl, the next, overflowing with any number of emotions.

Laura understood exactly what Carrie was going through. It had devastated Laura when her grandfather had died. He'd been her best buddy, especially the summer before they found the tumor. Experience had taught her nothing, she realized. She'd felt the same sense of loss, and yet she had no way to help her daughter's pain go away.

That evening, T.J. bounded into the kitchen while Laura

was preparing dinner. He grabbed a carrot and munched noisily. "How can Daddy be happy in heaven without us?"

Laura put down the knife she was using, and her mouth opened, though the words she sought would not come. She leaned on the counter and looked at the younger version of her husband. "Heaven isn't like Earth. There is no sadness and pain."

"Do you think Daddy asked God why he had to die?"

"Yes, your dad probably had a whole list of questions for Him." She wrapped her arms around her son and gave him a kiss. "I think God is telling Daddy the same thing that I remind myself of each day, that He hasn't given us any more than we can handle. Sometimes it's not easy to understand God's plan, but the Bible says we should trust in the Lord with all our hearts." Could she really expect her son to believe words she herself had questioned over and again in the past few months?

"Oh," T.J. said, accepting her answer with a childlike trust. Then he ran back to the playroom.

Laura stood, surrounded by the emptiness that her son's difficult questions prompted. "God, why isn't it that simple for me? Why can't I accept your wisdom with that same kind of trust?"

Later, while she was getting ready for bed, a raw and primitive grief overwhelmed her. Her entire body ached from uncontrollable sobs. "What do you expect of me God?" Stepping into the shower, she let the tepid water drip over her face and tired body. Inhaling deep, she leaned her head back. "How can I possibly raise these three children alone, God? They were all Todd and I could handle together."

The next weekend her best friend, Barb, and her husband Chuck came for dinner with their two kids. Realizing how much she'd missed entertaining, Laura had looked forward to adult conversation all week.

Barb snatched a mushroom from the salad, and Laura scowled.

"Don't start, Laura. My boss is driving me crazy. I'm almost ready to get back into child care," Barb proclaimed.

"Right." Laura laughed, still chopping vegetables for the salad. "If you want more chaos in your days, you are crazy."

"A doozy, huh? What happened?"

"Ty and Jeffrey's mom came and needed to talk just as the kids were getting up from their naps. I shouldn't complain, it's been months since she's stopped long enough to visit. I think she was afraid to bother me after Todd died." Laura checked the lasagna and filled the glasses on the table. Carrie escorted Barb's daughter, Kate into the room.

"Mom, you said we could have pop tonight," Carrie complained with an air of authority.

"After you drink your milk, you may." Carrie moaned aloud while Laura called the boys to dinner and continued her story. "Since a parent was here, the kids decided to test the limits. Carrie started playing the piano. The two-year-olds pulled all the toys off the shelves. Jeffrey left the basement door open when he went to find his lost dinosaur. Rachel moved like a centipede toward the stairs. Letisha just kept on talking. When I tried to get around her, I dropped Jacob's bottle, the top flew across the room, and formula splashed from the ceiling to the floor. I did reach the door before Rachel took a nosedive down the stairs."

"Is that all?" Barb said in a sarcastic tone.

"Of course not. T.J. and Chad burst through the door fighting and screaming. Then, to make matters worse, the phone rang, and the school principal called about a fight Chad had been involved in. I'm so glad it's Friday."

After dinner, Chuck turned on a movie for himself and the kids, suggesting Laura and Barb escape to the family room to visit. Laura sank into the sofa and leaned her head back.

"You need to take a break."

"Right, a vacation to my island paradise, huh?" She gave Barb a knowing glance.

She and Barb were more like sisters than friends. Barb knew Laura better than Laura did herself, and that in itself created some difficult situations. But what was worse, was Laura wanted to reach out, to talk, to feel again. And she knew Barb knew it, too.

"Talk to me, Laura," Barb said quietly. "You have something on your mind."

"Why do I bother trying to hide anything from you?" After a lengthy silence, Laura looked at her friend. "I have to learn to cope, as much for the kids' sake as my own," Laura murmured. "I have never understood how single parents deal with everything."

"I think they learn to accept help when it's offered," Barb suggested.

Laura straightened her back and lifted her chin. "I will not become dependent on anyone again."

"It's hard now, Laura, but it'll get easier. There are more important things than work. Let yourself relax every now and then. Even God took a day off."

"I used to enjoy throwing around the football, kicking a few goals and pitching a few home runs. Now there's no time or energy for that. It's a constant struggle to keep up with the day-to-day stuff."

"I'm sure it is. Something has to give."

Laura rolled her head from side to side. "But what? I can't ask any more of the kids. They're already starting to notice we've cut most of the fun day trips from our schedule."

"Then let's take the kids to the zoo one of these weekends."

"That would be good for us. Get outside, walk, and of course, I have to get some cotton candy."

"Now you're talking like yourself."

After they'd finished the dishes, Barb hugged Laura.

"What was that for?"

"I just have this feeling."

Laura laughed. "Don't do this to me. The last time you had one of your 'wonderful' feelings, I ended up sick for nine months."

"Admit it. You wouldn't know what to do without Chad keeping you on your toes."

"That's an understatement. At least that won't be the case this time. Maybe I'm going to win the lottery. Of course, since I don't play, I couldn't win."

"No, that's not it. I see a change in you." She looked at Laura, studying her. "You've become stronger."

"You mean more stubborn. It couldn't be physically, I haven't had time to work out or walk since before Todd died."

"I don't mean either. It's emotional. God must be preparing you for something."

This time, Laura laughed aloud. "Oh please. You're being ridiculous."

Barb wagged her eyebrows, then smiled. "And whatever it is, you'd better hang on to your hat, because it's going to take everything you've got, and more."

Chapter Five

Two weeks later, Laura, Chad, Jacob and Carrie sat on the portable bleachers cheering for T.J.'s team. Tears welled up in her eyes as she thought of Todd missing his son's first football game. *Oh, Todd. You were supposed to be here. Watching him, coaching him. Who's going to…?*

Laura's thoughts were interrupted when T.J. recovered a fumble and took off down the field. Laura jumped off the bleachers. "Go T.J.! Cut right!" She stopped yelling, suddenly remembering the baby beside her. She prepared to soothe him, but he slept through all the noise from the game.

The Mustangs had a strong offense, but their defense lacked the size to stop the opposition from scoring more touchdowns. They played hard, and Laura was proud of them.

Bryan walked across the field with his hand on T.J.'s slumped shoulder. "I promised T.J. I'd take you all for an ice-cream cone after the game."

Laura croaked, "Thanks, but I need to get home. Why don't we take a rain check? You did a great job, T.J."

"We didn't even win, Mom," T.J. answered, clearly disappointed.

"Can I go with Bryan, Mom?" Chad interrupted.

Bryan motioned Laura aside and pushed his son's stroller, smiling lazily. Laura tried to ignore the fluttering in her stomach. She cleared her throat before trying to talk again. Again, a raspy reply was all she could manage. "Not today, Chad."

"Sounds like *you* need a double-decker ice-cream cone. What's so important at home?"

Laura's voice was barely a whisper. She motioned to Carrie to tell him, but Carrie shrugged her shoulders. "I don't know why we can't go! You never let us have any fun since Daddy died." Laura watched as Carrie stomped away, a sudden stream of tears flowing. "All we ever do is work!"

T.J. and Chad looked at Laura, then chased after their sister. Laura turned to Bryan, guilt laying its burden on her again.

"Yours must have been the voice I heard encouraging the boys. I appreciate it."

Laura nodded, thankful that he didn't mention Carrie's tantrum. "Thanks for the offer, but I have cakes to decorate for a wedding shower. They'll be picked up in a few hours."

"A talented woman. Well, since you'll be busy for a while, why don't I take the kids for lunch and bring them home later? I'm sure you could use a little peace and quiet."

Laura shrugged. "I can't give in to her tantrum."

"Everyone's entitled to change their mind once in a while, even mothers. Take a few hours off."

Laura was puzzled by this side of Bryan. The career-minded executive was offering to take her children to lunch.

"Thank you anyway Bryan…"

"I believe it was you who said that this child care contract was like a partnership in parenting. That should work both ways. I may not be Superdad, but I can handle burgers in the park."

She wanted to argue, but recently coping with the effects of her husband's death kept her in a constant state of turmoil, and right now, her emotions were quickly gaining control. She met the kids at her van and sent them to meet Bryan.

When they arrived at the house an hour later, Laura was finishing the cakes. Without prompting, the kids thanked Bryan and got their mother's permission to go to the park.

"Be back in an hour. And be careful."

Bryan held Jacob, and sat across from her at the table. "The kids said your favorite is an old-fashioned chocolate soda. I hope they were right. I also brought you a burger and fries, in case you didn't take time to fix lunch." He looked at the cake and back to Laura. "Mind if I watch?"

"That's fine." Laura drank the soda, letting the ice cream slide slowly down her sore throat. "This tastes wonderful. Thank you."

He watched as she added borders to the cakes and put them into boxes. "You seemed to enjoy the game."

"I wanted to strangle a coach or two, to be honest."

"Present company excluded, I hope."

She smiled apologetically, "You did a great job with the boys, Bryan. Not all coaches share your philosophy, though."

"Warning taken. I've already talked to Kevin, but I'll mention it again. I've been meaning to talk to you about doing me a favor. The company has offered their block of seats for me to take the boys to a Bronco game. What do you think about helping?"

"Weekends are pretty busy at our house."

"I bet they are. I need one more chaperon, and I'm sure

having an experienced mother along would comfort the other parents. Carrie and Chad would probably enjoy it, too.''

She stole a glance at him. "I appreciate the invitation. It's been hard for the kids to understand some of the changes we have to make without Todd, but they'll get used to it. I'm sorry about Carrie's outburst.''

Bryan set Jacob on the floor and set a brightly colored toy in his view. "A daddy's girl?''

Laura nodded. "I just begin to think we're making progress, when something else happens. I can't figure out what makes her act like that.''

"Try not to let her get you down.''

"Easy for you to say.''

Jacob rolled into the next room. Bryan caught him and brought him back. "I think she's acting pretty normal for a pre-adolescent girl who's just lost her father.''

"It just seems I can't do anything right anymore. She argues with everything I say.''

"Maybe she's ready to make a few decisions on her own.''

"She's ten years old!''

"Ten going on twenty, right? I'm suggesting you start with small decisions, nothing monumental. Let the responsibility grow with her.''

"And what makes you an expert on raising kids suddenly?'' Leaning back in her chair, she crossed her arms defiantly.

He stood up, smiling with satisfaction. "I guess not as much as I thought. I think I've overstayed my welcome. See you Monday.''

As he walked out the door, Bryan overheard her muttering. "Uncomplicated, Bryan. Let's keep it that way!''

The next Monday Bryan watched in fury as Kevin pushed the boys, stressing the importance of winning even

more than before. After the practice ended and the kids
were gone, Bryan pointed out that they should be teaching
good sportsmanship, teamwork and skills, not just winning.

"It's the reason we play." Kevin turned and walked off.

"Where'd you come up with that?" Bryan flung the ball
into a duffel bag and zipped it closed.

Kevin's eyebrows lifted, and he pointed at Bryan.
"You're not going to tell me winning, at anything, isn't
just as important to you. Are you?"

Bryan faltered, unable to deny the accusation. "Who are
we here for, them, or us? Half of these boys haven't ever
touched a football."

"And what about the few, like T.J. Bates, who have the
raw talent to go all the way with this? Don't they deserve
more than what this team has to offer?"

"They all need the basics. Not one of them, including
T.J., are so good they can't strengthen their form."

"Winning is the goal, in case you've forgotten."

"One goal, but not the priority at this level. Didn't you
look at their faces during the game? They were having fun
out there whether we were winning or not. Let's not put
that fire out." Bryan couldn't believe they were having
this argument. For months they'd planned and anticipated
the fun of coaching these boys.

"If you think you can do a better job of it, the position's
yours. No problem."

"Oh, no, you don't! You're the head coach, I'm just
helping."

"Not any more. You don't like the way I'm coaching,
you do it. I'll just sit back and take a few lessons from the
pro."

Bryan opened the trunk and dropped the bag inside. He
slammed the lid, venting his anger on it instead of his
friend, who seemed to have changed his coaching philosophy overnight. Sure, they'd both been aggressive players,
but Kevin had never talked or reacted like this before. "If

you won't do it right, then I guess I'd better. Another week of your attitude, and we won't have a team left!''

''Then maybe they don't belong here in the first place,'' Kevin muttered, as he climbed into his truck and drove away.

Bryan discovered he'd fallen into another one of Kevin's schemes. This one was geared to show Bryan that kids were a lot more fun than hassle. It was as if his friend knew exactly what Bryan was thinking.

He also realized something Kevin didn't. Being a coach, and being a dad, were not synonymous. Just because he knew how to teach beginners football, didn't mean he would be able to transfer that talent into teaching his son about life.

Chapter Six

Bryan scanned the garage and walked back into the house. "Where'd you put the ladder, Kevin?"

"Still in the truck. What're you doing?"

"Mrs. Richards needs some help picking apples before the frost gets them. She's going to watch the baby, so don't worry."

Kevin met him at the front door. "Every time she sees me she offers to take care of him for us. Her ladder's a little rickety, so I'll run get another one from the warehouse and help."

Bryan stopped him. "Fine, but the pie's mine."

"You haven't seen her pies, bud." He opened his hands to show several inches. "If she asks, we want the Dutch apple."

An elderly woman walked across the driveway and reached for the baby. "It's such a tragedy about this little one's mother. I hope you found Jacob a good sitter. He needs a mommy." Jacob went without a fuss, while Bryan and Kevin smiled at one another.

"My secretary helped me find a wonderful child care provider. He's very happy there."

"It's not one of the big places that you see on those scandal reports, is it?"

Bryan laughed openly. "Not at all. Laura watches a few kids in her home. She's been doing child care for several years."

"You pick a sack of apples for her, too, then. Dutch apple as usual, Kevin?"

Wrapping his arm around the woman's shoulders, Kevin gave her a gentle hug. "You make the best, Lil. Need any other jobs done while we're here?"

"Bribery. So, one pie's not enough anymore, huh?"

Bryan had carried the ladder back to the yard and returned for the boxes to hold the apples, just in time to hear the woman's remark. He looked to Kevin, silently scolding him for begging for more. "I was joking, Kevin. One's plenty."

"Oh, pshaw. You two could use a few more calories. No wonder Kevy can't find a nice girl. Nothing to hold on to." Then pinching Jacob's cheek, she turned back to her house. "And your daddy shouldn't have any trouble finding you a suitable mother."

Once Lillian Richards was inside the house, Kevin pinched Bryan's cheek. "No trouble, at all. Bless her for not placing her spell on me!"

"I take it that means I don't need the extra calories, huh?"

The door opened again. "Kevin, I do need the deep freeze moved to clean under it, if you two wouldn't mind." The two men looked at each other and grimaced.

When Kevin returned with the second ladder, the jibing resumed. "Yup, all you need to straighten your life out is a wife." He roared with laughter.

"At least I can get one," Bryan returned.

"Thank heavens, I can't."

Bryan picked a rotten apple and threw it at Kevin, hitting him in the stomach as he reached to the top of the tree for more apples, the surprise knocking him off the ladder. As expected, Kevin popped back up, both hands loaded, and ready to fire.

"If you weren't so skinny, you wouldn't have even felt that."

"Boys," a high-pitched voice hollered. "The baby's diaper needs changing. I don't know how to use these paper things."

"He's your son," Kevin bragged. "I'm only the uncle. That means, I don't have diaper duty."

"Kevin, since you're already on the ground, why don't you give his daddy a break," Lillian called.

"Yeah, give me a break." Bryan chuckled.

At dinner that night, Kevin placed the meat loaf on the table and sat down. "The football team's doing great. You've taught them a lot, Bryan."

Sprinkling his food with salt and pepper, Bryan eyed his friend. "They're eager learners. And the game's still fun."

"Imagine that." Kevin chuckled, pouring himself an over-size glass of milk. The ragged University of Colorado shirt, left over from their college days, was evidence of his friend's dedication to the sport.

Bryan knew that Kevin wanted to rub it in that he'd staged the entire winning fanatic episode on purpose. He wouldn't give him the satisfaction of saying, "I told you so." In his own mind, there was no comparing coaching three days a week to being a father.

Jacob sat in the high chair next to the table, playing with a set of plastic keys while Bryan shoveled spoonfuls of strained fruit into his hungry son's mouth as quickly as he could.

"I have to be out of town Tuesday night. Do you want me to ask Laura to watch him?"

"I can handle it. Pick him up after work Tuesday, then take him back to Laura in the morning, right?" He scooped another bite of mashed potatoes into his mouth. "No problem."

Bryan finished his bite then added, "You'll go through his whole routine, won't you?"

"Yeah, yeah, bottle, play, diaper, eat cereal and fruit, play, then bed. We'll be fine."

"No, it's bottle, eat, bath, play, read a book, music, then, bed. Want me to write it down?" Bryan pulled a pen from his shirt pocket along with a pad of paper.

"I don't have to sing, do I?"

"Whatever you do, don't sing. You want him to sleep, don't you? Laura gave us some lullaby tapes. I turn them on before he goes down."

"No bottles during the night?"

Bryan shook his head.

"Piece of cake."

Tuesday night, Bryan called from the hotel to check on his son and Kevin. They were getting along fine. It was him that was having difficulty. He used to enjoy the traveling. Since his son had arrived, he'd reassigned the accounts that required overnight stays to the junior executives. He hadn't felt right flying off when he was just getting to know his little boy.

This account was different. The owner of the company had requested Bryan, and his boss had given him no choice in the matter. Though he was grateful that his superiors had given him time to adjust to his new circumstances, he'd realized that it couldn't last. Traveling was part of his job, an aspect that he could no longer delegate to others.

It created a difficult situation that he'd ignored up until now. Expecting Kevin to fill in as daddy wasn't fair. He'd already welcomed them into his home while Bryan looked for something to reinvest the money from his and Andrea's home into.

The arrangement was working well for both of them so far. When Bryan had learned about his son, Kevin discouraged him from finding a place of his own right away, claiming the adjustment would be easier with two of them. He'd been right. Bryan didn't know how he could have managed alone.

In the meantime, Bryan had invested his profits into the expansion of Kevin's construction company. At the rate business was booming, Kevin would be paying back the money ahead of schedule.

Bryan loosened his tie and kicked off his loafers, then turned on the evening news. After three reports of rising crime, he changed the channel, stopping to listen to the catchy children's tune. What was he going to do when he had to be away for a week, or like the job in Sweden, a month? Something had to change.

Chapter Seven

Thanksgiving reminded Laura that even with all she'd lost this year, she still had much to be grateful for. That still wasn't enough to ease the loneliness Todd's death had created.

Much about the day had been the same as always, family had gathered, the air was crisp, and the television continued to offer the traditional parades and football mania. Though everyone missed Todd, no one talked about him. That, too, had become a tradition in the short time since he had died. Pretending that everything was okay. That the pain, no matter how intense, would disappear if ignored.

It didn't.

Even the call from Kevin had been a welcome break. After hanging up, Laura turned to her mother. "Bryan's roommate just called. It turns out Bryan and Jacob stayed home alone today and Kevin seems concerned. Since we have so much food left over, I thought I'd take him some."

"I'm sure he'll appreciate it, honey. Your dad and I'll watch the kids. If he's a football fan, maybe he'd like to come keep your father and brother company."

"Can't hurt to ask."

Laura wrote down the address and got into the car. A few minutes later, she pulled into the driveway of Kevin's home. She grinned at the image of two bachelors living here. Gathering the plates, she climbed the steps and elbowed the doorbell.

Bryan answered after a long delay. "Laura! What are you doing here?" Before she could reply, Jacob tried to jump out of Bryan's arms and into hers.

"Happy Thanksgiving." She held up the plates. "I thought you might enjoy this."

Bryan motioned her inside. His eyes narrowed. Laura set the plates of turkey dinner on a coffee table, then took the baby and snuggled him close. "Hi, Jacob. Are you and Daddy having fun?"

"Just having a few beers and watching the football games," Bryan mumbled, reaching for dirty dishes strewn across the table.

"Sounds relaxing." Laura handed him another empty beer bottle, then offered him a warm smile.

"So, does your child care service always include complimentary, holiday dinners? Or am I a special case?"

Puzzled by his mockery, she replied, "If you don't want it, I'll be glad to take it home. I'm sure someone there would enjoy it."

"Did Kevin ask you to check on us, or was this your idea?"

She didn't know how to answer. If she claimed credit, he'd think that she had a personal interest in him. If she admitted Kevin had called her, she'd break the confidence he'd placed in her and possibly create problems between the two men.

Before she could answer, Bryan made the decision for her. "No matter," he said turning into the kitchen. "Thanks for your concern, but as you can see, Jacob and I are doing fine."

Laura heard the clamor of dishes and empty bottles. She

hugged Jacob, letting his small warm body soothe her nerves as she followed Bryan.

Watching Bryan from the doorway, his clenched jaw confirmed her suspicions. "What's wrong, Bryan? You haven't been the same since Friday...."

His dark eyes filled with a burning, faraway look.

"Bryan...?"

He dropped a baby bottle into the dishwater and raked wet hands through his hair, then slammed his fists on the counter.

"I guess I shouldn't have come. I just thought, well...I thought that I was a little harsh Friday night about you not calling to let me know you'd be late." She handed Jacob to him and turned to leave.

He took hold of her arm and motioned for her to go into the living room. "Don't go. We need to talk. I've been trying to figure out how to tell you."

Laura sat on the sofa and hid a toy rabbit from Jacob, urging him to find it. She raised her eyes to find Bryan watching them.

"If I've done something..."

"You haven't done anything. It's about Jacob. He'll be staying with my sister after Christmas." Bryan walked to the tall, narrow window and gazed into the fading sunset.

"Oh," she whispered.

"I expect to pay until you can find another child. I know this must be a difficult time to find a new client."

"You mean he's staying there permanently?"

He shrugged, lowering his head. "This isn't an easy decision."

"I'm sure it isn't. You're giving your son away?"

"It's best for him," he snapped.

"I know the adjustment was hard for you at first, but the roughest part's past. Are you sure about this?"

When he didn't answer, she knelt beside Jacob, who was reaching for a photo album. Rescuing the open book, she saw photos of Bryan and a woman standing before an elegant white stone fireplace. She wore a stunning cream sequined dress with diamond-and-emerald jewelry that matched her green eyes.

Jacob's mother was beautiful. Not that that should come as a surprise.

Laura turned the pages. In every picture Jacob's mother was immaculately dressed. Laura couldn't imagine this woman pregnant, let alone cuddling the little boy Laura had come to love.

She glanced at Bryan, who continued to stare out the window at the darkened sky, ignoring Jacob's happy squeals.

"I realize that your family was broken up just when it was starting, Bryan, but this seems so drastic. You and Jacob need each other now more than ever."

Laura felt her words of comfort were hollow. How could she possibly help someone else deal with his grief when she had such difficulty herself?

"The three of us were never a family." He grabbed the album from Laura's hand and flung it across the room. The leather-bound book crashed into the wall and tumbled to the floor.

Jacob wailed, frantically reaching for Laura. She swept him into her arms and bounced him on her hip until he calmed down.

Bryan turned away and began to clean up the mess, carefully replacing the pages in the binder.

"I'm a pretty good listener."

"We'll be fine."

"You think you're the only one who's angry about losing a spouse?" she said, her voice racked with emotion.

"I don't think you understand the situation." He glared, not at her, but past her, as if at an invisible enemy.

"I'm willing to try."

"You couldn't begin to understand, Laura. Your life is

so sheltered...." His bellow stopped midsentence. He dropped the album into an empty chair and jammed his hands into his pockets.

"Yes, it was once," she softly admitted. The guilt she'd been fighting blanketed her. Why was it that this man could infuriate her at the same time her heart swelled with feelings she couldn't understand?

"I didn't mean that the way it sounded."

Frustration fed the tension between them.

Bryan continued, "I'm just not cut out for fatherhood. You make parenting look so easy."

Laura closed her eyes, rubbing her aching temples, giving in to the tension that had been building all day. "Abandoned. Confused. Angry. Afraid." Her tone hardened. "Easy? I know what you're feeling, because I was there. I was Mrs. Todd Bates, wife, best friend, mother. Todd was everything to me."

"I'm not..."

"No, Bryan, let me finish. I'm tired of this pedestal you seem to have put me on. I have the same fears and frustrations you and every other parent has. And like you, I'm learning to face them—alone." She backed away and collapsed against a closet door.

He sat on the couch, his profile rugged and somber.

She swallowed hard, asking God to fill her with courage. She wasn't sure if Bryan believed in Christ or not, or whether he would even listen. What she saw as God's handiwork, others often saw as coincidences. Laura sat on the edge of the sofa.

"Bryan, there hasn't been an easy day since Todd died, whether we're talking children or not. As much as my kids mean to me, there are days I don't know how I can cope. Yet God placed them in my hands, to raise, to love, until He's ready to take us home. It's the same with my clients' children."

Bryan reached across the sofa and took hold of her hand.

The warmth and tenderness surprised her. "He gave you a very special gift, Laura."

She pulled her hand away, refusing to let herself feel anything for a man who could turn away his own child. "He gave you one, too, Bryan. A son."

"Right. And I'm doing a real bang-up job with him."

"It's no sin to be less comfortable with a baby than an eight-year-old. God made each flower different. Some tolerate heat, some last until the snow falls, and some are only pretty a few weeks in the spring, but God takes care of them all in His special way."

As he considered her minisermon, she continued. "It won't ever be easy without Todd, but I know now that I can manage. God answers our prayers every day, big and small." Tears, trapped by her stubborn will, fought for their freedom.

Laura let the silence lengthen before proceeding. "What is sending Jacob to his aunt really about?"

"Andrea was nothing like you."

"I can see that. So?"

Bryan remained silent, staring blankly at the wall. Laura waited. He picked up his son, then turned to her. "Until a week before I met you, I knew nothing of Jacob. Had no idea I was even going to be a father."

Laura gasped.

"She left me right after she found out she was pregnant, by my estimation. A year later her lawyer called and told me she'd died, and that I was a father."

Laura shook her head. "How could she...not tell you?" How could Andrea look into Jacob's beautiful brown eyes, touch his smooth olive skin, hold his long fingers and not think of his father, Laura thought.

Jacob grinned, and her tears broke loose with a reluctant laugh. "Good grief, he even smiles just like you, first one side, then a whole smile. He's a spitting image of you." Laura's teary gaze met Bryan's in a silent shared understanding. "What your wife did was terrible, Bryan, but it's past. Jacob needs you."

Bryan looked at his son as Jacob closed his eyes and rested his head on Bryan's shoulder. He picked up the thermal blanket, walked down the hall, and returned empty-handed.

When he came back, he again tried to explain the unexplainable. "I need time to work through this. It was so sudden. One day I was giving a 110 percent to my job, and the next, I'm trying to figure out how a baby thinks.

"My career is ready to take off, that'll mean more traveling, longer hours. It's all hitting at once. He deserves more than I have to give him."

"In a blink of the eye, Jacob will be ready for footballs, computers and girls. Where will you be? Still in the office, climbing that corporate ladder. For what? A son who doesn't even know you?"

Bryan wondered how she could read his mind and verbalize his fears after knowing him only three months. Already she'd made a difference in his son's life. In his too, if he'd admit it.

"Don't let whatever happened between you and your wife ruin what you and Jacob can have."

"I don't even know what happened between us, Laura. One day she was here, the next she was gone! And a year later, her son is creating total havoc in my life."

"He's not just her son!" The words ripped impatiently out of her mouth.

Bryan turned away. Laura had no idea what she'd just said. Had no idea how many times he'd hashed over dates, events and documents in the last few days, struggling to overcome doubts that he was Jacob's biological father. He needed time and distance from the baby to come to terms with Andrea's betrayal.

"Isn't there anything I can do to convince you, Bryan?"

He shook his head. "The decision's been made. Cass and her husband will be able to give him everything I can't."

"Everything you won't, you mean!" Laura stood and paced the floor. "Tell me that you don't love the idea of raising that little boy, Bryan—of coaching his football team, of sharing an ice-cream cone...."

"Stop it, Laura. This isn't your problem."

As if he'd totally worn her out, she clipped each word. "Put the past behind you."

Thinking of the many times he'd seen that dreamy look appear in her clear blue eyes when talking of her husband, Bryan realized she was as guilty as he. "Is *that* how you manage?" He turned and faced her, his voice thick with sarcasm. How different his life would be now if his wife had ever felt for him what Laura had for Todd.

She looked as if he'd slapped her. "I do the best I can, but I couldn't have made it through the past few months without God."

"I think I burned those bridges behind me a long time ago."

She lifted her chin, meeting his gaze straight on. Two deep breaths, and her anger was replaced with a serene confidence. "He doesn't keep score, Bryan. He knows your needs and is just waiting for the invitation to help."

"Sometimes, it's just not that easy...."

Jacob started crying, yet Bryan hesitated. Laura looked down the hall, then back to him. He could see the panic in her eyes, almost feel her heart racing, trying desperately to scheme a way to mend his rotting soul.

"There's a Sunday morning singles' class I've been attending. I was reluctant at first, but it's been very helpful. If you're interested...let me know."

She turned and walked out the door.

"Don't hold your breath," Bryan grumbled.

Chapter Eight

"Why do we have to go to another football game?" Carrie complained.

"It's not T.J.'s game, Carrie. It's the Broncos'. At Mile High Stadium, like on T.V." Laura poked the needle through the canvas and pulled the floss taught, then crossed the square to complete the stitch.

"It's still football."

Laura took a deep breath and counted to ten. After the way she'd lectured Bryan the week before, she figured she owed it to him to try his advice on parenting. "If you want to stay here, that's fine. You could go to Lisa's house while the boys and I are gone. I'm not making that decision for you. Just let me know your answer so I can let Bryan know how many tickets we'll need."

Her daughter straightened her back, the whiny attitude replaced with interest. "Bryan's going with us?"

"T.J.'s entire football team is going. They needed a parent to go along, and Bryan was nice enough to ask us."

She'd been ready to say no after their discussion on Thanksgiving day. But he'd come in the door the following Monday morning and admitted that she'd hit a nerve.

While he hadn't agreed to go to church with her, he seemed curious. For his and Jacob's sake, she vowed to do anything she could to convince Bryan to keep his son.

At the game a week later, Bryan absentmindedly handed a granola bar to one of the boys. He watched Kevin and Laura come down the steps with refreshments. Kevin leaned provocatively close, and she blushed in response to whatever he'd whispered in her ear.

Laura handed the tray of snacks to Carrie, who was sitting next to Bryan. As she stepped over several boys, tiptoeing through their gear, Laura lost her balance. Bryan jumped up, but it was Kevin who grabbed her around the waist and helped her regain her footing. Bryan's glare brought a raised eyebrow and mischievous smile from his friend.

This day couldn't end a minute too soon. It had been pathetic. The Broncos won, T.J. and the rest of the team had had a great time, Chad was enthralled with everything, and even Carrie appeared to have enjoyed herself. None of that mattered. It was Laura that had been the center of his attention. There was no doubt in his mind, she'd had a great time, too. Why wouldn't she? Kevin didn't taken his attention from her the entire game.

Daylight quickly faded into darkness during the last quarter. As they left the stadium, Kevin caught up to Bryan. "Great game, huh? Say, I've been thinking, Laura shouldn't drive back after dark with a bunch of kids to handle."

Bryan had thought the same thing, but reasoned that she had more experience dealing with a car full of kids than he did. Still, her van had been acting up lately and she might need help. He glared at Kevin. "Well, I guess that leaves you to do the noble duty then, doesn't it? I have to drive the company van."

Kevin smiled. "A man's gotta do what a man's gotta do."

"When did you become so chivalrous?" Bryan grumbled, and continued to lead the group back to the parking lot.

Laura helped the kids load their backpacks and accepted Kevin's offer to help with the kids. She followed close behind Bryan's van until they were on the interstate, then let the distance between them grow.

They arrived at the school twenty minutes earlier than expected, but streetlights illuminated the grounds. The kids raced to the playground as Kevin joined Bryan.

"That is one terrific woman," Kevin said.

Bryan watched his friend's gaze return to Laura, who was sorting through the scattered gear left in her van. As she leaned over the seat, he knew exactly what Kevin was thinking.

"Quit playing your games, Kevin. Not with Laura."

"Who says it's a game?"

Kevin tossed his coat into the company van, then returned to Laura, appearing to be offering his help. Bryan continued to supervise kids and greet parents. When Laura leaned over the middle seat, Kevin moved closer to her, blocking Bryan's view of her completely.

While they waited, Bryan threw the football with the boys, keeping one eye on Laura's van. He fought the temptation to see just how accurate his throwing arm was after all these years.

Why do I care? A woman is the last thing I need complicating my life right now! Forget her. In just three more weeks, Jacob will be with Cassandra, and everything will get back to normal.

He realized how much he had come to respect and admire Laura Bates. She was compassionate and sensitive. Charming and intelligent. Dignified and beautiful. And how he'd tried to ignore his growing feelings for her. Even reminding himself of Andrea's betrayal didn't taint the warmth he experienced when Laura was around. Their conversation from Thanksgiving day played over and over in his mind like a stuck record. If there'd been any doubt before, it became clear that day. Nothing meant more to Laura than her family. She'd never understand his decision.

Three weeks. If I can just survive three more weeks.

After the other parents left, she approached him.

"Thanks for the tickets, Bryan. We had a great time."

"Glad you could come. You and Kevin certainly seemed to enjoy yourselves."

"He's something else."

The smile on her face could have been considered admiration, could have been contempt; he wasn't sure.

"I'd be glad to fill you in on what makes him tick." Bryan wanted to warn her about Kevin—how he toyed with women, how he loved them and left them. *What a fool you'd be to fall for him, Laura Bates.*

"I already know what makes a man like him tick. Thanks anyway." She stepped back as Kevin joined them. "See you in the morning. Bye, Kevin."

"Later," his friend replied with the obvious intent to see her again.

Bryan watched Laura drive away, then got into the van and slammed the door. "Hands off, Kevin!"

"I never touched her," Kevin claimed, raising his hands, pleading innocence.

"You know what I mean."

"Thought you weren't interested."

"My wife just died!"

"Andrea's been out of your life for over a year. You're free to start dating again, and Laura seems like as good a place to start if you ask me."

"I didn't ask you, but that hasn't stopped you from throwing interference, has it? We have a professional working relationship. Nothing more."

"Right. That's why she brought you Thanksgiving dinner. Did she take any of the other families dinner?"

"Just admit that your stunt didn't work. You know as well as I do, that if any of the other families had been in the shape I was, she would have done the same. Laura takes care of everyone. That's as far as her feelings for me go."

"The question is, for how long?"

Bryan stared straight ahead, simmering with jealousy. She was a wonderful woman, possibly one who could blow Kevin's chauvinistic attitudes all to pieces, but in the end, it came down to the fact that he had no right to stop Kevin, and no intentions of exploring his own feelings for Laura.

He was about as interested in a wife and three more children as he was in eating quiche. Though if given a choice of kids, T.J., Carrie and Chad wouldn't be so bad. In fact, they were just what he'd hoped for so many years ago.

The next weekend he overheard Kevin on the phone. "Afternoon Laura, what do you say we take in a movie?"

Bryan stopped to listen.

"You never know, I could be the man of your dreams."

After a pause, Kevin cleared his throat.

"Well, when you change your mind, let me know. Goodbye, Mrs. Bates." Kevin hung up, mumbling to himself, "Imagine that woman trying to develop a conscience in me!" Kevin walked into the kitchen, obviously surprised to find Bryan was cleaning out the refrigerator.

"What are you doing now?" Kevin growled. "Next thing you know, you'll be cleaning closets and washing windows!"

"Laura is quite a lady, and she rattled you. I haven't seen a woman do that to you in a long time." Bryan razzed his friend, hoping he'd give up the matchmaking attempts.

Kevin had been the first one scheduled to make the trip to the altar, and the scars of being jilted still hadn't healed.

Yet, as sour as Kevin was about marriage, he seemed to think a family would take care of all Bryan's problems.

"Don't worry. No woman's going to get to me." Kevin turned to leave and called back over his shoulder, "But Laura Bates has gotten under your skin, friend, and it has nothing to do with 'professionalism.' May as well admit it."

"Not on my life." Bryan insisted. "We're down to two weeks."

"Fool," Kevin muttered as he closed the door to the den.

It had been a long day, and an even longer week. Bryan had left the office early to work out before picking Jacob up from Laura's. She looked up from the picture book she and Jacob were reading.

"Rough day, huh?"

Rough is losing a major account, this goes way beyond that. He grunted something in response and looked at his son.

"Bryan? You okay? Can I get you something, do something?"

"Yeah, go for a drink with me."

Laura didn't seem to need any prompting to see that he was upset and needed someone to listen. "Sure, I'll find someone to watch the kids. Would you like to leave Jacob here?"

"If you don't mind."

An hour later, Bryan and Laura sat in his sports car at a drive-in restaurant drinking their second round of root beer floats.

"Not that I mind the small talk, Bryan, but I don't think it's football that's upsetting you."

Bryan leaned his head back onto the leather seat, realizing that this woman's compassion threatened to fill his emptiness with emotions and aspirations he had long laid to rest. If they'd only met a few years earlier, or never at all. Especially not now.

"Maybe we should have made this a stout instead. Then at least you could cry in your beer."

"It's bad enough sober, it doesn't need help."

"Wouldn't you feel more comfortable talking to Kevin?"

His gruff response raised her eyebrows.

"Is there something I can do to help?"

She's not Andrea! Give her a chance. You trust her with your son's life every day. What do you treasure more than that? "Do you think I'm a terrible father for sending Jacob to my sister?"

She didn't even hesitate.

"No. I do wonder what's so painful that you feel it's necessary, though."

He stared at her. Why did he feel so comfortable talking to this woman? Was it her faith that gave her the strength to go through what she had, and remain so strong and appear content even when she claimed to have experienced the same emotions as he struggled with daily?

A package had arrived that afternoon with snapshots of Jacob right after his birth. Pictures of a woman he'd once loved, a woman he thought he'd known. The enclosed note had said, "One day, Jacob will want to know about his mother...." Bryan had never seen the blond-haired man before, and yet there he was, standing next to his wife and newly born son.

As if she hadn't noticed his lapse of attention, Laura was still speaking. "A terrible father wouldn't have thought about the benefits his son would have elsewhere. He'd do it simply because it made his own life easier."

Bryan shook his head, dispelling the notion of telling her everything. She'd talked about forgiveness. She hadn't a clue what she was suggesting he forgive. He took a long swallow, licked the foam from his lip, then dried it with the tail of his T-shirt.

Laura's eyes widened. If he weren't so irritated, he'd find it amusing that she thought him too sophisticated for such a juvenile habit. He smoothed the damp spot of his favorite college T-shirt, hoping to repair his image.

"I'm going to spend the day with Jacob tomorrow."

"Good." She looked out the passenger window. "It'll be good for you to spend some time with him before..." her voice caught, then she continued "...you go to your sister's."

"He has a checkup with the pediatrician, then I'm going to get him a few new clothes. Even though she'll have custody, I do plan to take care of the bills."

They were quiet. Bryan considered sharing the many reasons for his decision, but decided against it. He would get past it—alone. Once this was over, he'd put his feelings for Laura aside, and move on with his career. As much as he tried to tell himself that she didn't matter to him, he couldn't stop pushing her. "You don't agree with my decision."

"It's not my place to agree or disagree." Her voice was even. Calm. Disappointed?

Why it mattered to him what she felt, he couldn't say. They'd met merely four months ago over a common cause, caring for his son. And when it came to child rearing, the woman was certainly opinionated enough. She didn't understand what demands his job would involve, long hours, traveling....

Laura's soft voice pierced the silence. "Bryan, I won't tell you what to do. You have your reasons and priorities."

"Is that supposed to make me feel better?"

Her surprised expression was followed by a stammering attempt to explain that they were nothing alike, had nothing in common, that it was only natural that she would handle it differently because she was a woman, and the list went on. Somewhere amongst blushes and flailing hands, Bryan realized she was honestly trying to get her foot out of her mouth.

He'd been a fool to think she'd somehow absolve him of his guilt. He couldn't help but wonder if the forgiveness she talked about was him forgiving Andrea? Or her forgiving him?

Chapter Nine

Jeffrey's mother walked into the playroom with a basket of Christmas cookies. "Laura, I came up with an idea. Instead of you doing all the work for the Christmas party this year, all the families want to help. I suggested that we all go to the mountains and cut Christmas trees, then come here and help you decorate."

"It's nice of you to offer, but I know how busy everyone is. We'll manage."

"Everyone's already agreed. They think it sounds fun. We'll each bring something to eat, and the gift exchange has already been organized."

Laura smiled, choking back the urge to cry. "You are all so wonderful. I haven't even been able to think about it yet."

"I don't doubt it. I wish we could do more to make it easier. After all, you give our children so much."

She hadn't argued with Letisha any more, just accepted this as their way of helping her deal with yet another aspect of her grieving. Barb kept telling her she needed to learn to receive as well as give. It wasn't easy.

The cleaning was done, the kids were asleep, and silence echoed through the house. Laura pulled out a Christmas album and turned the stereo on. "I'll be Home for Christmas" came on the stereo. She closed her eyes, remembering last winter when Todd had returned from his conference....

"Leave your wet boots next to the door so you don't track snow all over," she'd reminded him. Todd had ignored her as usual, with that playful smile on his face. He removed his jacket and wrapped his strong arms around her. Their lips met and his cold hands teased the small of her back. The cold touch that usually annoyed her was more like striking a match....

Laura dried the tears as the song ended and wrapped her arms around herself. She wished this was just another of Todd's business trips, and that he would walk through the door and annoy her all over again.

But it wasn't, and Laura knew it was up to her to continue the Christmas traditions she and Todd had begun. Lighting the house, decorations, choosing presents for children less fortunate. She and the kids would make gifts and cookies for friends.

Friends... Her thoughts immediately went to Bryan and Jacob. The baby would only be coming two more weeks. While Laura knew that his aunt would love him and meet all his needs, she still regretted the separation between father and son.

And selfishly, she mourned her own loss. Through her own need, she had given her heart away as a mother would to an adopted child. She hadn't realized it until it was too late. Hadn't felt it happening, until Bryan had announced that Jacob would be leaving. And suddenly, she felt like a mother bear, wanting to fight for her cub. But each day, she reminded herself that she had no right to intrude.

She'd never become overly attached to any child in her care before. When she realized how much she loved Jacob, she had reasoned that since he'd been without a mother, she must have taken over the emotional commitment. Since Todd's death, nothing had been quite the same for her. Especially not her emotions.

Laura looked at the boxes she and the kids had brought down from the attic earlier that evening, hoping to forget that she only had a few more days with the adorable brown-eyed child. Hoping to forget the baby who needed stability, love, and his father.

Yet simply glancing at the box of decorations carried her mind back to another time, a happier time, thirteen years earlier, when she and Todd had cuddled in front of their Charlie Brown Christmas tree. Each year they'd added more homemade decorations to this collection of memories. Laura carefully unwrapped each treasure and wept.

"I have so much, Lord. Help me learn to celebrate instead of mourn. I don't understand why you left me alone to raise the children...but I trust you. Forgive my anger. Help me shed this shield of armor and live again, to serve you better. Show me what you hold for our future, Father."

Laura woke hours later to a beautiful morning, determined to make it a fun day for the children. She would not allow her self-pity to ruin their celebration. After breakfast Carrie made hot chocolate, while Chad and T.J. brought the sleds to the back of the van. The families arrived as scheduled and finalized plans.

She closed the front door, making sure it was locked.

"Would you mind if we ride with you?" the deep voice said in her ear.

Turning brought her face within inches of Bryan's. "With me? I mean us. No, I don't, I mean, of course you can."

"I thought the kids could help entertain Jacob."

"They'd like that. Oh, Bryan, I haven't told them he's leaving yet. I want to wait...."

"Still hoping I'll change my mind?" he guessed.

She felt her smile disappear. "I just want to wait until after Christmas. I don't want them to worry...that..." She stepped back, needing to collect her own thoughts. "You're welcome to ride along. Kids, get into the van," she called. "Why don't you get Jacob's car seat, and I'll get some toys."

Bryan left, looking as if he wanted to throttle her for getting her hopes up. The expression had disappeared by the time he returned.

The kids, as expected, loved entertaining the baby, and the distraction was refreshing for Laura. Even her conversation with Bryan was a pleasant change from the routine topics regarding life's challenges.

She was enchanted by his slow, deliberate speech as they discussed everything from politics to sports. The soft conversation swept her from the cold emptiness of reality to a dream where his voice, deep and soothing, warmed her like a blanket....

"Have you considered dating?"

It was as if he'd dumped a bucket of ice-cold water over her, shattering her rosy illusion. "What?"

"You have a habit of answering a question with another one. Did you realize that? What's wrong with the question?"

"It depends on why you're asking." She recalled Kevin's invitation, which Bryan probably knew nothing about, since he was asking about this topic in the first place.

"Why does that matter? You either have, or haven't."

"I haven't, then." Giving advice on moving on with life had proven much easier than following it. And she was in no condition right now to discuss that subject of dating, particularly not with Bryan. Laura glanced at him, then back to the road. "We should be almost there. Kids, don't leave this van without your gloves."

Laura continued with a list of warnings and reminders, filling the time before pulling to a stop behind Russ's white truck. Bryan glanced at her as if to say "you can't avoid the question forever."

They stopped and opened the doors. Carrie pulled a back carrier from the van and handed it to Bryan.

"Thanks. How about giving me some help getting him into it."

"It's easy, Jacob loves riding in it. Mom uses it a lot. Don't you have one?" Carrie asked incredulously.

"No, I don't."

"Well you should get one. My dad always carried us in it when we went fishing and hiking. Chad used to pull Daddy's hair, and he'd howl like a coyote. It was funny." Laura watched as Carrie showed Bryan how to adjust the straps.

Couldn't have planted a better seed if I'd tried. She hoped the roots of fatherhood dug its claws in deep, and soon. There wasn't much time left. More than anything, she wanted Bryan to change his mind. For himself, and Jacob. She couldn't imagine Bryan's life without his son.

By noon they had all found trees and were sledding and playing in the snow.

Laura felt a snowball hit her arm and turned to see Chad wide-eyed with delight. After tossing one back, she ran behind a tree for cover. Letisha had taken Jacob while Bryan helped load the trees onto the pickup.

By the time the men had finished, several parents had joined the friendly battle. Laura had dodged numerous snowballs and soon became the prime target.

Bryan checked on Jacob, who had fallen asleep on Letisha's back. "Thanks for watching Jacob. Let me relieve you."

"I'm fine, Bryan. Go join the fun," Letisha suggested.

"Thanks. Looks like the kids need some help." He called Laura's children over and formed a huddle.

"No fair, Bryan. You can't help them." Laura stopped to catch her breath.

"Just offering a few suggestions," he said, popping up out of the huddle momentarily. The kids laughed, then scattered.

Letisha retreated, offering the toddlers a snack in the van. As soon as the kids were safely inside, Laura smashed Bryan in the jaw with a snowball as he was bent over to make a snowball. He jolted upright. His brown eyes seemed to dare her to try it again, which she immediately regretted when the next frozen lump left her glove and plastered itself on his jeans.

"Oh, now you've done it, Laura Bates."

"Beginner's luck," Laura said as she backed up. "No, Bryan." She felt a tingly sensation, then turned and ran.

"No Bryan, what? You expect mercy?"

She laughed. "Forgiveness."

"Retaliation is more fun." Bryan tackled her and she fell into the powdery snow. Still holding her down, he playfully threw handfuls of fresh snow at her.

Laura begged for help, but none came. His gaze seemed to look right through her.

From her children she heard resounding applause and merriment. "Yea!"

"Get her, Bryan!"

"Ye ha!" Russ added a few more raucous cheers for the cause.

Bryan helped her up, then turned her in front of him.

Laura realized what he was doing, yet couldn't pull loose. "Oh, no, you don't, let me go."

"How can I take you seriously when you're laughing?" His strong hands wrapped around her middle. "You brought this on yourself. Come on, kids, this is your chance to get your mom." Carrie was the first in line. Bryan ducked as Carrie nearly hit him in the shoulder. "Hey there, remember who you're after. Aim low. Not at the face. We don't want anyone getting hurt."

They all took their shots. After several misses and a few

hits, Laura was able to knock Bryan off balance, and they both toppled back into the snow, laughing.

Laura wriggled free, brushed herself off, and headed for the van. Bryan caught up with her, his words warming her, even as she fought the reaction.

"You okay?"

"Why wouldn't I be?" She told herself to keep focusing on the van, but her eyes betrayed her. She couldn't resist smiling back at his half grin. "I'm fine. We haven't had a snowball fight in years. I probably shouldn't have done it with the little kids right here."

"I think they knew it was all in fun."

"I didn't mean to hit you in the face, you bent over at the wrong time."

He rubbed his jaw, playing it up good. "Beginner's luck, my foot." When he finished the sentence with a smile, Laura relaxed. Bryan helped her brush snow off the kids' clothing and made sure everyone was buckled in before they headed home.

Between the kids' interruptions and Jacob's crankiness, Bryan never had a chance to bring up the discussion on dating again.

The caravan of families went to Laura's home for a late lunch. Afterward, when the younger kids were put down for naps, the rest started decorating the house.

Two of the fathers helped put the tree in the stand, while the other three worked on hanging the lights from the eaves. Laura watched, close to tears, as her house was transformed for the holidays in the true spirit of Christmas.

When they had finished, Bryan placed a hand on her shoulder and escorted her inside. "Thanks for helping us through these past few months, Laura."

"I was only doing my job." She hoped the words sounded more truthful than they felt.

She looked up at him, but a splash of color on the ceiling caught her attention. She was stunned to see mistletoe above her. "Who did this?" Laura stretched, but couldn't reach the sprig.

No one claimed responsibility, and Bryan laughed as she pulled a chair across the room.

Letisha led Russ to the entryway and gave her husband a loving kiss. "I vote you leave it up."

"You would," Laura said as she playfully pushed them aside.

Letisha protested. "Aw come on, spread a little Christmas joy, Scrooge."

"I'll be glad to send it back home with you, Letisha." Laughter filled the room, and the attention shifted back to decorating. A warm strong hand pulled her away from the chair as she stepped up. "Bry-an," she growled.

"Leave it, or I may have to throw you back into the snowdrift," he whispered.

The twinkle in his eyes said she wouldn't be alone. She forced a polite grin. "I don't get mad, I get even."

"Even better."

Impaled by his steady gaze, Laura was amazed at the delight she felt. Jeffrey called her, and to Laura's relief, Bryan let her go. "I'll help you get the kids up."

"Thanks anyway," she managed to say. "We have a routine. It won't take long." Laura took extra time getting the little ones ready, hoping to regain her composure before she returned.

The party culminated with the exchange of gifts. She received a month of a cleaning service from one family, several certificates for local restaurants, a therapeutic massage, and a sweatshirt with a pair of dolls on it. Laura gave each of the children their gifts, hand-stitched ornaments and a bag of their favorite books. It had been a day full of fun, and everyone was tired.

Bryan was the last to leave. After he managed to get Jacob into his snowsuit, Laura walked with him to the door.

"It was a fun day. Thanks," he said.

"It was, wasn't it? We'll enjoy the dinner certificate. Not cooking is always a treat. And thanks so much for teaching my kids the art of snowball fights."

"You never know when it may come in handy."

"Have a good evening," She noticed him grin, then look up at the mistletoe. Before she could back away, he wrapped his free arm around her, pulled her closer, and kissed her. It wasn't just a brotherly peck, but a long, tender kiss.

When he let her go seconds later, she stumbled backward.

Bryan looked as surprised as she felt.

"I'm sorry, Laura. I didn't plan that."

Laura couldn't speak. *What do you say after a kiss that makes your heart do flips?*

"Are you mad?"

"Mad? No. Surprised...confused maybe. It's been forever since anything like that happened to me."

"Yeah, I know."

"What do you mean, you know?" she said sharply.

"I mean, me too, since I reacted that way. I'm sorry." Bryan opened the door, and backed away.

Fighting the heat that was rushing through her, she forced herself to hide her true reaction. "Don't worry about it. It was nothing."

"Right. Nothing. I'll see you tomorrow."

Laura closed the door behind him. Her heart took too much time to resume its usual speed, and it took several slow deep breaths to eliminate the light-headedness. *I must be lonelier than I thought, if one careless kiss could affect me this way! He didn't even mean anything by it. It was just the mistletoe. A man like Bryan couldn't be interested in me. Could he?*

Laura sent the kids to bathe and get ready for bed. After reading a chapter from *The Christmas Stranger,* she straightened Chad's covers while the other two went to their bedrooms.

"Mom, can we adopt a new daddy?"

"You don't adopt a daddy, Chad." She grinned. He missed his daddy, there was no doubt, but how could Laura ever hope to replace such a wonderful husband and father?

"Why not?"

She tried to explain, but he didn't understand.

"Bryan could be our daddy," Chad suggested.

Laura's hands covered her mouth and she let out a long sigh. "Bryan is a friend, but I don't think he's quite right."

"He's a great football player. And he's strong. I like wrestling with him. He's fun."

Forcing herself to sit instead of pacing the room, Laura struggled to remain calm. "Is that what's important to you?" She brushed the hair from her son's brow. Laura felt so strange talking to her son about finding another father, especially so soon after Todd's death. She'd expected this at some point, but definitely not yet.

Her son was reciting a list of desired qualities he wanted in a father. "Well, he has to like sports, and fishing. Daddy liked those, and so do I. Bryan's taller than you, huh, Mom? The dad has to be taller than the mom."

Laura hated seeing her kids so lonely. They missed Todd as much as she did, but the comparison wasn't even near the same—a daddy and a husband. "Dad's aren't always taller, Chad. But, I'm not ready to find you a new daddy yet. And when I am ready, I can't just go out and pick one...."

"Why not? I asked God to help us find just the right one."

"Well," she replied, "I need to know a lot about a man before I could marry him." Laura gave up the fight and paced.

"Like what?"

"Like if he believes in Jesus. If he likes children. All kinds of things."

"Bryan goes to church."

She froze. "What?"

"I saw him there last week. And he likes us just fine. I'll ask him if you want me to."

He went to church? Our church? "It's just not that easy, honey. I'd need to know that whoever I consider marrying loves all of us before I could marry him. And Bryan…well, I don't want you to say anything to him about being your daddy. He has enough to worry about with Jacob. Okay, Chad?" Laura's voice was stern.

He made a face and grumbled, turning away from her.

"Chad…"

He looked back at his mother. "But Mom, he's just right."

"No Chad. I know you like Bryan, but you have to promise me you won't ask him."

He ignored her, and she repeated the demand.

"Okay."

Laura groaned. "You go to sleep now. I love you very much. Maybe someday, honey…but not yet."

She tucked T.J. and Carrie into bed and tried to finish writing Christmas cards, but her thoughts returned again and again to Bryan's kiss—and Chad's longing for another father. Her head rested against the high back of the couch as she gazed at the twinkling lights on the Christmas tree. She recalled the ease with which Bryan had joined with the other families, and the warmth with which they'd welcomed him.

The news that he'd gone to their church had also surprised her. Not that she'd expected him to go with her really, but she would have been glad to have introduced him to some of the other members, had she known he was there. At the time, she wouldn't have thought anything of being seen with him, but after today she wondered…

Her finger touched her lips. As much as she wanted to stop picturing herself kissing him, she couldn't. His kiss was so sweet and gentle, and wonderful....

What am I doing? Bryan's a client! And I kissed him back. I must have seemed starved. What in the world must he think?

The snowball fight. He must have thought I was flirting. She stood up and marched to the phone, ready to set things straight. Then she set the receiver down. *It was only a kiss, Laura. In just a few days, he'll be out of your life anyway. Just forget it.*

She straightened the kitchen, then folded laundry, but her mind wouldn't let it go. After all, she reasoned, kisses like that didn't happen just any day. How long had it been since Todd had kissed her with such enthusiasm?

Laura crawled between the cold sheets and turned out the light. She recalled the day she had interviewed Bryan. In his double-breasted suit and silk tie, he looked more like a stockbroker from Wall Street than a computer analyst in a rural town like Springville. He'd been self-absorbed, and rigid, and about as comfortable holding his baby as dancing the ballet.

Over the past four months, he'd changed. In recent weeks, he'd even helped put toys away before they left, took the time to tie a child's shoelace, and he'd even replaced Rachel's frilly hair ribbon once.

Refined, punctual and thoughtful were traits that described Bryan Beaumont. Listing his assets wasn't the wisest thing to do right now, she reminded herself. She was a new widow, and he was still grieving his broken marriage. And in just a few weeks, he'd be giving his son away. There was no way she'd let herself be remotely interested in a man like that. No way.

Laura closed her eyes. Suddenly she sat up and clapped her hands to her face. "Oh no," she whispered. "God, you can't be answering last night's prayer already. Not so soon…"

Chapter Ten

William hen Bryan saw Laura at church the next morning, it was clear that she planned to avoid him. He'd thought about not coming today, but decided it would be a perfect opportunity to let her know he'd been coming to church without getting into a lengthy explanation. After that kiss, he figured she'd be curious about his motives, but doubted that she'd question him here.

Bryan had called his secretary the day after Thanksgiving to find out which church Laura attended. He'd blamed her for the two nights of insomnia he'd suffered after that holiday visit. No matter how he tried to deny it, somehow, she'd reached right past his defenses and touched his soul. It wasn't a comfortable feeling, and he'd come to church to prove, as much to himself as to Laura, that he didn't belong here.

Convinced that he'd blown it for good during his wild college years, Bryan had shoved his faith aside. It wasn't until recently that he'd remembered a verse from Psalms that a Sunday school teacher had recited over and over: ''For as far as the east is from the west, so far does He remove our transgressions from us.''

He figured that must be why he was here for the third week in a row. It felt right. Just as right as holding her had felt. He was overwhelmed by the changes he'd experienced in the last month. First reestablishing his relationship with Christ, then releasing his anger toward his wife, and now, in the midst of everything, were these confusing feelings he had for his son's caregiver.

Nothing would have pleased him more than to deny the attraction. If only she wouldn't have reacted so perfectly. Her feelings for him were as jumbled as his were for her. He'd seen the apprehensive joy in her eyes during the snowball fight and the way his teasing had made her shy away during the party. She felt it, too. Yet she'd been as shocked as he by the passion of the kiss they shared. He'd seen it in her eyes.

Knowing it wouldn't take much for Laura to overreact to his being here, explanations were the last thing he wanted today. He didn't want to see the satisfaction on her face. Because along with that satisfaction would be the expectation to change his plans for Jacob as well. And he couldn't try to explain that to her again. Every time he did, his reasons sounded more and more lame, even to himself.

Bryan couldn't explain why he'd kissed her, either. It was impulsive. It made no sense at all. He thought everything through very carefully before making any move. Even when it came to women. Especially when it came to women. The only thing he'd decided, was that Kevin had finally gotten to him.

Because Laura was everything Andrea wasn't.

She was gentle and wise and beautiful with a simplicity that could easily be overlooked. Her inner strength enhanced her femininity. She was accustomed to being depended upon, yet still fought to be self-reliant. The guilt of enjoying his kiss must be eating her alive. He couldn't help but wonder if her shoulders ever tired of the burdens she carried.

Bryan watched her climb the stairs ahead of him. As she rushed ahead of him, her heel caught in the folds of her skirt. When she landed, he helped her to her feet.

"No need to run, I don't see any mistletoe," he teased, taking advantage of the crowded doorway to whisper in her ear.

"I wasn't running," she said indignantly, "and I'd rather you forget what happened yesterday." She walked into the classroom and poured a cup of coffee.

He followed. "No harm done. I'm sure it was only that you were carried away in a wave of holiday spirit."

"Me?" She spun around and looked up, fixing her crystal blue eyes on his. They were full of challenge. "That's not funny."

"Yes, it is. Lighten up."

She cast him a wary glance. "Chad says you've been coming to church for a couple of weeks. Why didn't you say anything?"

He shrugged his shoulders. So he was wrong. He should have known she wouldn't shy away from the issue. "I didn't want to let you down if it didn't feel right."

"Let me down? I don't want you here for any reason besides your own faith." Laura glanced around, and Bryan, too, noted the curious glances they were receiving. After all, he was a newcomer, and she had been a widow less than a year. For some reason, it pleased him to see her friends watching out for her.

"Another good reason not to tell you." He'd been thinking a lot about his future lately, and he regretted that he'd totally ignored his faith. His parents had set a great example; they'd never missed a Sunday sitting in the fourth pew of their small town church. The songs had changed, but the people hadn't. There were times when watching families around him, that he could almost feel his father's hand upon his own shoulder, just as he had twenty years ago. It had been a long time since he'd felt such peace in his life.

Their banter was interrupted as the leader started class with a simple prayer. The class discussion was on the difficulty of creating traditions during the holidays as a single or in a single-parent family.

"Changing traditions isn't always a matter of sentiment," Laura suggested. "Todd and I have taken the kids to see the lights and nativity at the civic center in Denver since they were babies. It's something I want to continue, but I wouldn't feel safe driving through that part of Denver alone, let alone walking up there like we did."

Others shared their sentiments and ideas to keep the holidays special when life circumstances change. After class, Bryan lagged behind the others as they moved into the fellowship hall for refreshments. He hesitated with the sudden idea, unsure how she'd receive his invitation after yesterday.

"Hi, Bryan."

"Morning, Chad. How're you today?"

"I'm okay. My mom said you have your hands full with Jacob, and I shouldn't bother you, but…"

"Chad! Will you go find T.J. and Carrie for me, please?"

The boy looked as if he'd been caught with his hand in the cookie jar as he turned and ran down the hall. Laura watched her son disappear around the corner, seeming relieved.

Bryan wondered what the boy wanted to ask him. Knowing Chad, it was bound to be from the heart. From day one, Chad had tugged on Bryan like no other child had ever done. He was the kid no one could miss. He knew what he wanted, and always had a plan on how to get it.

While Laura filled her foam cup with coffee and added cream and sugar, Bryan made his suggestion. "Why don't we take the kids to see the Christmas lights in Denver tonight? I hate to see you and the kids miss a family tradition over a technicality so easily resolved.''

Laura stared at the cream as it blended with her coffee. ''I don't think that's a good idea. It's been a really full weekend. I have to do laundry and get groceries and…''

''I promise it won't happen again.''

She struggled with the mixed emotions. Even though she knew she shouldn't have enjoyed his kiss so much, it was difficult to deny that she'd come this morning half in anticipation, half in dread of just such a statement. Consoling herself that any woman would have been flattered to have been kissed by an attractive man such as Bryan, Laura brushed an invisible speck from her prairie-style skirt.

''Think about it. I'll even throw in dinner, since we'll have to take your van.''

She started to protest, but Bryan disappeared. Carrie and T.J. joined her while Laura was talking to an ex-teammate of Todd's. Chad returned a few minutes later with Bryan and Jacob in tow.

Bryan's scrutiny of the man beside her didn't go unnoticed, but she had no time to dwell on it, as Chad interrupted the conversation. ''Mom, Bryan wants us to go to Denver to look at the Christmas lights with him tonight. Can we? Pl-ea-se?''

Laura excused herself from the other gentleman, then turned to Chad. ''I have a lot of work to do today, Chad.''

Her son urged Laura to bend down and whispered loudly into her ear, ''Please Mom, then you can ask Bryan…''

''Chad! Go get another cookie,'' she snapped, noting the grin on Bryan's face. She turned to Carrie and T.J. ''You two may get some juice and a cookie, too.''

When the three children were gone, she turned to Bryan. ''It's hard enough saying no without the guilt they lay on me.'' She glanced at Jacob, content in Bryan's arms and remembered her vow to do anything to keep Bryan and Jacob together.

"I'm sorry, didn't think of that."

The trip to see the spectacular Christmas display at the civic center and the skyscrapers all lit with sparkling lights had always been one of Todd's favorite traditions with his children. And if she was lucky, Bryan would share that same joy with his son. Todd would approve of this mission.

"This has nothing to do with yesterday."

"Nothing."

"If you're sure you don't mind going."

"I wouldn't have offered."

Laura picked Bryan and Jacob up late that afternoon. They stopped at an Italian restaurant in the downtown area for dinner. Her children had chattered nonstop, barely eating a strand of spaghetti they were so excited. Laura apologetically offered to pay for the wasted meals.

Bryan refused, claiming it was worth it to see them happy. She thanked him and asked him to drive since he was more familiar with downtown Denver.

As they rounded the curve to pass the display of lights, Laura looked back at Jacob, noting the distance between father and son. "Would you mind finding a place to park, Bryan? We like to walk past. It's so much more meaningful up close."

He smiled as if he were dealing with a temperamental child. Finding a parking place took nearly half an hour, then it was a twenty-minute walk to the civic center. Laura refused to let Bryan take a turn carrying Chad, who repeatedly claimed to be tired.

The plan was for Bryan and his own son to bond and create memories, not to complicate her own son's feelings for the man. As they approached, the music grew louder, grabbing Jacob's attention. When the baby turned and saw the lights, he squealed with delight. Laura held her own children close to keep them from interfering.

Bryan lifted his son higher, pointing to the different displays. Jacob turned and kicked with excitement, alternately nuzzling his father's shoulder.

Tears stung her cold cheeks, and Laura turned away, hoping he'd missed the wistful gaze that had passed between them. Several minutes later, they returned to the van, joining the piped-in Christmas tunes. She drove, following his directions through the downtown area, keenly aware of his scrutiny.

She waited until the children had fallen asleep before venturing into a conversation. "Thank you for coming, Bryan. As you could see, it means as much to the kids as it did Todd and myself."

"I had a nice time. I'm glad you accepted."

"Me, too." She attempted to keep the conversation going, but all she received were simple answers, and the van fell into silence as the disc jockey rambled on about shopping and children's dreams of presents.

Today's snowstorm was just another in a series of storms to pass through the state in the past two weeks. Seeing the magic of the holiday through the eyes of the children warmed her heart. They'd sung songs, painted, and read Christmas stories that morning, and after nap time, Laura took the preschoolers outside to play. They'd only been out a few minutes when the rambunctious four-year-old yelled.

"Bryan! Snowball fight."

She looked up from the snowman they were building to see Bryan in an Italian suit. Laura mentally confessed how out of place he looked here among the children.

A slight dimple on one cheek preceded his smile as the three-year-old girl with pigtails lifted her arms for Bryan to pick her up. He lifted her high above his head then held her in the crook of his arm. Rachel laughed.

Laura was stunned, not only by the action, but by the look of pleasure in his eyes. He tickled the little girl and set her down. Laura admonished herself for holding on to the hope that Bryan would change his mind about being a father.

"Sorry kids, no snowball fight today."

"Hi. Are you early, or is it later than I thought?"

"Both. I decided I'd put in enough hours this week. With the holiday everyone was taking off early."

She brushed the snow off the little one's clothes before going inside, and served dinosaur-shaped crackers and juice.

Bryan set Jacob in the high chair with a handful of cereal, then straddled the chair backward. "What do you say to a walk this evening?"

She tried to ignore his boyish mannerisms and concentrate on the suit that confirmed how different they really were. *After today, we'll have nothing in common.* "It'll be dark soon. I can't leave the kids home alone."

"I planned to go to the health club. They have child care there, and we won't have to deal with the weather. How does an hour sound?"

There was no use prolonging their relationship. He hadn't changed his mind at all. "I'm not a member."

"You can be my guest. Besides, you owe me one, remember? One last chance to pay up."

Last chance. She'd wanted to talk to Bryan about Jacob, to see if there was any hope he'd change his mind.

It had been a busy week and she could use some time away from the kids before the long vacation ahead. Weather reports predicted another arctic storm descending on the area, bringing subzero temperatures. There had been snow on the streets for a week, and cabin fever was taking its toll on her patience. She'd promised the kids she would take them swimming tonight, and wasn't sure how they would accept the change of plans.

"I promised the kids we'd do something tonight, but we could go after that."

Carrie and Chad ran in the front door and around Laura, already in the middle of a high-speed chase. "What's going on?"

"He told Devon I like him." The girl broke into tears.

"Chad. We've talked about teasing your sister."

Chad tried to escape his sister's angry grip. "We're going swimming tonight, Bryan. Can you come with us? We want him to, don't we, Mom?"

Laura grabbed each child as they ran by and pulled them apart, not sure how to mend her daughter's broken heart. At the same time, Laura was aware of how rude it would be to un-invite Bryan under the circumstances. "Bryan has other plans tonight."

Bryan took Jacob's snowsuit from the coatrack and spread it on the sofa. "Sounds great. Bring your swimsuits, and we'll take the kids to the pool after our walk. It looks like they have energy to burn."

"I couldn't impose on you like that. I'm sure I could find a sitter for later."

"Don't bother. Pool's right there." Bryan zipped Jacob's jacket, and pulled the infant's hood up.

Laura struggled for another excuse to turn down his tempting offer. As if he sensed her true feelings, he interrupted her thoughts. "Meet us there. Kids, help your mom get ready." Chad slapped Bryan a high five and ran to his room to change. Carrie and T.J. exchanged smiles, then disappeared as well.

Laura felt as if she'd just been ambushed.

Chapter Eleven

Laura wore a pair of paint-spattered sweats and an oversize T-shirt that Bryan figured had been Todd's. Why, even dressed like that, did she look so darned cute?

After the kids were settled, they went to the indoor track, immediately falling into a matching stride.

He couldn't shake the feeling of gloom that pressed on his heart. "You looking forward to your vacation?"

She shrugged. "We haven't been to Todd's parents' cabin since he died. I don't expect it to be easy. You?"

"I think you know the answer to that."

"I'd like to think I know the answer, but I don't."

Bryan couldn't explain why he hesitated to tell her his reasons. As a child care provider, there was no doubt in his mind that Laura was trustworthy. But as a friend, his heart still needed reassurance. That would take time.

"I believe that you want to understand, Laura."

"I can imagine the pain you're feeling, and I don't blame you for being angry, but...Bryan..."

"Laura, I admire your dedication to your children and your job. This is all so new to me. My job will be demanding more and more time. I think it would be different— No, I know it would be, if Jacob had a mother to…maintain a balance in both of our lives. With Cassandra and her husband, Jacob will have everything. He'll have sisters and a dog and all the attention a child deserves. I want more for my son than a part-time father who knows nothing about being a parent.''

"You're wrong, Bryan. Unfortunately, I do understand."

"Unfortunately?"

"There's never been a more challenging time to be a parent than now. Past generations could at least claim ignorance, but not us. There's a class for every stage of a child's life. We have no excuses, and yet, when it comes right down to it, it all boils down to one thing. Love. You love Jacob. I know you must."

He nodded. When he'd seen Laura and Kevin at the football game, he realized how much more he wanted in his life. Yes, he wanted a family, had always wanted one, but Andrea had taken his son, and his trust. He wondered if that could ever be repaired.

"Do you ever think about a family?"

"Of course I do. With three children, it's never far from my mind."

"I mean…a dad for your kids…a husband."

Laura faltered. "I'm not looking for a dad, or a husband. Being the sole breadwinner and a mother is plenty to handle."

"What if the right man came along?"

"You're beginning to sound like your roommate. To be honest, I'm growing fond of setting my own schedule, making my own decisions.…" her voice trailed off. "Sometimes being single isn't so bad," she said softly.

Liar. It stinks, every blasted minute of it. "You don't want to remarry?"

"I didn't say that. I mean, I hope one day that the right man might come along."

"Have anyone particular in mind?" He tried to get her

to look at him. She had to be feeling what he was. He
wanted to see the fear in her eyes.

"I haven't been looking." Laura stared at the floor, obviously determined not to meet his glance.

"What about Kevin?"

"Kevin?" Laura finally looked up and laughed, seeming
almost relieved. "Thanks anyway, but I'm not interested in
being set up. We'd better take the kids swimming before it
gets too late."

Bryan watched her hurry off the track and disappear
through the locker-room doors. Did she mean what she'd
said? Or was she as afraid to become involved as he was?

Laura stepped into the pool area and dived into the water
before the boys arrived. Carrie sat along the edge, working
her way into the tepid water. She was still faltering when
Chad and T.J. jumped into the water, ready to play.

"Bryan went to check on Jacob. He told us to come on
in," T.J. informed her with obvious pleasure at having been
given the responsibility of passing along the message.

"Mom, they splashed me!" Carrie stomped over to her
towel and sat down.

"We came here to swim, Carrie. Just get in and have
fun. Let's not argue." She looked at the locker-room door,
nervously waiting for Bryan to appear.

"I hate swimming...."

"Carrie..."

Chad threw a plastic ring and Laura dived to get it. As
she came up from the bottom, she looked right at a brawny
form diving into the pool and popping up out of the water
inches from her.

"Hi."

Before she could say anything, Bryan scooped her up
and let her go with a big splash.

She came up and spit out a mouthful of water. "Bryan!
How dare you?"

"You're wet anyway, Mom," Carrie mimicked from her sanctuary.

Laura paused, pushing the wet hair off her face. "Yes, I am, aren't I?" Then, turning to Bryan, she whispered, "Watch out, I get even."

Something had changed between them in the last week. She wasn't at all sure that she liked or even knew what it was. When he was near, she was anxious. And when he was gone, he was in her thoughts more than not.

The kids saw Bryan's antics and begged for his attention. Laura smiled mischievously, letting them drag him away. After swimming a few laps, she waved goodbye. From around the corner of the locker room, Laura watched as Bryan persuaded Carrie to join the fun. Chad and T.J. were ruthless with him. Carrie watched longingly. She wondered who would be more worn out by the end of the night—the kids, or Bryan.

Inside the locker room, she stepped into the Jacuzzi bath. She closed her eyes, imagining Bryan relaxing in his chair, watching a football game. There would be no Italian suit, no expensive shirts and ties, no fine leather loafers. Just a man in a soft T-shirt and jeans. The vision was so clear that Laura had to remind herself that an astute executive like Bryan would never be content spending his evenings helping kids with homework, making dinner or repairing broken toys.

No. There was no room in her life for a man who couldn't make time for his own son, let alone someone else's. Perhaps Bryan was right after all—Jacob would be better off with his aunt.

Before she became light-headed from the high temperature, Laura went to the nursery and returned to the pool with Jacob. After getting Bryan's approval to take Jacob into the water, Laura stepped in and let him splash around.

"Mom, watch this! Bryan taught me to dive without getting out of the pool." Carrie showed off her new skill, obviously indebted to Bryan for his guidance. When she surfaced, Laura noticed the change in her daughter's attitude.

This, is crazy. Allowing my children to become attached to a man I can't have. I should never have let any of us get this close to any client, especially a man who wants no part of fatherhood.

She couldn't fault Bryan alone. She'd vowed to show him how wonderful parenting could be, without considering the downfalls. Now and then, she'd seen a hint of satisfaction and pure joy in his eyes. From her own perspective, it had been worth the effort, but had she done so at the expense of her own children's hopes and expectations?

Laura complimented her daughter and prompted the children to get ready to go. After some grumbling about not being tired, then rubbing their eyes, even Bryan admitted it was time to get Jacob home. He took the boys to the locker room and met Laura and Carrie in the lobby after they were all dressed.

As the kids raced to the van, Bryan said, "Let me take you and the kids for dinner."

"Thanks anyway, Bryan. We stayed later than I'd expected."

"You don't want to have to cook now." As if he knew her next argument, he continued. "At least let me buy you some burgers."

"I'm sure you have a lot of packing to finish before you leave tomorrow." She picked up Jacob and gave him a long hug and kiss. "Have a Merry Christmas, Jacob, Bryan." She zipped his snowsuit and handed him to Bryan. "Goodbye, Jacob. If there's anything I can do to help, Bryan, just call."

"I can't thank you enough."

"I just did my job." Laura turned to the van, her eyes fogged over with tears.

* * *

It was their last night at home. As Jacob snuggled, Bryan tentatively drew him closer.

He remembered this desperate need to hold and be held from the night his father died. Bryan rocked his son, looking at the child's tiny fingers next to his own.

Jacob had a crooked finger on his right hand just as he did. How had he missed it before?

The infant reached his hand up and touched Bryan's whiskers.

Bryan grinned as his son frowned and pulled his tiny hand back, then repeated the process. It became a game, and Jacob laughed as Bryan growled, bending his head close so his face was easier for Jacob to reach.

"I haven't the foggiest idea what to do Jacob. I wish everything had been different for you."

Bryan remembered his own father lathering his face, raising his chin and stroking the razor until there wasn't a spot left that wasn't smooth. His dad would slap on aftershave then gently take Bryan's cheeks in his big strong hands and pretend to share the masculine aroma. It'd been years since he'd thought of his own childhood.

Could he deny his desire to be a father and raise his son? Was Laura right? Would he regret his decision later? Yes. He already did. Why else had the past month been so difficult? For the first time in over a year, Bryan faced the darkness that had controlled his every waking moment since Andrea walked out of his life. His dreams of a family had gone with her—or had they?

Jacob pushed the bottle away and Bryan helped his son stand up on his lap. He imagined the two of them playing dinosaurs, crashing Matchbox cars, and throwing a football in the park.

This little guy who looked just like him, would grow into a boy, then a man. And he should be the one responsible to help his son make that journey.

Watching Jacob's angelic face as he fell asleep, sucking his bottle again, tears filled Bryan's eyes. "I'm sorry, Jacob. I do love you, Son." He held Jacob close, set the bottle on the dresser, then carried his son to his crib and pulled the blanket over his small arms.

Bryan grinned as Jacob's pursed lips began sucking again. "You're the luckiest kid in the world to have Laura as a part-time mom. She's a very special woman."

Bryan opened the suitcase and removed the stacks of tiny clothing from the dresser. He finished folding the laundry, added it to the bag, then zipped it closed.

In the months after Andrea moved out, she had taken everything that had meant anything to him. Including the hope of having his own family.

Without telling him, she'd taken his son.

The child that had meant commitment.

Responsibility.

Family.

Jacob Alexander Beaumont. Bryan eyed the birth certificate. Andrea had named their son after both grandfathers, and wrote Bryan's name on the birth certificate. "Why, Andrea? Why didn't you tell me about him?

"You used to say, 'Love conquers all,' Dad. I gave her all I had, but it was never enough. If it wasn't good enough for her, how could it ever be enough for our son?"

Chapter Twelve

Moonlight glistened across the glacial valley. Another storm had left its mark on the already buried terrain. Nearly five feet of snow had kept the kids busy sledding and building a snow fort for the past week, but the isolation had crushed Laura.

Meal after meal, food lay on her plate uneaten. The days were haunted by memories and nights she spent pacing the cabin floor. She had to get away. Laura wrote a note and left it on the table, then drove to the property where she and Todd had dreamed of building their own cabin one day.

Not only had memories of Todd here at his parents' cabin become more than she could handle, but the guilt over her feelings for Bryan plagued her, too. *Why did I let myself get so close to another man devoted to his job? My kids have already lost their father, and now Bryan. How could I put them through that kind of pain again?*

I failed again. I couldn't save Todd, nor could I convince Bryan of his value as a father. How do I explain to the kids that Bryan chose to give his son away? And Jacob. How will he feel as a young man, to know that his father didn't want him?

She stopped the van at the west entrance of the acreage and shifted into park, feeling the repeated anguish of loss and the torture of guilt eating away at her. Helplessly she murmured, "Why do I keep losing the people I love? Please, God, make it stop. You promised not to give me more than I can handle. Surely you can't expect more of me than this."

After a lengthy conversation with God, she shifted to drive and a quarter of a mile later, turned onto the gravel turnout. The road was impassable, but she watched the sun rise over the mountains from the van. The spears of light glistened with morning frost.

During Laura and Todd's years of college, weekends were spent here, in the seclusion of the southwestern Colorado mining town. Originally, there had been six one-room cabins on the once operating dude ranch. All but two had burned down during prohibition. As their family had grown, Todd's grandparents had built a larger, modernized cabin.

Laura had always loved stepping back to another time: cooking on the woodstove, carrying water from the spring, lighting the lanterns, and even the outhouse up the hill had held a unique charm. It was always good to go home to modern conveniences.

Surrounding her was evidence of hardship and perseverance. Abandoned structures—some barely standing—with sod roofs, gnarled tree limbs, and broken wagon wheels served as historical monuments right there on her land. Somehow generations had survived under much worse conditions than she was being asked to do.

"Saying goodbye to you is difficult, Todd. Here, of all the places we shared and built our life together, is the hardest. I know you don't want me to cry. I miss you. I need you. I can't do this alone."

After her admission, she felt free. Free from the expectations to take care of others. Free from the guilt of finding

Bryan so attractive. Free from everything. Momentarily at least.

She dried her tears, pulled a bag from her pocket, and stepped out of the van. She strapped the snowshoes to her boots and trekked through the forest, silent except for the brushing of her own shuffling feet. Clusters of naked aspen trees stood rigid against the bitter cold, while neighboring ponderosa pines boasted of warmth and protection from the harsh elements.

In the next pasture, a herd of elk watched her intently. Laura turned away, wanting this time alone, not even to be shared with God's majestic creatures.

Inhaling, the bite of crisp fresh-cut pine-filled air brought calm to her stirring emotions. Before she could cry, she removed a glove and opened a self-sealing bag. Her lips pressed together, forcing a smile. "What better way to carry a sportsman's ashes than in your favorite container?" Laura blotted her dripping nose. "I thought you'd approve." Uncontrollable laughter choked away the tears.

Thank you, God, for the healing balm of laughter. For the reprieve from this intense pain.

As she scattered Todd's remaining ashes across the land that would have someday been theirs on which to build their own cabin, Laura felt renewed strength. "The roots of love were planted here, blossomed, and will live forever."

Laura hesitated, tears trapped beneath the fear of change. She was past mere survival, but could she honestly move ahead? Being Todd's wife had been wonderful, but it was time to accept that she was no longer Mrs. Todd Bates.

Taking one last look across the valley, Laura wiped her eyes and forced herself to walk away. "I'll always miss you, Love."

Later that evening, she sat in front of the woodstove warming her feet. Her brother-in-law brought her a cup of cocoa topped with a handful of marshmallows. "Thanks, Marc. What's up?"

"I was about to ask you that question. You've been pretty quiet this week. Guess it doesn't take a genius to figure out what's wrong, does it?" He took the book from her hand and turned it right-side up.

"Probably not."

"Darn it, kiddo, you aren't the type to sit and wait for life to pass you by. Some people are meant to be alone. Not you. Are you getting out any?"

"With work and the kids..." Laura hedged, avoiding the subject of her personal life.

"When *do* you plan to start dating?" Marc asked.

"Good grief, you're blunt." She turned and stared into the fire.

"You and Todd had the best marriage I've ever seen. I would think you'd want that again."

"Don't you think I can make it on my own?"

He chuckled. "You could do whatever you set your mind to, Laura Bates. None of us doubts that."

Laura forced herself to smile. Even her family thought of her as Laura Bates. Or had they always? Had she been the only one who had linked her own identity so closely with Todd that she couldn't see her own? "Maybe I don't think I'd be that lucky again."

"And maybe it wasn't luck. It takes a special woman to devote herself to her family the way you do. A man would be lucky to catch you."

"I'm not looking." Laura was quiet, unable to stop thinking of Bryan, and that careless kiss. The kids came through the kitchen singing Christmas carols at the top of their voices.

"'I saw Mommy kissing Santa Claus...'"

Laura cringed. There'd been a sack of small packages left in the driver's seat of the van the morning they were to leave. At first, she'd assumed Barb had left them, but by the time they'd reached their destination, it was clear that Bryan had played Santa. Why they'd picked that song out of all the ones on that tape, she wasn't sure. But one thing she did know, was that some day, she'd get Bryan back for this.

Chad thinks he's found a new dad. She laughed at the sound of her own words. *It sounds so cold, so clinical, like the guy should fill out some kind of application, or submit a résumé of his qualifications.*

"What about this Bryan I keep hearing about?"

"Oh, Chad…" She groaned. "He was just a client."

"Was?"

"He's leaving Jacob with his sister. I guess some men just can't handle both a career and the responsibilities of a family. Getting involved with a him would be disastrous."

"Cut the excuses. Tell me about him."

Laura felt herself blush. "He's nice, but he's…" She swallowed hard, trying to forget how easily she could fall for him. Concentrating on his lesser qualities, she blurted out a description she hoped would quiet Marc's curiosity. "He's an athletic, dedicated, self-assured, workaholic. You know, a real charmer. Not my type."

Marc smiled. "Sounds okay to me." Laura didn't respond, and he continued, "I suppose someone should set Chad straight if you aren't interested."

"Would you talk to him? Please."

"I already have. His description of Bryan was a bit more…friendly."

"Marc, don't get any ideas. I can manage on my own."

Marc laughed. "And heaven help the person who tries to get in your way!" He lifted her chin and looked into her eyes. "Todd wouldn't want you to be alone, Laura. If you like the guy, see what happens. As for Todd's mom, she'll come to accept it—eventually. We all will."

"I won't ever love anyone the way I loved Todd."

"We know that, kid. It may not be easy at first. Ruth

doesn't even realize that she's sentenced you to spend the rest of your life alone. She doesn't mean it literally.''

''You're defending her, just like Todd did. Sometimes the similarities between you two are so clear it hurts.''

''And about now, Todd would ask if you've changed your mind about Bryan.'' Marc leaned back on the couch and put his feet on the coffee table.

''No,'' she said, pushing his feet down. *The last thing I need is a man whose career takes precedence over being a father. I don't need him! I don't need anyone.*

''If it were Kayla, I wouldn't want her to spend a day without someone to love her and care for her.''

''You don't understand what it's like, Marc. I needed Todd. I depended on him. You haven't had a part of your existence ripped from your life.''

''And maybe God has brought someone else into your life. Someone who needs you. Someone you might be able to depend on as well.''

She walked to the window and leaned her head against the log. ''It's just not that easy.''

''Nothing worth having is.''

Two days later, Laura dropped each of the kids off at their friends' houses, then drove to Barb's office.

''Surprise. How about going for lunch?''

''I thought you were at your in-laws' until tomorrow.''

''Cut the trip short,'' Laura said nonchalantly. ''I have a couple of hours free. How about it?''

''We've hardly even talked this past month. Sounds great.'' Barb clocked out and grabbed her coat.

They walked down the street to their favorite restaurant. Red-checkered tablecloths and bleached muslin curtains gave Laura the feeling of stepping back into a country café.

''How was your visit with Todd's family?''

''Fine.'' She didn't want to tell Barb how difficult it had

really been, mainly because she didn't want to refresh the feelings of guilt that the week had created.

"For being 'fine' you sure look exhausted. You usually come back with a skiing tan. What's up?"

"We didn't go skiing. I'm fighting a cold."

"You sure you're okay?"

"It's nothing." She rearranged the silverware and took a drink of water.

"Okay, you don't want to talk about it. I'll drop it for now, but you're not off the hook yet."

"Gee, thanks for the favor."

Barb's smile was as fake as the reprieve Laura had just been given. "Why don't you and the kids to come to the New Year's Eve party at church with us tomorrow? It would be good for you to get out."

"I'm not in the mood for partying, Barb, but thanks for the invitation."

As she'd suspected, the smile disappeared immediately. "Oh, come on. You should meet some of the new members of the congregation. Where else do you expect to meet people?"

"People? I assume you are referring to the tall dark and handsome kind of people, in particular. I don't even feel single, let alone available, Barb." Laura shoved the food around on her plate, hoping Barb wouldn't notice that she'd only eaten a few bites of her meal.

"Even when Todd was alive you had no problem admiring God's masculine creations. It's been almost a year, Laura." A look of disapproval mixed with exasperation completed Barb's protest.

"Eight months is not almost a year. Not to worry, I still admire. But it's different now." Laura tried to ignore the six-foot-three image of Bryan trying to take over her thoughts. "Someone may think I'm interested, and I'm not."

Barb laughed. "I never thought I'd see this day."

Chapter Thirteen

Bryan had hoped Laura would be at the church party, but he enjoyed himself despite her absence. She was right, this had to be for him, not her, or anyone else. He was the one that had messed his life up, he needed to make it right with God.

There were games, refreshments, a cake walk, and for the more serious-minded, a rigorous game of Bible trivia. After enjoying the lighter activities, he joined a group in the chapel for prayer requests and a time of praise and worship. Bryan was touched by the experience, and right before the close of the evening, felt the desire to renew his own commitment to God.

He'd left several messages on Laura's answering machine in the past week, but since she hadn't returned his calls, he figured that she was fighting her feelings as much as he had.

When she answered the phone, he grew concerned. "What's wrong, Laura? You sound terrible."

"Just a cold. No big deal." She paused. "Sorry about

not calling you back. But I'm still feeling a little under the weather.''

"Don't worry about it. Do you need anything? I'd be glad to run to the store, or take the kids so you can rest.''

"We'll be fine.''

Stubborn as a mule. "I need to talk to you. Could we meet?''

"I can't.''

"Could I come over for just a few minutes, after the kids are in bed?''

"I don't think that's good idea, Bryan.''

"I have a surprise. I want you to help me celebrate.''

"Congratulations, on whatever success you're celebrating. I'm sure you'll climb the corporate ladder with lightning speed now.''

There was total silence on both ends of the line. It hurt that she'd thought the worst of him, that she wasn't the least bit interested in talking to him, that she'd obviously given up her faith in him doing the right thing. One day, he'd prove her wrong.

"I'm sorry, Bryan. I'm not in the best of moods. I feel terrible....''

"No problem. Just one quick question. I'm in another bind. Do you or don't you have an opening? If not, could you recommend another child care provider?''

"What?''

He'd finally caught her attention. "Do you or don't you have room for Jacob? I realize I gave up his spot, but I was praying it would still be available.''

He smiled, imagining her satisfaction, picturing her jumping out of her chair, thinking of those crystal blue eyes fogging over with tears that she would refuse to shed.

"You didn't...? He's here?''

"I've left several messages. I need someone for tomorrow. Do you or don't you have room?''

"Of course I do. What happened to change...?''

"I don't want to waste your time. You get some rest. I'll see you in the morning."

After two weeks she'd hardly said a civil word to him. The cold weather seemed to have filtered into Laura's body. Oh, she'd been very professional, and doted on Jacob just as always, but she wasn't the same. What steps they'd taken as friends were now covered with ice.

She slammed the van door closed and opened the hood. "Just what I need today. It's not enough that I have kids to take to school, Chad's glasses to find, and an appointment, but now the van won't start." Laura looked at Bryan and rolled her eyes. "And I suppose you want to play hero! No thanks. I know a dead battery when I hear one."

"Just thought I'd offer. I don't know what your problem is lately, but far be it from me to interfere!" Bryan walked toward the house, barely able to make out her grumbling.

She turned and kicked the tire. "Darn you! You couldn't break down when I just taking a drive. No-o-o, you have to die when I need you! Real dependable!"

Seconds later she turned to Bryan. "I would appreciate a hand pushing this heap out of the driveway, if you—"

"I'll take Jacob inside, then let's see what we can do." A few minutes later, Bryan fiddled with a few belts under the hood, paying no attention to his expensive suit. "Didn't your husband tell you that cars are like women? The more temperamental they get, the sweeter you have to talk to them?" He smiled to himself, knowing without looking at her, that she was probably beet red at being overheard in a rare moment of weakness. "Get in and steer." When she'd shifted it to neutral, he began pushing. "Do you have jumper cables?"

"Of course I have jumper cables," she said in a clipped tone. Laura put the vehicle in park and ran into the garage.

Watching from the corner of his eye, Bryan admitted to himself that he'd come to admire her, right down to her feisty temper. Most of the women he'd dated over the years wouldn't have known how to open the hood of a vehicle, let alone what to do once they got it open.

At one time, he'd enjoyed the helpless games women had used to catch his attention. No more. Experience had taught him that the more helpless the woman, the more she demanded. The independent type was looking mighty appealing.

When Laura returned, she attached the cables to the van, trying to prove that she didn't really need his help. It was just another one of those weak moments when she wanted something else in her life, and again, God seemed to be showing her how much things had changed.

She wanted to be independent, and here she was accepting Bryan's help.

She wanted someone to lean on, and the one man who was making that offer was off-limits.

She wanted to feel free and happy, yet held tight to the fears from her past.

Bryan pulled his car close and took the cables from Laura.

"Don't use your car to jump it, Bryan, use mine."

"No need to weaken the battery on your only other vehicle when it's going to sit out in this cold all day."

"But..."

"It's fine, Laura. Don't worry about it." He attached the cables to his car and revved the engine, drowning out her voice. Laura put her hands on her hips, then turned and started the van.

A few minutes later, Bryan detached the cables and returned them to her. "There, a little help didn't hurt so much did it?"

"I guess not. Thanks. Have a good day." She wouldn't let herself look at him, but managed a weak smile before returning to the garage. *So he helped me out. So he brought Jacob home with him. So what!* Thinking he'd left, she slammed the garage door down, when a gentle voice right behind her made her jump.

"Garage doors are out of my league, just for your information. Send Carrie out and I'll drop her off at school so you can get back on schedule. If the van gives you more problems, call me. I've got a light schedule today."

"Stop it, Bryan! I don't need your charity."

"Oh, everything has a price, Laura. Question is, are you willing to pay it? A simple walk with me this evening might cover my bill. We haven't talked in a long time."

She hesitated, pulling in the reins on her emotions, feeling like a giddy teenager being asked to go to the prom.

"Everyone deserves a second chance, don't they?"

"I'll see how the day goes. If it continues like this, you won't want to be around me."

"If it continues like this, you'll need a marathon to relax. Now get to work, and send your daughter out. One testy woman in a family is enough." He smiled slowly—that half smile that affirmed his confidence, that made his lips look so tempting, that told her she was in big trouble. Laura ran into the house and sent Carrie out.

Laura returned from taking kids to school, quickly changed the baby's diaper, and had just started feeding Jacob when the phone rang.

Barb's cheerful voice greeted her. "Laura, why don't I stop by later so we can have lunch today?"

Laura twirled the cord around her finger as Jacob devoured his formula. *Why today? This woman knows my life better than I do sometimes.* "I would love that, but I can't, I have an appoi—" She stopped short.

"An appointment? With the doctor?"

"Don't sound so pleased. It's just my yearly exam."

"I'll bring lunch over so we can talk while the kids nap. See you about one." Barb hung up.

She didn't want to be with anyone today, but knew her friend wouldn't take no for an answer. Laura remembered

Barb's comments about how worn-out she'd looked after Christmas vacation. Todd's family had even noticed.

Laura didn't want to worry anyone, but she was concerned. She hadn't had her monthly cycle for several months. Now that it was time for the appointment, she dreaded going. Laura wasn't sure she could handle any more bad news right now.

Waiting impatiently in the examination room was unusual for Laura, and feeling her body become tense when the doctor came in the door was absurd. Emily Berthoff was a close friend.

As her doctor, Emily asked Laura routine questions, examined her, and expressed concern with how Laura was doing after Todd's death. "Being in the same singles' class at church gives you an unfair advantage, Emily. Next time I'll make the appointment with one of your partners."

Emily laughed. "I'll be sure to make a note here for them to consult with me on your case, then. Really Laura, I don't think it's anything to be alarmed about, but we'll keep an eye on it." She continued to try to soothe Laura's fears while giving her an injection. "If things don't return to normal within a couple of months, come back in."

On her way home, Laura picked up the preschoolers and stopped at the drive-in to get burritos for the kids' lunch. They ate lunch, and went down for their naps.

When Barb arrived, she again commented on how tired Laura looked. "I know what you're digging for, so here it is. I'm under too much pressure, as if I couldn't figure that out. My iron count is very low, and my periods have stopped, probably due to stress."

"What did Emily recommend?"

"Gave me a shot of hormones, told me to take vitamins, iron, eat better and get more exercise and rest. I'd like to see her rest around here."

"Are you still having nightmares?"

Laura nodded. "I've realized how protected my life was, and I liked it that way. Now it's just me."

Barb reached for her hand and Laura continued. "Not that I didn't realize that before, but lately... Today, Chad lost his second pair of glasses, then the van wouldn't start, and I bit Bryan's head off when he offered to help. I was a mess by the time I reached the doctor's office. I should have rescheduled. I'm not usually this tense." Her voice broke, as tears threatened to fall. She refused to give way to the weakness.

"It's been building for weeks now, Laura. You can't keep up this pace. For starters, I'm going to take the kids tonight. I want you to do something for yourself."

Chapter Fourteen

Bryan hadn't forgotten his offer by that evening. "What about that walk, then maybe a deep dish pepperoni pizza."

"The kids are gone for the evening. That sounds nice."

Trying to hide his shock, he paused before responding. "Great. I'll see if Kevin can put Jacob to bed and be back in a few minutes."

Half an hour later Bryan led the way to the track, and sat down to change shoes. "How was your doctor's appointment?"

"Who said I went to the doctor?" Laura asked, hanging her jacket in a locker. She inserted a quarter and took the key.

"Women never say they have to see the doctor when it's the gynecologist, it's always 'an appointment.' When the women at work need time off, if it's the dentist, they say so, if it's the hairdresser, they say so, but when it's the gynecologist, it's 'an appointment.' Need to talk about it?"

Laura blushed. He loved making her turn red as much as an eight-year-old boy loves tormenting his sister. But somehow, it wasn't the same. "I'd rather not."

"Okay," he said lightly. "How was the rest of your day?"

"Same as usual. Yours?"

Bryan laughed. "I see you're not going to loosen your grip tonight. What do you want to talk about?"

"Not work. Anything else."

"Okay. We've missed you in class the last few Sundays."

"I decided to try something else for a while."

"A different class, or a different approach on life?"

"Please, not more lectures on my changes this month."

"I'm not the only one who's noticed, huh?"

When she didn't answer, he went on.

"How about a movie this weekend?"

"You don't have to try to cheer me up, Bryan." Laura walked faster, but he kept pace with her.

"I'm not just trying to cheer you up, I could use an evening out, too." Bryan wasn't sure why she'd come tonight, but it was progress. "I enjoy being with you."

The past month had gone by quickly. In addition to his job, he'd felt the insatiable need to work on his relationship with God. Through the process of forgiving his wife's betrayal had come the realization that he wanted to include a woman in his life again. Specifically, the one woman who'd shown him what was missing in his empty, day-to-day existence.

He didn't notice right away that she had stopped, and walked on. Then he turned around. She studied him.

"Why does it surprise you that I want to spend time with you?" He had stepped closer.

Her eyes widened.

She felt a lump at least the size of a tennis ball go down her throat.

Laura had resisted silly daydreams where Bryan was concerned. It wasn't that she didn't consider herself to be attractive, but her choices included a hairstyle that required minimum time, little to no makeup, and rarely took time for an exercise routine. There was barely enough time in her life for the necessities. A man like Bryan belonged with someone beautiful, or stunning, or at the very least, pretty.

She'd come tonight because she knew the exercise would be good for her, and adult conversation sure beat another night of television.

Bryan interrupted her thoughts. "Your friendship has brought me through the toughest months of my life. You cared enough to give me your honest opinion. I value that. Not many people care enough to stick their necks out for someone else like you have."

"Laura? Is that you?"

Laura turned hesitantly. "Steve." She threw her arms around the blond-haired man, sharing a tight embrace. "I thought you quit running."

"Didn't expect to see you here, either. How're you and the kids doing?" Laura noted Steve's attention shift to the man standing possessively behind her.

"We're getting along fine." She felt Bryan close the space between them. "Steve, this is Bryan Beaumont, one of my clients. Bryan, Steve was Todd's best friend."

Laura watched as the two men scrutinized one another, then obligingly shook hands.

Steve's gaze shifted between Bryan and Laura. "Jaime mentioned getting together for dinner sometime."

Feeling like a noose was being wrapped around her neck, Laura changed the subject. "Sounds fun. How's the baby?"

"Jaime says he's like me. Can't figure out what she means."

Laura laughed. "Want a few ideas?"

"Steve, our court's open," a short barrel-chested man yelled.

"Hey, call if you need anything. Anything." He nodded toward Bryan before he left.

Once they were alone, she heard an edge to Bryan's voice. "Am I only a client, Laura? I thought I might be at least a friend."

"Steve knows my clients are friends."

"You know what I mean," he growled.

"Bryan, it's only been a few months since my husband died. If the truth be known, I shouldn't have come tonight. I'm not interested in a relationship. And even if I was, I'm not at all your type."

"What is my type?"

Laura noticed Bryan's jaw tighten and the muscles in his neck tense. She looked away.

"Just what is my type?" he repeated.

"Never mind."

"No. I'd really like to know what kind of woman you think I need. You've obviously spent time thinking about this."

"No, I haven't. I guess, I mean you're not my type."

He turned his head and laughed. "And why not?"

"Well you…you're…I mean…"

"My reputation? My interests? What?"

"I don't know. I picture you with someone more like the chic, gorgeous, career-oriented…" Realizing she was describing Andrea, she stopped.

"I could have all the gorgeous women I ever wanted, but maybe I don't want that anymore…not that you're not…you are." Bryan realized his mistake, and jerked his head, muttering to himself. "This is another fine mess you've gotten me into. I hate being set up like that!"

Laura, relieved that he hadn't taken offense to her mistake, laughed and took off running.

"Oh, come on, Laura. Talk to me." Bryan immediately caught up with her, running side by side for nearly a lap before he pulled her out of the way of the other joggers.

"Laura, I don't want to return to the way things have been this month. I can't take your cold shoulder. I won't."

Laura panted, leaning her head back, as if in exasperation. "I shouldn't have come tonight."

"Don't give me that garbage again."

"This was a mistake. We're getting too close."

"Too close? We're friends. What's the great sin in that?"

"It can't help but make our working relationship difficult. I let that happen with a mother once, and it not only cost us our friendship, but it almost ruined my business. I have three children to support. I can't afford to lose everything."

"It won't happen."

"It could. You're upset with me already and we haven't even made the mistake of dating! I have three kids and run two businesses which doesn't leave much time for anything or anyone else."

Bryan crossed his arms in front of him. "I don't agree. It doesn't have to interfere. I'm glad to include the kids."

She acted as if he'd slapped her.

"No. Leave the kids out of this, Bryan. I think we'd better skip the pizza."

Never had there been a more stubborn woman in Bryan's life. She declined his invitations for dinner, insisting that she didn't want to compromise their working relationship, so he threatened to end it. Then she claimed to have meetings and kids' commitments. If it wasn't that, she had cakes to decorate, or laundry to do, or any other excuse she deemed convenient.

Bryan wondered if it was still too painful for Laura to think of being close to a man again. He'd heard only good things about her husband, and it appeared they had a strong marriage. If it had been like his, full of lies and endless expectations, he could understand her wariness. But it didn't seem to be that at all. So why didn't she want another relationship?

He knew the pain she had experienced.

He knew how frightening it was to let someone inside when his heart had been broken. He was glad that Laura had been the woman who'd pulled him through.

Time.

She needed time.

Could he wait?

If he wanted her, he'd have to.

It had been a long week and he was ready to kick back and watch the basketball playoffs after bathing Jacob and getting him to bed. He pulled into Laura's driveway, surprised to see no signs of the boys outside. Inside, she and Jacob were cuddled on the floor looking at a book. "Man, it's quiet in here. Where are the kids?"

Laura jumped to her feet and lifted Jacob into her arms. "The other parents came early, and my three went with Todd's mom and dad for the weekend. How I'm going to make it through two days of this peace and quiet, I don't know."

Jacob dived into his dad's arms, and Bryan returned the affection with a baby-size bear hug, complete with a throaty growl, which made Jacob laugh.

"Great. Why don't we go out for dinner and a movie. You won't have to worry about—"

"Thanks, but no." Laura turned and put the book on the shelf.

Bryan probably should have left well enough alone. He should have turned and walked out the door and never looked back. But he didn't. He took her hand and held it tight. "You know Laura, maybe it's time you think about getting on with your life." Unconsciously, his fingers twisted the diamond ring on her finger.

If Bryan thought he had seen rage before, he was mistaken. She jerked her hand away from him.

"Obviously your ring didn't mean to you what mine does to me!"

"It's getting rather awkward asking you out when you're still wearing your ring as if you're married. Give yourself a chance to live again, Laura. No loving husband would want his wife to be alone. Not even Todd."

"I don't need a man to take care of me. I can take care of the kids myself...and...you have no idea how Todd would feel." Tears began to fall. "I need a friend, I don't need a...a..."

Bryan fought to hold his temper. "I don't believe I was offering more than dinner and a movie."

"Get out! Now."

Bryan picked up Jacob's coat and bag and left, slamming the door behind him. He buckled Jacob in his seat and put the car into reverse, squealing the tires as he backed out of the driveway.

Chapter Fifteen

Bryan rang the doorbell. There was no answer. The house was dark, inside and out. It was only nine o'clock and both cars were in the driveway. She wouldn't be in bed this early. He pounded on the door, his concern growing. When she didn't answer, he walked to the side of the house and saw light escaping from the basement. Instinctively, he stepped close and looked in the window.

Music was booming—Boston. Not exactly what he'd expect from Laura, but nothing she'd done today was what he would have anticipated.

The shiny fabric of the leotard magnified her jerky movements. Her skin glistened with moisture. Bryan watched through the gap in the curtains until she set the weights down, then knocked on the glass.

Laura screamed. For an instant, it was quiet. Then she yanked the flimsy curtain aside, holding a small barbell above her head. When she recognized him, she lowered the weight and pushed the window open. "What are you doing out there! You scared me half out of my wits."

"Sorry. We need to talk. May I come in?"

She put one fist on her hip and wiped her forehead with

the other hand, nearly hitting herself with the weight. "We may as well get this settled. Meet me at the back door."

A few minutes later, Laura unlocked the door and waited, hand splayed on her hip, as he walked by. She had put on an oversize shirt before coming to meet him.

"You look great...working out, I mean your form...I mean your style was good, even if it was careless," he growled.

What is it about you, Laura Bates. I haven't been this tongue-tied since junior high. "I mean..." Was she blushing, or red from her workout? Laura wiped her forehead repeatedly, avoiding eye contact.

"Do you always peep in women's windows?" Laura interrupted.

Again, Bryan was caught off guard by her cold reaction.

"Only when I'm desperate. I came to apologize. When you didn't answer the door, I got worried. Listen, our conversation today got way out of hand...."

She bit her lower lip. "That's my fault. I'm sorry."

"I had no right to expect you to take your ring off just for me. I was out of line." Bryan shoved his hands into his pockets.

Laura lowered her head and tugged on the hem of the shirt, then motioned for Bryan to sit down in the chair across from her. She sat, pulled her legs close to her body and slipped the fabric over her knees. "So, why are you desperate? I thought you could have any woman you wanted."

Sarcasm cut through his ego like a razor. Trying to remember the speech he had practiced for the last hour, Bryan paced the floor. "I'm not desperate, I mean, I am, but not the way you think. I mean...that's not why I'm here! You're trying to get me into another mess, but it won't work this time."

Laura stretched her long legs out in front of her, crossed her arms in front of her and waited, keeping her features deceptively composed. How, after all these years, could one woman unnerve him like this? Bryan sat again, propped his elbows on his knees and churched his hands together. "I don't want to live with this tension between us, Laura. I can't lose you…as Jacob's child care provider, or as a friend. You've been so much help to me, and I only hoped you might be ready to think about dating."

Her eyelids lowered, revealing long lashes, moist and dark against her fair complexion. She'd been crying.

"Don't take it personally, Bryan."

"When a woman turns me down as many times as you have, I can't help but think there's something I'm doing wrong."

Laura looked down at her wedding ring, fingering the modest diamond. It was as if she wore her love for her husband as a protective veil.

"This ring has been on my finger for nearly thirteen years. I don't feel single. I don't want to go through all that dating stuff again. I know you're trying to help, but I can't…"

Bryan wished he had the strength to comfort her with a smile. She was everything he'd imagined, compassionate and emotional, spirited and loyal. A woman like Laura was a rare treasure. "I hope that when you're ready you'll let me know."

"No! You need someone…" she waved her hands, as if they would supply her with the words she needed "…someone who is able to give you and Jacob all she has to a relationship. It wouldn't work, Bryan. I can't date a client. I have three children," she exclaimed, as if that explained the world away.

"Whoa. Wait a minute, Laura. I'm not out looking to fill any position. You are very special, and I want to know you better. You're a fascinating, beautiful woman."

Laura looked away, her face bright red now. "Thank

you, Bryan, but as I've told you before, I don't think I'm
your type."

"There are plenty of ways you could mean that, most of
them probably aren't favorable. I won't try to deny that
I've made a lot of mistakes in my past, but this time, I'm
waiting for the right woman."

Her eyes widened. "Oh."

Bryan knelt in front of her and took her hand. "I want
to be your friend, Laura. If nothing else comes of it, I'll
settle for your friendship." When she hugged him a moment later, he was almost too surprised to react. But when
he wrapped her in his arms and felt her body relax, he
thought he'd die of pure pleasure. She was a woman who
needed love more than she would admit.

"You are our friend, Bryan. Thanks for coming back,"
she whispered, her voice soft and alluring.

"I'm glad I did." Bryan felt the tension leave her body,
and a much different tension grip his own. He wanted to
hold her like this forever, to take her pain away, but the
moment was soon over. He couldn't leave. "You should
never lift weights alone. Why don't I show you a few pointers so you don't get hurt?"

"I don't usually lift, but thanks for the warning. I needed
to push myself tonight, to work off the anger. I was just
messing around," she said, shrugging her shoulders. Laura
walked to the door and gripped the doorknob.

"You don't mess around with weights. Come on,"
Bryan said, keeping his voice stern. "I'm not about to let
you take foolish risks like that."

"No, it's okay." Laura backed away, but he took her
hand and waited. She looked at him, her blue eyes reflecting his own fear, pain and unquenchable warmth.

"It's not okay. You shouldn't have them in the house
without knowing the proper way to use them. It's dangerous."

"They're kept in a spare room behind a locked door. The kids don't go in there without me."

"You should learn the proper way to lift to prevent injury. If not your own, it could be T.J. Or Chad. Or even Carrie, for that matter," he said, squaring his shoulders. "I can be stubborn, too." They stared at each other in silence.

"Fine. Show me, then." Laura led the way to the weight bench.

Somewhere along the way, he'd shed his wool jacket, and was now unbuttoning his shirt. Bryan slowly pulled it off his solid shoulders, and neatly tossed it over the back of the chair. He straddled the bench, pulling the legs of his slacks up, then reclined.

Laura felt a lump go down her throat, and fought to restrain the groan that wanted to release itself. Instead it came out as a mere whimper.

Bryan smiled, and she felt herself blush, knowing he'd seen and heard her reaction. As his muscles tightened, a wavelike motion rolled across his stomach. He effortlessly lifted the weights Laura had struggled with, explaining proper form and the best technique to benefit each muscle. Then he got up and motioned for Laura's turn.

She stared blankly at him for a moment, then refused. His hand was planted on his hip, and the cock of his head silently dared her.

"Come on, it's your turn."

"You know, I did just fine all by myself!" She started to walk away, but he pulled her back.

"I'm not making a move on you."

"I didn't think that."

"That's why your face is bright red?"

Laura yanked her arm away from Bryan. She hated the fact that she had let him in tonight, that he was so darn attractive. She tried to convince herself that if he weren't drop-dead handsome, she'd have no problem resisting his charm…or maybe if she wasn't so lonely…. That didn't work, either.

Laura pulled the shirt over her head and threw it on the floor, thankful that she'd chosen leggings and a modest leotard instead of one of the many skimpy styles most women were wearing now. When she was ready, Bryan placed her hands on the bar the proper distance apart. She barely heard his voice, her thoughts focused on his strong yet gentle hands touching hers. A flood of images of him flashed through her mind—him holding Jacob, playing football with her boys, the snowball fight, that kiss….

Laura found herself vacillating between adolescent eagerness and sheer terror as confusion ripped through her. *God, why did you bring Bryan back here? If this is a test, I'm failing.*

She tried to pull her thoughts back to the weights and Bryan's instructions, but his voice was fuzzy. "Would you start the record? It helps me pace myself."

"Boston's an interesting choice." He turned to the stereo. "I prefer the theme to *Rocky*…"

Metal hit metal with tumultuous thumps.

Bryan turned, instinctively reaching for the source of the noise. Laura had curled into a protective ball and rolled safely away. After replacing the bar in the cradle, Bryan knelt down beside her. "Are you okay?"

She nodded. "Todd always listened to *Rocky* before his games. When you said that…" Laura let out a ragged breath.

"Go ahead and cry, Laura. You're going to be fine." Bryan wrapped his arms around her, brushing loose tendrils of hair off her face. He didn't let go until the tears had stopped. "Sure you're okay?"

Laura nodded. "Aren't you going to say 'I told you so'?"

"Not a chance. Feel like trying again? A good workout always helps clear my mind."

She hesitated. "I'll give it a try."

Bryan never again moved from the head of the bench and pushed her until her body ached. When he reached out a hand to help her up, it took an excruciating effort to stop the forward motion from carrying her body into his arms. Steadying herself, she headed toward the stairs. She lifted a foot, and her legs gave out.

Bryan swooped her into his arms and started up the stairs. "That was downright careless, Laura. Why didn't you tell me you'd had enough?"

Laura kicked and pushed away from him. "Put me down! I just bobbled a little. I'm fine."

His grip tightened. "You fainted! How long has it been since you ate?"

"What?"

"When did you last eat something…anything?"

"Lunch…no, it was…" Laura rested her head on the arm of the couch after Bryan set her down. "Snack? No…"

"Great, you don't eat, you lift weights alone and you probably don't get enough rest, either! Do you see what I mean about lifting alone being dangerous? Thank God I came back. I was right to worry."

"The kids are usually here."

"They don't count, and you know it. Those weights are history."

"N—"

"I mean it, Laura," he yelled.

She'd never seen Bryan this mad before. Right now she was far too vulnerable to allow herself to be affected by his outburst, but his protectiveness was definitely flattering.

"Go get dressed so I can take you for a decent meal." The tone of his voice was neither gentle nor compassionate. It was clearly an order.

"I'll get something later," she said weakly and turned to her side, curled up and closed her eyes.

"I'll believe that when horses fly," he muttered.

She felt the corners of her lips twitch as the fatigue took over. *Call it like it is, Laura. It feels good having someone over five feet tall here, who cares if something happens to you, who cares enough to give you an order. It feels even better that that person is Bryan.*

When she opened her eyes a few minutes later, he was gone. She heard noises coming from the kitchen. "What are you doing?"

"Fixing you dinner. Stay put."

She hadn't the strength to go anywhere, even if she did want to run away. It wasn't long before he stood before her and handed her a plate.

"What is it?" She sat up slowly, steadying herself so she wouldn't pass out again.

"Roast beef, ketchup, cheese, tomatoes, lettuce and avocado, with a sprinkle of alfalfa sprouts on top."

Laura looked at the sandwich apprehensively. "How do men come up with such interesting combinations?"

"It must be our lack of inhibitions." His boyish grin made her smile in return as she took a bite.

It wasn't bad. Once Laura had finished the sandwich and soda pop, Bryan left. No kiss, no fight, no innuendo of romance, which Laura found almost disappointing.

The doorbell rang and the door creaked open. "Ready, Laura?"

"Be right there." Laura finished making the bed and walked down the hall and around the corner.

"Good grief, what happened to you? You're pale as a ghost."

"Don't say it. Let's get out of here. I need to talk."

Barb put her hand on Laura's shoulder. "What in the world has you so upset?"

"Chocolate."

"Chocolate?" Barb cocked her head.

Laura nodded. "Yeah, chocolate. As in a gaze as warm

as hot chocolate, hair as dark as chocolate truffles, and a smile as tempting as chocolate mousse.''

"A *man?*"

"Oh, Barb, this can't be happening."

"You're kidding me. Who?"

While they drove for the next forty-five minutes, Laura told Barb everything about Bryan Beaumont, then waited for a lecture. "Well, say something." Laura glanced at her friend.

"He sounds incredible. This is wonderful." Barb pulled into the parking space and turned the car off.

Laura got out of the car and slammed the door. "It is not wonderful. I can't date a client. He's not even my type. Oh Barb, what am I going to do?"

"Your type? I didn't know you had one. Just for the record, you're not into handsome, successful, attractive men?"

"You know what I mean. What do I have in common with a man who wears Italian suits? Put Todd in slacks and a button-up shirt and he thought he was ready to meet the queen." Her thumb automatically began twisting the wedding ring around her finger as she thought of the conversation that had started the argument between her and Bryan. She knew there was no reason to wear it any longer, but it gave her comfort. It kept men at a distance…all but one. The one that knew her too well.

Bryan's words had stung more than she was willing to admit. She did miss the closeness of a man, the comfort of strong arms around her, even that musky scent of perspiration after a hard workout. Again, remembering those special times with her husband moistened her eyes, and she pressed her lips tight, willing the tears back.

Barb started walking away from the car. "It worked on you, why not the queen?"

"You're a big help!" Laura ran to catch up with her spirited friend.

They wandered aimlessly through the shops, admiring the jewelry, the home decorations, and the latest fashions. Laura found herself in the dress department running her hands over a black silk evening dress. *I haven't had a reason to wear anything this formal for years. What am I doing here?* Then Laura heard a giggle behind her and turned around.

"Now what would Bryan think of this?" Barb held up a red evening gown and smiled.

Laura felt the heat rush to her face. "He wouldn't be thinking of me. Besides, I'm not even ready to think of dating yet."

"Sounds like you'd better start."

"Not likely." Laura shoved the red dress aside and mumbled. "I was looking for something I could wear to church."

"Then I guess this is out." Barb put the outrageous dress away.

Laura blushed again, trying to ignore Barb, and regarded the elegant black dress with a sigh. "It is pretty," she said absent-mindedly.

"You'd look great in that style. You should try it on just for fun," Barb prodded her.

"Where would I wear something like this?" Laura insisted.

"Even Todd would want you to stay in touch with this part of you, Laura," Barb said softly.

Laura swallowed a lump of emotions. "But Barb, there's hardly a day goes by without me thinking of how much I miss Todd. Then Bryan does something stupid like kissing me. I feel so guilty. I wish they made a pill to turn off hormones."

"Sexuality is one of God's creative gifts. He made you the way you are—feminine, sensual, motherly. One of your responsibilities to your children is to teach them that, and the appropriate way to express it."

"This is crazy. Nothing will ever come of any of this. I'm acting like a lovesick teenager." Laura pushed the dress back into the rack and strode purposefully toward the escalator. Barb silently followed.

Why didn't my mouth follow orders when I interviewed Bryan? The minute I saw him, I knew I was in trouble.

Before returning home, Barb and Laura went for lunch and a short hike in the mountains. It had been a pleasant day, and when she arrived home, she was tired. It was a weariness that came from fresh mountain air, and Barb's wonderful sense of humor.

After a hot bubble bath, Laura put on her pajamas and crawled into bed. She realized she had been denying her feelings, afraid she may never have what she had with Todd again. She closed her eyes. "Thank you God for all my friends, for their understanding, for their encouragement to live again, for their sense of humor at all the right times." Still afraid to verbalize her attraction to Bryan, she added, "Please give me the courage to carry on without Todd."

The next morning, Laura overslept and missed Sunday's class. She woke to the doorbell's chime. She pulled on her robe, stumbled down the hall rubbing sleep from her eyes, and opened the door.

She had to be dreaming.

A warm smile met her as she looked into Bryan's chocolate eyes and leaned against the frame of the door with her arms crossed over her chest.

Bryan's eyes sparkled. "Now I see why you weren't in class today. We missed you."

Laura looked at the pickup in the driveway. Kevin waved. "Did you come to gang up on me?"

"Nope. I'm not into sharing. We tried to deliver this yesterday, but you weren't here. Either that, or you were hiding. Would you hold the door open please?" Bryan turned and walked down the driveway. The next thing Laura knew, a huge box stood in her living room.

"What's this?" Laura's puzzled look deepened.

"Exercise equipment. No more loose weights."

"Get it out of here. I've never even used those weights before, and I don't plan on doing so again."

"I know you won't, because as of now, they're out of here." Bryan raised one eyebrow as he glanced at her. "Would you go get Jacob and bring him in please? This is going to take me a while to put together. Isn't it, Kev?"

"A few hours at least." Kevin made no attempt to hide his smile. "Cold feet, huh?"

Laura looked down at her stocking feet and gave him a scowl. "I don't want that thing!" Laura stood with one hand on her hip and the other pointing to the box.

"I don't recall asking. Now, go get Jacob. Please." Bryan put his hands on her shoulders, turned her around, and gave her a gentle push toward the door. "You aren't going to win this argument, Laura, so save your energy. Kevin, I'll see you later."

Chapter Sixteen

Later that week, Laura heard the front door open. Glancing out the family room window, she saw Bryan's car in the driveway. As she stepped around the corner to the living room to greet him, she noticed her sons huddled close together on the floor. Bryan walked over to join them.

"Hey guys. What're you up to?"

"Nothing."

"Nothing, huh?" There was a pause, and Laura saw Bryan confiscate a magazine and fan through the pages, quickly snapping it closed and rolling it into a log. "This is nothing, all right."

Laura had been so busy with the preschoolers that she hadn't checked on the boys after they'd had snack. Now she knew why they had been so quiet. She heard Chad's slang comment about the pictures, which came out sounding more like something a teenager would say than a six-year-old. Since no one had noticed Laura, she backed around the corner, wondering how to handle another difficult situation.

She heard Bryan's deep voice soften. "Where'd you boys get this?"

"From Joey. It's his dad's," the boys said in unison.

"Does his dad know Joey gave it to you?"

T.J. looked at his younger brother. "He has lots of magazines. He doesn't care if we look at them."

"Maybe he doesn't, but I don't think it's a good idea."

"Why not?" Chad asked.

"You're way too young to be looking at…women's bodies."

The two boys looked nervously at each other. "Joey says they're sexy," T.J. mumbled, shrugging his shoulders.

"Well, maybe."

Bryan wiped his brow, rubbing his eyes as he finished.

Chad looked right at Bryan. "But why can't we like girls? Did you know my mom's a girl?"

"Yeah, I noticed. It's not that we can't like girls, it's natural.…"

"Don't you like looking at girls?" Chad interrupted.

"Sure I do, but not like this. What makes a woman really beautiful is what's in her heart. Pictures like these make us see only of one side of a woman, and there's so much more to love about them. Isn't there?"

Both boys looked puzzled.

"For example, your mom knows just what to say to make you feel better when you get hurt. And she cares enough to fix your favorite meals, and she's always thinking of others. That makes her special, as well as beautiful. Isn't that right?"

T.J. looked down as Bryan handed the magazine to him. "I guess."

Chad took the magazine from his brother's grasp and shoved it back at Bryan. "You take it so Mom won't find it."

He held his hands up in front of him. "Oh no, I'm not getting caught with this."

Laura wanted to chuckle at his chicken attitude, but covered her mouth and took a deep breath instead.

"Think you should talk to your mom about Joey?"

The two boys looked sick.

"What's wrong? Chad, T.J.?" Bryan again squatted before the boys and looked at them.

"Mom doesn't like Joey's family. We weren't s'posed to be there. She'll get mad if she finds out," T.J. admitted.

"Don't tell her, please, Bryan. We won't do it again."

Bryan remained quiet for a few minutes, then looked from one worried boy to the other. "You're asking me to lie to your mother. I won't do that."

Chad and T.J. frowned at each other. "You're going to tell on us?" mumbled T.J.

"No. I'm not. I think it would be much better if you boys told your mom about this yourself. If you'd like, I'll stay while you do."

"You will?"

"Sure. And we'll let her decide what to do with the magazine."

"Great," Laura complained silently. "Why in the world do you have to be so admirable, Bryan?"

A week later, Laura closed the door as the last toddler left. Marc and Kayla had taken her three kids for the weekend, and this time, she had prepared herself for a quiet weekend at home. She started a bubble bath and pulled a book off the shelf. As she stepped into the tub, the phone rang. Laura grabbed a towel and ran to her bedroom. "Hello."

"Hey there, Laura. This is Kevin. I have a proposition for you. I have two tickets to *Phantom of the Opera*. What do you have going tonight?"

"'Hey there? What do you have going tonight?'" Laura imitated. "This is how you beg for a stand-in—for tonight?"

"I was under the impression that you had no desire to

date, so I decided not to insult you by making you guess as to why I'd be rude enough to call on such short notice.''

"Wise choice. I appreciate you not assuming you could buffalo me." She thought a moment, then continued. "As a matter of fact, I'd love to see *The Phantom*. Just so you understand—this isn't a date."

"We'll see how it goes, then make that decision. Dress formal, we have orchestra seats. Since we don't have much time, I'll pick you up in half an hour and take you out for dinner afterward."

"Half an hour! You're not asking much. If I didn't want to see it so much you'd be going stag." Laura jumped into the tub and bathed. On the way to her bedroom, she stopped to get her dress from the guest room closet, immediately thinking of the New Year's party she and Todd had attended. She suppressed the memories that the royal blue sequined dress evoked, as she didn't have time to deal with them now.

Laura pulled her hair into a ponytail at the nape of her neck and added a bow, just finishing when Kevin arrived. On her way down the hall, she stepped into the dress and reached for the zipper. It caught and wouldn't budge.

"Just great!" The doorbell rang again. She had no choice but to answer. "Come on in Kevin, I'm almost ready." As she spoke, she backed away from him, her arm twisted behind her to hold the dress together.

"What's wrong?"

"My zipper caught. I'll go fix it and be right back."

"Turn around and I'll zip you."

"Not a chance." Laura backed away. "Why in the world do designers put zippers in the back?"

Kevin smiled. "So you need help getting in and out of them." After several minutes, he called down the hall. "How are you doing?"

"Lousy. It won't move and I can't get the dress off."

"We don't want to be late. Come here and I'll work on it. I'm great with zippers."

"I'm sure you are," she mumbled, realizing she may have no other choice. She slipped on her pumps then added her jewelry. Before heading to the living room, Laura gave it one more try. *Please God, fix this thing. NOW.* Laura twisted her arm behind her and it zipped right up. Relief escaping her lips, she closed her eyes and lifted her chin. "Thank you, Father."

Kevin looked at Laura approvingly, adding a catcall, which helped her relax. "Next time you'll be at the top of my list, lady," he said. The corners of his mouth turned up.

Laura fought the urge to smile back. "There won't be a next time. I'm just being greedy, I want to see the show."

"It's admirable of you to be so honest, but you sure could use some pointers on starting off a date...excuse me, an evening."

"No smart remarks, buster." She poked his chest. "I can't believe I even agreed to this...outing."

Kevin chuckled. "But you did. So let's get started, shall we?" He took her coat from the back of the chair and offered her a hand. "It's warm in the truck, I don't think you'll need this yet."

Laura agreed, then transferred a few things to her evening bag and locked the door behind them. Kevin opened the door of his short-bed truck. She looked over her shoulder, a feeling of panic surfacing. His hand was waiting to help her up. As he hoisted her into the seat, Laura grumbled, "I'm sure you love this, don't you?"

"You bet. Especially when the dresses show gorgeous legs like yours."

"You're incorrigible."

"Thanks." He closed her door, then climbed into the driver's side of the cab.

"That's not a compliment." Laura laughed, surprised

that being with Kevin was so painless. He had a one track mind. As long as she knew where he stood, she was okay. "Thank your um...date...for my ticket."

Kevin glanced to her. "I doubt I'll get the chance."

"Why am I not surprised? Did you hear from Bryan this week?"

"Bryan?"

"Yeah, Bryan, your friend with the adorable little boy? Remember, he's been gone on business."

"Why would he call me? We're a little old for checking in with each other."

"Excuse me. I was just wondering."

They were interrupted by the buzz of Kevin's cellular phone. He answered. "Hey there. How was your week?" He paused, noting Laura's I-told-you-so smile, then added, "Hold on a minute, I'm going to put you on the speaker, the traffic is terrible." Kevin pushed the button and set down the receiver, smiling back. "The house sure was quiet without you two. How did the little guy do with Andrea's folks?"

"He did great. Her parents and I had a good talk when I dropped him off Sunday. Keeping in touch with them is going to work out."

Laura felt a warm sensation as she heard Bryan's voice. She had missed both of them more than she wanted to admit.

Bryan continued, "I can't believe how much I missed the little tyke in those four days. I swear he grew two inches while I was away. Laura was right, there's nothing like those little arms reaching out for me after being apart. Say, I just wanted to let you know I'll be home earlier than I expected tomorrow. I hated to catch you in the middle of a hot date. You have plans tonight?"

"As a matter of fact, I'm on the way to see *The Phantom*..." Kevin grinned as Laura shook her head and put her finger in front of her mouth to quiet him "…with Laura."

There was a long silence. Bryan's voice lowered. "Laura's with you? Now?" he said, practically growling.

"In the flesh." Kevin smiled as if sharing their own private joke.

"Ready to date now are you, Laura?"

Laura gave Kevin a dirty look. "This isn't a real… Well, Kevin's date canceled, and he didn't want to waste the tickets. I'm a greedy stand-in, aren't I Kevin?"

"She's a mighty fine lady to…" Kevin cleared his throat "…stand in for me."

Laura snapped, "Will you stop it!"

Bryan interrupted, "I've heard all I care to. Laura, enjoy your…date. Kevin, don't do anything I wouldn't do." His voice was thick with sarcasm.

"That wouldn't be any fun. See you tomorrow."

Laura swung her hand and hit Kevin's arm. "You didn't have to make Bryan think we planned this!"

"I don't sneak around behind my best friend's back."

"I didn't mean you should, but this isn't a…"

"Date. That's exactly what it is, Laura. If you have a hang-up with it, you'd better deal with it, quick. If I have any say, this won't be the last time I ask you out."

Laura's eyes must have shown her surprise.

"Why so shocked? Worried about what Bryan will think?"

Laura remained silent.

"He's not happy, I'll guarantee it. Why'd you come tonight? To make him jealous?"

"Of course not! My personal life is none of Bryan's concern."

"Maybe not, but he'd like it to be. Why are you set against dating him?"

She had no choice. It wasn't that she didn't want to, but

under the circumstances, she couldn't. She shook her head slowly. "I can't date a client."

Laura considered why she had agreed to go with Kevin. Yes, she had needed to distract herself from spending another night dreaming about Bryan. Yes, she was sick of watching movies at home alone, and she wasn't about to turn down a chance to see *The Phantom of the Opera* performed onstage. And yes, maybe it was time to consider dating, just for fun. She knew dating Kevin would never lead to anything serious.

Dating Bryan, on the other hand, would be dangerous. He was the type of man she could fall for, and hard; the kind of man to whom she could give her heart and never want it back. Dating Bryan would be serious business, and that was exactly why she had to take her mind off of him. She'd already experienced the only broken heart she planned to have in this lifetime.

Kevin laughed. "You two are hopeless. I'm sure grateful I won't let any woman get under my skin."

The two sparred up to the opening of the curtain, then all the way through dinner. Hours later, Kevin walked her to the front door of her house and reached for her keys.

She pulled them back and turned to Kevin. "Why did you really call me?"

"That's right to the point." He paused, then added, "Maybe I got a little curious. What is it about you that's made Bryan change so much?"

Laura looked at him in disbelief and stood a little straighter. Over dinner she had quickly found out Kevin was as loyal a friend as anyone could ask for, protecting Bryan's privacy, yet incredibly concerned about his happiness.

"It was fun to get out. Thank you, Kevin." Laura stepped closer to the house.

"The fun doesn't have to end here." He touched her arm.

"Oh yes, it does." Laura turned and unlocked the door. "Let's go skiing tomorrow."

She jerked her head around, trying to hide her surprise at his suggestion. "Skiing?"

He put his hand on the door frame behind her. "Quit hiding behind that shield, Laura. You aren't the play-it-safe type any more than I am." Kevin stepped closer to Laura and lowered his head toward her, his eyes focused on her lips. "Go with your guts, lady, let's have some real fun."

"Good night, Kevin."

Before he could move, Laura was behind the closed door. In bed, she tossed and turned. Kevin had known just what to say. She was tired of playing it safe and running from life, but she was still hesitant about getting involved with anyone, and obviously, Kevin was too. *Maybe it will help me take my mind off Bryan.*

Right now, nothing sounded better than flying down an icy slope with the wind in her face, chasing away thoughts of Bryan Beaumont. Laura picked up the phone and dialed. When she heard Kevin's sleepy voice, she had second thoughts, but forged ahead with her plan to move on with her life.

"Hello, Kevin?"

"Yeah," he growled.

"I'm sorry. Were you asleep?"

"Actually, I was just wondering how you got out of that dress all alone. You know I'd have been glad to help." He paused, "Do I dare ask what's keeping you awake?"

"Let's go skiing."

Chapter Seventeen

It had been a perfect day. The lines were short, snow was falling, and the mood was light. Laura had packed their lunch and been ready when Kevin arrived. They were among the first on the slopes that morning and had stopped just long enough to eat. Most skiers were leaving before the pass closed. Kevin came to a stop next to Laura. "You ready to head for home before this storm gets any worse?"

"One last run before the lifts shut down. I've been away so long. It feels too good to stop now."

"Aren't you tired yet? I can't believe it's been six years since you skied. The way you acted when I suggested it, I assumed you would at least be a beginner, and I'd be able to impress you."

"You didn't tell me you used to be an instructor, either. Race you down," she challenged.

"Let's take one last easy run."

"Chicken. Who's playing it safe now?" Laura smiled.

Kevin shook his head in disbelief. "If that's what you want, you're on, lady."

The race was close. Laura was about to pass Kevin when she saw a shadow coming out of the trees.

Another body slammed into hers.
Sliding.
Couldn't stop.
She heard screams.
Her ski caught in the snow and was ripped from her boot.
The pain was instantaneous.
She stopped with a jolt.
Everything turned black.

Once Kevin crossed the finish line at the base of the slope he looked back. Laura was nowhere in sight. He waited, searching for her to come around that last curve.

"Where in blazes is she? She couldn't have passed me."

He turned and noticed the ski patrol in an organized commotion. He moved closer, overhearing a report of two injured skiers. They needed another rescue basket sent up the slope.

Kevin started toward the lift to go back up and find Laura, but the lanes were closed for the day. He wedged his way up the mountain as fast as he could.

When Kevin saw a woman wearing a ski patrol uniform headed down the mountain pulling a rescue basket, he gasped. Laura's blue jacket and brown hair were showing from under the blankets. "Laura?" He skied closer. "Laura!"

"Kev…" she moaned.

Kevin followed the ski patrol down to the lodge, giving them what personal information he could. Then he watched, in shock, as they loaded her into the ambulance. An hour later, he paced the emergency room waiting area to hear some news. Finally given permission to see her, he walked up to the bed, startled by her weak voice.

"You won this time, Kevin, but next time, you won't stand a chance." She turned her head and closed her eyes.

"Laura!"

"She'll be fine, we gave her a sedative to keep her

calm," the doctor said from behind him. He explained Laura's injuries and the need to keep her overnight.

When Laura woke up, Kevin was beside her.

"Hey there, lady."

"Hey there, yourself. Only a bullheaded chauvinist would go to that length to win a race."

"And only a sassy lady like you could come out of an accident like that with only a mild concussion and a few strained ligaments."

"Where am I?"

"At the hospital. The doctor wants to keep you overnight. Bryan is gonna be furious."

"It's none of his business. Besides, it was an accident. Or did you hire the hit?" Laura grinned.

"Don't get funny, lady. I thought maybe if I pushed you and Bryan a little, you'd see the obvious, that you two belong together. Truce?"

"For such a chauvinist, you have a good heart, Kevin."

"Hey, watch it! I have a reputation to keep up." He feigned anger, then smiled. "Get some sleep, Laura. It's going to be a long night."

Saturday afternoon, Bryan pulled into the driveway and carried his sleeping son to his crib. After worrying about Kevin and Laura's date the previous night, he was anxious to give his friend a piece of his mind.

Bryan ran up the stairs to Kevin's den. "Kevin, what do you think you're up to, taking Laura out?" The room was empty. He went back down the stairs to find Kevin's bed crumpled and looking like he'd had another of his wild nights. "Surely Laura didn't...she wouldn't...not with Kevin. Not *my* Laura."

He dialed Laura's number, then Kevin's cellular number, but neither answered. He waited impatiently all afternoon, and into the evening, then tried calling both again. No answer.

"Kevin, we've been friends ten years and you've never pulled anything like this. Why now when I was just beginning to trust her?''

Bryan and Kevin had agreed years ago that their private lives were none of each other's business, but nonetheless, he was perturbed that Kevin didn't call when he didn't come home that night, and furious that his best friend had made a move on Laura.

Bryan's anxiety worsened when she didn't appear at church the next morning. Hoping to placate his imagination, he drove by her house after the service was over. Kevin's dark green truck was parked in her driveway.

"How could you, Kevin?" Bryan parked the car, grabbed Jacob, and headed for the house, anger smoldering hotter with each step. The front door stood wide-open allowing snowflakes to gather on the carpet.

"Laura? Kevin?" Bryan walked on in, closing the door behind him. He put Jacob in the high chair and handed him a cracker from the diaper bag. Following the sound of Kevin's voice down the hallway toward the bedrooms, Bryan stopped momentarily when he heard Laura.

"How does this feel?" Kevin asked gently.

"Ohhh."

Her voice was soft and sensual.

After a moment's hesitation, Bryan stepped around the corner and into Laura's bedroom, expecting to see anything besides Laura in a pink sweat suit, hair strewn across a pillow, and her hands locked around Kevin's neck as he helped her lie back.

"Thank you, Kev…" Laura slurred.

"What did you do?" Bryan exclaimed.

Both Kevin and Laura looked up in surprise. Laura broke into a weak laugh. Kevin looked at her, then back to Bryan.

"I know how this must look, Bryan, but it isn't what you think," Kevin said quickly.

Laura giggled, tears rolling down her cheeks. "An incredible weekend. Kevin broke my zipper...." She fur-rowed her brows. "No, he fixed my zipper...in the middle of the night...he stayed with me. Such a sweet guy." She sat up and threw her arms around him, kissing his unshaven cheek. "Oh, my head, no, my leg hurts...."

"Is she okay?"

"Yes, she's okay!" Kevin growled. He took Laura by the shoulders and pushed her back onto the pillow. "You stay put, lady, before you get us into more trouble!"

Laura giggled, then smiled and closed her eyes.

Bryan took a step toward Kevin, his hands firmly planted on his hips. "How could you, Kevin?"

Chapter Eighteen

A few hours later, Laura stirred. Bryan brushed the curls from her forehead and examined the knot.

"How're you feeling?"

"Bryan. What are you doing here? Where's Kevin?" She looked down at her arms and frowned. "Where'd this sweat suit come from? What's going on?"

He let out a deep breath. "The nurse dressed you in it before you left the hospital. Need anything?" *At least that confirms Kevin's story.*

Obviously confused, she shook her head. "Hospital?"

"Feeling okay?"

"I'm fine. What's going on?" She tried to pull the covers higher, then seemed to notice her elevated leg.

Bryan stood up and stuffed his hands into his pockets. The smile disappeared. "So, what's going on with you and Kevin, Laura? Why did you go out with him when you've refused me countless times?"

She didn't answer.

"Well?"

"I thought he'd be a lot safer."

"Safer! Than *me?*"

Laura frowned, running her long fingers over the lump on her head. "You don't have to yell. Don't take it personally, Bryan. I mean, being with Kevin is easy...."

Bryan lowered his voice. "Fine then, if it's Kevin you're interested in, I'll..."

"I don't care a hoot about Kevin! I mean, not that way. I went out with Kevin for fun."

Bryan walked around the bed and sat in the window seat. "So I'm no fun now. You could at least give me a chance."

"I can't." Laura wished this whole weekend had never happened. Why had she been so weak and gone out with Bryan's best friend? Of all the crazy things she'd ever done, this was among the stupidest. "I missed the slopes, it's been six years since Steve and I skied. I needed..."

"Steve, the one from the spa?"

"We were skiing partners for ten years."

"Didn't that bother your husband?"

Laura nearly choked on her laughter. "They were best friends. Steve and I grew up next door to each other. He introduced Todd and I."

"Oh." Bryan stood and leaned against the door. "I've tried to be patient, Laura. Do you or don't you care for me?"

"Of course I do, I couldn't watch Jacob if I didn't," she said flippantly, sidestepping his question.

Bryan noticed the way Laura avoided looking at him. Even after a day with Kevin she still wouldn't admit she missed the companionship. He could have pushed the issue, but from the little information he'd dragged out of Kevin, it sounded as if he would have to test his patience.

"When did you get here?" Laura asked.

Bryan looked into those beautiful blue eyes, and his anger faded. She may not have admitted she wanted him to stay, but she didn't kick him out, either. "You don't remember?" Half a smile greeted Laura's frown.

"Oh, no. What did I do?" Laura grumbled.

"You said yes."

"To a date?" Her eyes opened wide. "I did not."

"You said you didn't remember anything." Bryan walked to her bedside and sat down.

"So you plan on taking advantage of my amnesia?"

He shook his head and chuckled. "I've never taken advantage of a woman, and I've never had to stoop to this level to get a date. However, I don't think you're in any position to say no. After one date with Kevin, you should be ready for just about anything," he teased.

Laura sat up in the bed and yelled, "What did that jerk tell you?"

"As much as it killed him to admit it, he said it was purely platonic."

She fell back onto the pillow. "Oh, my head..."

"Here's your prescription. I'll get you some water."

Laura pushed the bottle away. "I can't take that stuff. It does weird things to me."

"I think you mean you do weird things when you take it."

"Same diff. Would you please help me up so I can get some aspirin? Didn't Kevin bring me some crutches?"

"You won't need any, I'm staying right here to make sure you take it easy until your brother-in-law brings the kids home tomorrow. By then, hopefully, you and that brace will be working together."

"How do you know about my brother-in-law?"

"Marc isn't it? He called..."

"You talked to Marc? You didn't tell him about the accident, did you?"

"I thought it beat the options, under the circumstances. Explaining my presence when you were too drugged to answer the phone might have gotten me into another heap of trouble."

"Oh man, today's Sunday, isn't it? I was supposed to

go get them.'' Laura threw the blankets off and started to roll across the bed toward the phone.

Bryan touched her shoulder. "Will you relax? No one's going anywhere. While you were sleeping we got at least ten inches of snow, and it's still coming down. You and Kevin barely beat the storm here. You don't remember any of that?''

Laura looked puzzled. Bryan raised the lace shade on the window, revealing snow-covered trees. "School's already been canceled for tomorrow.''

"Well, I still have to work. I can't afford time off.''

"It wouldn't hurt you to give that leg one more day of rest before you have toddlers hanging all over you, but if the kids really have to come, I'll take care of them.''

Laura looked at the ceiling and closed her eyes. "Good grief, Bryan. You can't stay here. I'll call my sister.''

"Help yourself.'' He handed her the receiver and dialed the number as she recited it to him.

Tracy couldn't get through the snow. Laura tried Barb, but they had a house full of company stranded by the storm. After the two rejections, she slammed the phone into the cradle.

"Don't you dare say I told you so! Where's Jacob?''

"Taking a nap in the other room. Before the storm settled in, I picked up a few things. I'm going to finish dinner, then we're going to have a talk.''

"Talk?''

"Yeah, talk. We have a few things to settle. Need anything besides aspirin?''

She shook her head no. "They're in the hall closet.''

Laura pretended to read while she listened to pans clanging and Bryan's chipper whistling. After what seemed like forever, he returned to her bedside with a dinner tray and two aspirin.

"This looks delicious. You like cooking?'' Laura admired the noodles covered with stroganoff, French bread, fruit salad and broccoli spears on her plate. Alongside he had placed a tall glass of milk and a single red rose.

"When I have time. Do you?"

"I'm a mother, I cook all the time. I love it," she said defensively, remembering a previous conversation they'd had about opposites attracting. *I am in* big *trouble.*

They sat on her bed eating dinner between spurts of conversation, when Bryan reached across to her radio. "Let's see what kind of music you like to fall asleep to."

She covered the radio with her hand just as his came to rest on top of it. "And what makes you think I fall asleep to music?"

"You do, don't you?"

Laura couldn't prevent herself from smiling. "Okay, so I like to go to sleep with the music on. So what?"

"Oldies? Soft rock? Classical?"

Laura turned it on. Oldies played. "Classical? Really." She made a face and laughed.

He smiled. "I love it when you laugh. You work too hard at keeping up your defenses. Relax. Even if I agreed to leave, I couldn't get anywhere in my car now."

"Not a very practical car, is it?" Laura grimaced as she readjusted her leg and turned to fluff her pillows.

Bryan did it before she could reach them, and motioned for her to lie back. "Not much is in this weather, but it has its advantages. Think you might want to try taking a spin in it with me sometime? I understand you're ready for some fun again."

"Bryan, don't."

"What's so wrong with dating me, Laura?"

She looked into his eyes. It was still there, that longing that kept Laura at arm's length. She pulled her gaze from him and stared at her lap. She couldn't let him see her fear. "We work together. We're nothing alike. I don't want a commitment."

"And you think I do?"

"Don't you?"

She could see him thinking. Was he considering the question, or wondering if she could handle the truth? Whether he'd admit it or not, Laura could see that he wanted a family more than anything. "Is that what dating is to you, a commitment? Last time I checked, dating is a way to get to know someone, before making a commitment."

Bryan touched her chin gently, and Laura knew she should push him away, but she couldn't. It was as if, even for a moment, she wanted to allow herself to forget about the pain she was feeling in every other part of her body and concentrate on how wonderful his touch felt. For just a moment, she wanted to live dangerously and let herself want Bryan.

He leaned closer and their eyes met. "Laura, I can't promise you anything. But I don't like you taking crazy risks like you did yesterday."

"I didn't take any crazy risks, as if it's any of your business. I went skiing, like I have hundreds of times before, and will again."

"I didn't mean it that way. You can do what you want."

She pulled away. "Thank you. The pain of losing Todd is enough for a lifetime, Bryan. For me and the kids."

"I understand that. A wise woman once told me to put the pain behind me and go on with life. It seems she could stand to follow that same advice."

The look in his eyes was so sincere that she almost agreed. The lump in her throat dislodged and she was close to reaching out to him, to kissing him, to giving in to her feelings. *Why is he always right here when I'm most vulnerable?*

Jacob started crying and Bryan backed away, collected their dishes and walked out. As he left, Laura threw a pillow at the door. "Why'd you have to remember every cotton pickin' word I said?" she mumbled.

After Bryan had told her good-night and retired to the guest room, Laura slid from the edge of her bed. She cringed as she put weight on her leg, hugging the wall for extra support. Once in the family room, she immediately fell into the chair and sighed, realizing how exhausted she was.

As she reached for her Bible, she noticed a book on the table with Bryan's briefcase. It appeared Bryan was serious about his relationship with God. She held the book for a long time, fighting the temptation to open it and read any notes he might have written in the margins. In the end, her curiosity went unanswered, and Laura returned to her room.

All of her preschoolers stayed home with their parents the next day, leaving her alone with Bryan until her kids arrived late in the afternoon.

When Marc showed up, Laura was at her wit's end. Bryan had been wonderful—catering to her needs, keeping her entertained with old movies, cribbage, backgammon and his charming personality. In general, he had torn her opinion of his priorities all to pieces. As Marc hugged Laura goodbye, he gave her the last thing she wanted: his approval.

Chapter Nineteen

Bryan shuffled through the stack of papers on his desk for at least the tenth time. His mind was far from work, as it had been in the two endless weeks since Laura's accident.

There was a knock on the office door.

"Come in." He glanced up at his secretary, then continued his search. "Is there something I can help you with, Vicky?"

"Are you missing something?" She held up a folder.

Bryan groaned. "I've been looking for that all afternoon." He reached across his desk for the folder, seeing a look of concern in her eyes. As Vicky sat in the chair across from him, he settled back into his own to brace himself for her pending lecture. "Is there anything else?"

"So far, I think I'm the only one who realizes your mind's not completely here. What's going on? These mistakes are totally out of character for you, Bryan. Even after Andrea left you, your work was faultless."

How could she tell? Of course, they'd worked together seven out of the eight years he'd been with the company, when he was fresh out of college. She had worked for his boss before he retired, then for Bryan when he was promoted.

Vicky was a terrific secretary, but she was more than that to him. She was like an older sister when it came to his personal life, helping him through his relationship with Andrea, their wedding, the separation, Jacob's arrival, and here she was again, as if on cue.

Vicky interrupted his thoughts. "I'm here if you need a sympathetic ear."

"It's probably too soon," he continued as if they were already in the middle of the conversation.

"For what?"

"Dating. I've been out a couple of times since Andrea left, but there's someone I'd like to date...seriously."

"So, what's the problem?"

"She's convinced we shouldn't see each other, but I can't give up. I didn't expect I'd ever trust a woman again. I mean..."

"I know what you mean. No offense taken. She sounds like quite a woman."

"After she went out with Kevin a few weeks ago, I thought I'd gone totally insane. He claims he wasn't seriously making a move on her, but I find it hard to picture any man not seeing how terrific she is. They both insist it was platonic. And worse, I believe them."

Vicky didn't say a word.

"Her leg is doing better, and..."

"Laura?" She gasped. "You sure that's a good idea?"

Bryan closed his briefcase and walked across the office to the window. "No, blast it, I'm not sure of anything anymore. Believe me, I've tried to get this notion of Laura and me together out of my mind. It's no use. What if we fell in love, Vicky? Is it right to deny each other happiness? Is it right to deny our children a family and loving parents?"

"Marriage? You've really thought about this, haven't you?"

"She's changed my life."

"What if it doesn't work out? I assume you've already considered the effect that could have on Jacob, let alone her children. They've already lost one father."

"So what do I do? Look at this." He held up the incomplete report, "I'll be out of a job within a month if this continues." He put the file in his briefcase and shook his head. "I know this is lousy timing for both of us, but surely we can work through that."

He'd never felt this emptiness before. Even when Andrea first left him, it hadn't been like this. He'd filled the hole with his career, and everything had gone smoothly. Until he met Laura Bates.

"I've never seen you quite like this." Vicky looked at Bryan and smiled.

"What's that grin about?"

"In all the years I've known you, you've rarely been rejected. And I can't begin to count the broken hearts around here before you finally settled down with Andrea."

Bryan cocked his head at the older woman. "You don't need to dig up those skeletons, Vicky."

"Laura's quite a woman, isn't she?"

"To say the least. She's strong yet vulnerable, determined yet sensible, intelligent, confident and has more artistic talent than all the women I ever dated put together. And I'm getting the impression she's a bit too courageous at times. It's enough to scare a grown man."

"You mean the accident? Well, she likes a challenge, but she's not careless. I'll never forget when Todd asked her to stop skiing...."

"Asked her to stop?" Bryan tried to remember exactly what she'd said about Todd and Steve. He was certain she didn't mention this. "What about it?"

"The older two kids were born during ski season, so she had no choice to make. She'd found out she was pregnant with Chad just before ski season opened. She was a great skier, so it wasn't all that dangerous, but Todd was worried she'd get hurt and lose the baby. It wasn't easy for her to stop. Now, with three busy kids, I doubt she gets the chance to do much skiing.'' Vicky shook her head and laughed. ''I never dreamed I'd start a torrid romance by referring you to Laura.''

Bryan leaned his head back against his chair. ''She's going to drive me insane.''

''Oh, I hope you'll survive, you poor man. Good luck, Bryan, but don't get discouraged. It could be she just needs more time. Todd's death shook her up pretty badly.''

Bryan looked at his watch, jumping to his feet and rushing out the door as he spoke. ''It's six o'clock! She's going to have my hide. Sorry I kept you late.''

''Good luck,'' Vicky said with a knowing grin.

''Thanks, I need it,'' Bryan replied.

Bryan pushed the speed limit to Laura's house, still unable to divert his thoughts from her. Each night he recalled how gently she held Jacob, how helpless she had looked crippled in bed after her skiing accident; but mostly, he thought of how he'd love to hold her in his arms the way he had the night they lifted weights.

''I'll give it one more try, and if she turns me down, I'm giving up.'' He pulled into the driveway. ''Okay, if she says no, I'll wait another month. I can't believe I'm doing this,'' he mumbled as he walked up the steps. He rang the doorbell and walked in as usual. It was now or never.

Laura was hobbling around, trying to get the kids ready to go. She stepped over the doll Jacob had taken back out of the toy box. ''Hurry up, kids. Please. My meeting starts in half an hour!''

Bryan noticed that she had changed from her jeans to dress slacks and a cashmere sweater. It was the first time since the accident that he'd seen her without the brace.

Their eyes met as she handed Jacob to him in total silence. He took a deep breath. ''Sorry I'm late. Laura, I know you keep saying we're just friends, that we're nothing alike, that you don't want to ruin our working relationship, but I want to get to know you better. I'd like to take you to dinner. Nothing heavy, just a night without kids. You hardly have a leg to stand on after your date with Kevin.''

"Very funny."

He glanced at her leg, smiling. "How is it?"

"Better." She looked into his eyes and took a deep breath. "The kids'll be gone for the weekend. It sounds nice."

"Nice. Not fun?"

Laura grinned. "Okay, it sounds fun. As you can see, I'm running behind schedule right now. Let's talk about it tomorrow."

Bryan smiled boyishly. "Yes?"

"Yes. Don't make an issue out of it. It's just dinner, to make up for being late, again."

Cool it Bryan, it's a start. His confidence reinstated, Bryan told Laura goodbye, and started out the door.

The phone rang, and Laura waved goodbye to Bryan.

After Bryan was out the door, he lifted Jacob's hand and gave him five. "I can't believe she finally said yes. Wo-ha!" Jacob chortled, as if understanding what his father had just said.

Jacob looked at his dad with a serious look on his face. Bryan grinned and patted his son's back. "You're too young to worry about women." He tried to imagine Jacob, asking to borrow the car to take a date to the drive-in movie. "I hope you don't have to go through what I did to find the right woman, son." Jacob was still watching his father, looking more puzzled than ever. "I can't believe I'm talking to an eight-month-old about dating."

Chapter Twenty

Laura had heard wonderful reviews of the lavish restaurant Bryan picked for dinner. After a hectic day, she'd taken time for a bubble bath to try to calm her nerves. It didn't help.

One outfit after another was tossed aside for some reason or another. "I should have bought a new dress," she grumbled aloud.

The doorbell rang. "Of all times to be early, you picked tonight!" She pulled out the last dress from the closet and pulled it over her head.

There was a knock on the bedroom door, and Laura froze. Barb called out her name, and Laura opened the door to find her best friend and Barb's daughter Kate, who was going to baby-sit. "You scared me to death! I thought Bryan was here."

"You forgot to pick Kate up, so I thought I'd bring her and see if you needed a last minute pep talk."

"I'm a bundle of nerves. Does this look okay?" Laura brushed a string from the front of her dress and turned to look in the mirror. The deep purple linen dress would never go out of style.

"Perfect. Skip the jacket, though."

"I don't want him to get the wrong impression." Laura went to put on her makeup while Barb hung up the dresses that were strewn from one end of the room to the other.

Barb lifted her eyebrows. "It's a date, not a business meeting. He'll approve."

Laura again considered adding the flowered jacket. "I can't believe I'm doing this! I'm a thirty-year-old mother of three, and I'm going on a date."

"It's not that uncommon, unfortunately."

Laura pulled out the pearl earrings and necklace that Todd had given her for their tenth anniversary. She ran her fingers over them, cherishing the memories, then put them on.

"You look fabulous."

Again the doorbell rang.

"I'll just wait here, I didn't mean to stay until Bryan arrived."

"Sure you didn't. You'd have hidden in the bushes if you had to."

"Okay, so I did hope I could see the two of you together. It feels just like waiting for Kate to go on her first date. I want you to have a great time."

"I don't even remember feeling this nervous when I was sixteen. I didn't like the dating routine the first time around, and I like it even less now."

"You'll be fine," Barb assured her. "You told me yourself, first and foremost, Bryan is a good friend. There's nothing to worry about."

When she walked out to the living room, Bryan was introducing Jacob to Kate. He turned and saw Laura walking down the hall and did a double take.

Bryan's eyes met hers, then glanced at her apprecia- tively. Her soft curls were swept away from her face, showing off the pearl necklace around her graceful neck. His gaze settled on her tentative smile.

He handed Jacob to Kate and walked over to Laura.

"You look gorgeous." He smiled. "Are you going to do okay on those heels?"

"I didn't think about that. Maybe I should wear something lower. I'll be right back."

As he talked to Kate, he heard voices drifting down the hall. Laura introduced him to her friend.

He turned to the woman at Laura's side. "Hi, Barb. I didn't realize you'd be helping with Jacob."

"I'm not. I just came for moral support."

"She's that close to backing out, huh?" He looked into Laura's eyes, which looked almost violet in contrast to her dress. He couldn't help but see the uncertainty she was feeling.

"I am not chickening out. I've given you plenty of chances to change your mind. Now you're stuck for the evening." Laura smiled, feigning confidence.

"You two get going. No need to hang around here."

"Jacob's dinner is on the high chair...."

Barb scowled, motioning impatiently for them to leave.

After starting the car, Bryan kissed Laura's hand, pleased to see her blush at the simple gesture.

He hadn't noticed until this moment how little she did to enhance her beauty. She was always pretty, but tonight, with makeup, polished nails, and hair elegantly styled, she looked absolutely striking. "You look radiant tonight, Laura."

"Thanks. You look pretty handsome yourself."

He put the car into gear. "No need for formalities. If you haven't noticed, I'm already impressed."

Bryan pulled up to the restaurant a few minutes later. Turning the car over to the valet, he escorted Laura to the door. Inside, Laura glanced briefly at him as he helped her

with her coat, then let her gaze settle on the exquisite surroundings.

"This is not what I call a simple date. It's so elegant,"
she whispered.

He leaned close and spoke in her ear. "From what I hear,
it blends ambience with Colorado hospitality. I hope you
like it."

The host interrupted. "Good evening. A table for two?"

"Reservations for Beaumont."

"This way, Mr. Beaumont, madame."

After the waiter had seated Laura, Bryan seated himself
in the chair next to hers and listened while the waiter re-
viewed the chef's specialties and suggested an outrageously
priced wine.

"You don't have to go for broke here, Bryan. I'm not
picky."

"That's one of the things I like best about you, Laura.
You never put on pretenses, even when you're dressed for
the kill."

"I told you the Sports Connection would be fine, I could
have worn jeans."

"I'm glad you're not in your jeans, you look fabulous
in that dress."

"I did not agree to dinner to be teased."

"Too bad. I love watching you blush."

She laughed. "I feel like a fool going through this dating
routine again." Laura wondered if there would be other
men, other dates, and if they would be as unsettling.

Laura watched as the sun's coral glow sank behind
Long's Peak. She closed her eyes, letting them adjust to
the dim light.

"We've become good friends, haven't we Laura?"

"Yes, we have. You've been a tremendous support."

"You, too, but I hope this isn't a date of gratitude."

She tensed. *Just when I thought I could really do this,*

he has to remind me of his honorable intentions. "Of course not," she said quietly.

"Then relax and enjoy yourself."

A reflection of the flickering candle danced in his eyes. Chocolate, she thought. His eyes were so warm, they could turn her broken heart into marshmallows—and melt every one. Laura turned to look at the purple glow fading behind the silhouette of the mountains, catching Bryan's gaze in the reflection of the window. The waiter brought the appetizer and filled the water glasses.

Bryan held up his goblet. "To beginnings."

She forced herself to meet his heartwarming gaze. "To friendship," Laura added. Their goblets rang in agreement.

Bryan put a spoonful of lingonberry sauce on the wedge of Camembert cheese and topped it with a sprig of fried parsley, then raised the tidbit to Laura's lips.

Laura reluctantly opened her mouth for the bite, annoyed that he could make sharing their food feel so natural. She closed her lips around the bite and let the morsel melt in her mouth. "Mmm, that's delicious."

Bryan grinned lazily as he prepared his own, and from there, the conversation flowed easily throughout dinner. Laura steered their discussion to the kids and work, and as far away from 'them' as she could.

They listened to the musicians playing a tune from the sixties. Bryan looked at Laura, and they both smiled. She'd noticed at some point in the evening that even their silence had become comfortable.

"Dance with me?"

"I'm not sure my leg is ready."

"Liar. I saw you playing basketball with T.J. and Chad yesterday. I promise to take it easy." Bryan stood, held out his hand and led her to the dance floor. The lights were low and a fire crackled in the massive stone fireplace. A flame licked a pocket of pitch and exploded like firecrackers.

Laura jumped. Immediately his arms, filled with tenderness and security, folded like a blanket around her. Laura knew she couldn't resist this man if he didn't stop being so wonderful. *How can being with another man feel so nice?*

When Bryan pulled her closer, Laura found herself wishing the song would end, yet missing him already. She closed her eyes, realizing her senses were working overtime to memorize everything about Bryan: the spicy smell of his cologne, his firm muscles underneath the wool jacket, and the gentle reassurance of his fingertips on her waist.

Laura opened her eyes to the reality of his presence, his probing gaze, the lock of brown hair that had fallen onto his forehead, and the smiling lips that invited her to kiss them. They swayed in unison to the soft rhythm.

After a few dances, the tempo picked up and Bryan backed away, leading her aside. "I imagine your leg is ready for a rest."

Overwhelmed by the peacefulness in her heart, she simply nodded.

"It's still early. Would you like to go for a drive, or catch a movie? There's a concert at the civic center." Bryan helped her into her coat and led her to the car.

"There's a movie I've been wanting to see, since I don't have to rush home to kids."

"Are you going to tell them about tonight, or am I the reason they're conveniently gone?"

"No, I'm not, and yes, you are, sort of. I suspected you'd ask me again."

He lifted his eyebrows. "Suspected? Or Hoped?"

She felt herself turn pink, thankful that the sun was down. "I think a lot of you, Bryan, but I can't stand to see them hurt again."

"How do you plan to protect them forever, Laura?"

"Forever?"

"Life without trust and love is pretty lonely. I have no intention of hurting any of you."

"I only meant, I don't want them to get their hopes up. It's obvious that they like you, but kids have a way of making mountains out of molehills."

"Such as?"

"We're already walking a tightrope here, Bryan. I'm only trying to lessen the pressure. Trust me. When we've both accepted that this…this…"

"Attraction? Magnetism? Obsession?"

"…is merely loneliness, you'll be glad the kids' emotions aren't involved. We'll find it easier to say goodbye." The car was quiet except for the drone of the tires beneath them. Laura slipped her hand to the edge of the seat, stroking the soft leather.

"I trusted your advice about Jacob, thank God, or I'd have lost my only chance to be a father, but I don't know what to say about this."

She smiled, mostly to herself. "I'm glad you don't regret your decision. What Andrea did will always hurt, but it's not your only chance to have a child."

"That's kind of hard to do without a wife, and right now that option is looking pretty bleak. The only woman I'd even consider, doesn't want me personally involved with her children."

Laura blinked away the tears, unsure how to respond to his admission. Before she could say anything, the car stopped and Bryan led her into the theater. He held her hand throughout most of the movie, and she wondered if he knew how tempted she was to get up and run away from him. Away from life. Away from love.

After the movie, Bryan drove to her house in silence.

He reached across the car to stop her from opening the door. "Wait, and I'll help you get out." She didn't argue when he put his hand on her waist as they walked up the driveway. "May I come back after I take the sitter home?"

There's nothing to be afraid of. Laura nodded.

Kate briefed them on Jacob's evening, then accepted Bryan's offer to drive her home.

Laura answered the ringing telephone, relieved that it wasn't her in-laws, who were watching the kids. "Barb...I can't talk now. I'll call you tomorrow.... Yes, it was very nice...."

Laura looked up and saw Bryan come around the corner. He leaned his shoulder against the door frame. One hand was jammed in his trouser pocket, and the other was resting on his hip in an incredibly masculine stance. "Good night, Barb." She hung up. "Barb's..."

"No explanation necessary, Kevin'll grill me, too."

She returned his smile. "Would you like some tea?"

"Sure. I'll just check on Jacob while the water's boiling."

"Just a second and I'll join you."

Bryan took Laura's hand and held it while they admired the sleeping child.

"He's grown so much."

For a long while, Bryan said nothing. "You should have incarcerated me for being willing to send my own son away."

"It was tempting." She pulled on his hand to get him to look at her so he'd know she was teasing. When he did look, she saw his moist eyes. "You didn't do it, Bryan. That's all that matters now." She tightened her hand around his. "Come on. Let's go have that cup of tea."

"You go ahead, I'll be along in a minute." When she went to the living room with the tea, Bryan was seated on the couch. He had removed his jacket and loosened his tie. She felt a twinge of panic as she realized he wanted her to sit next to him. She handed him his cup of butter-rum tea and sat in the stuffed chair across from him.

Bryan appeared disappointed by her silent message.

They talked for a while, then Laura hinted that she

needed to get up early the next morning for church. Bryan
took her cue, got Jacob from the crib, and wrapped him in
his blanket. Before he left, Bryan kissed her lightly on the
lips. "Thanks for the wonderful evening, Laura. I really
enjoyed it."

"I had a nice time, too." She smiled, wondering how a
simple peck could evoke such a powerful reaction. *How
can I feel this way so soon after Todd's gone? And how
can I feel this way about Bryan? He's nothing like Todd.*

After locking the door and turning out the lights, Laura
went to bed, but tossed and turned. She rolled over and
looked at Todd's picture staring at her from the nightstand.
She knew that he would want her to move on with her life.
They had always agreed they would be open to fall in love
and remarry if either of them died. It had been easy to say
at the time—they still had each other.

Thoughts returned her to the security of Bryan's arms.
Romantic music played, and a gold-and-crystal teardrop
chandelier showered over them as they danced. Childhood
dreams of dancing with Prince Charming couldn't even
compare to tonight.

Laura closed her eyes. Bryan's large hand gingerly
stroked the dew from the crystal goblet, and comforted her
when she was startled by the fire. She felt his whisper in
her ear, and smelled the cologne that still lingered in each
breath she took.

Her final undoing was standing with Bryan over his
sleeping baby, sharing emotions so deep that they had
brought tears to a grown man's eyes. What was it that
Bryan was feeling? Joy? Guilt? Regret? Whatever it was,
she'd felt something in her heart change at the sight of his
tears.

Chapter Twenty-One

"Beep! Beep! Beep! Beep!"

She fumbled for the button to turn the alarm off, knocking a lotion bottle off the nightstand in the process. When the electronic chirping stopped, she dropped her head into her pillow and slept for ten more minutes, when the snooze alarm rang again.

As usual, her early morning thoughts turned to Todd, who always woke cheerful and ready for the day, teasing her unmercifully about the way she set her alarm earlier than she needed to get up and let it go off several times before she got out of bed. Even then, she wasn't really awake until after a shower and a second cup of coffee.

A night owl since her teens, Laura had always stayed up until the wee hours of the morning. It had only gotten worse after the kids were born. Those precious hours were her reprieve from the demands of motherhood.

Now, the nights were too quiet, too lonely and much too long. She no longer slept soundly as she once had, dreams of Todd waking her regularly. Dreams so real she'd reach out to touch him, and find herself clutching his pillow instead. This morning was no exception. She threw his pillow across the room and stumbled into the shower.

She returned to her bedroom. The purple dress on the chair turned her thoughts to Bryan. He'd been quite clear about his feelings, and his honesty had done more than just startle her. It was more like a potent sense of shame that Bryan's admission thrilled her.

What would Todd think of Bryan? Was he the type of man Todd would want raising his children? Would Todd have trusted his wife to Bryan's care?

Before she could answer, the phone rang. "Laura, I have to apologize. Marc and I thought the kids were asleep. They overheard us talking."

"So. What's the problem?"

The voices that greeted her next were not Kayla's, but Carrie's. "How was your date, Mom?"

"Did you ask Bryan if he will be our daddy?" Chad added. Her feeble refusal didn't even convince herself.

"Did you kiss him?" T.J. yelled from the background.

"We had a nice time. And the rest is not up for discussion. I'll see you this afternoon and then we'll go to the zoo. Gregory and his parents are coming too, remember. Let me talk to Aunt Kayla."

Standing beside Bryan, Laura saw Barb coming toward them. "Not now Barb, I'm not ready to announce it to the whole congregation."

"Be nice to me, or I might!" she teased. "I just came over to invite Bryan to go to the zoo with us. And Gregory suggested we stop for pizza afterward."

Laura looked at Bryan, who seemed to catch Barb's intentions immediately. "That sounds fun, but it's up to you, Laura."

She knew he wanted to accept, and silently admired his yielding to let the decision be hers. "They already know about last night. You're welcome to join us if you'd like."

"I'd like."

Barb smiled. "See you at our house, say, twelve-thirty?"

It was a warm day for winter, but still cool enough to require coats. Laura had rushed home to change and get the van ready. When Bryan and Jacob arrived, they added baby gear, then drove to Chuck and Barb's house.

Chuck slapped Bryan on the shoulder and laughed. "You sly dog, you didn't tell me the woman was Laura Bates!"

"Bryan, what's he talking about? You know each other?"

"Chuck invited me to join the men's prayer group a couple of months ago. We should get going."

"You never mentioned it before," she said quietly.

"Didn't know I was supposed to clear it with you." His eyes were warm and teasing, as if he liked the thought of being accountable to her.

"I didn't mean it like that. I was just surprised."

Laura found herself wishing the kids were along so they would provide a distraction, as Jacob had fallen asleep in his seat before they even arrived at her house.

In the moments of silence, her thoughts returned to the men's prayer group. Laura couldn't help but wonder if they'd been praying for her? And exactly what had Bryan asked for? Suddenly she felt the fear of being hurt all over again. Was his interest in his faith sincere, or was he only using it to find a new mother for his son?

Just blocks before they reached Marc and Kayla's, Bryan asked. "Why'd you change your mind about telling the kids about our date?"

"It was changed for me."

"Did they mind?"

"Did they mind? You know they didn't." That was the problem, or at least part of it. From the day Bryan Beaumont walked into her life, her children had been captivated with him.

Laura introduced Kayla and Bryan, trying to ignore

Marc's look of approval. She pushed to leave right away, half afraid her brother-in-law would ask Bryan his intentions. She'd already figured that out. Bryan wanted a housewife and mother for his son. A woman who could "maintain a balance" in their lives.

Bryan waited until the kids were engrossed with the Dall sheep climbing on the artificial rock mountain to whisper into her ear. "What's bothering you, Laura?"

It unnerved her that he could read her moods so easily. "All of this is too much. I'm just not ready," Laura said. "Last night was wonderful, but I…can't." She began to walk. Bryan took her hand. She wished she had the strength to pull it from his tender grip.

"I've never been so comfortable with any woman, and I hoped you felt the same. Is a little relaxation, fun and a friend to listen to too much to hope for?" He continued to hold her hand as they walked behind the others.

She couldn't even answer.

The kids rushed up to them, begging to ride the miniature train around the children's zoo. Bryan handed Chuck some money for Laura's children's share and asked Chuck to meet them in the bird sanctuary after they were done. He took Jacob from the stroller, and asked Laura to join him.

Outside, a dozen penguins played. "I wonder what that penguin has in mind?" Bryan whispered in her ear as they watched two penguins nuzzling.

She laughed as the female walked away. "His name must be Kevin. He's getting the brush-off."

"I think you're right. Smart female." Their eyes met in an understanding gaze. "Now if that had been a goose instead, she'd know his intentions were honorable."

Laura blushed.

"Because geese mate for life."

"And they most often live in solitude after a mate dies."

"Thankfully, we're not geese."

"Stop it, Bryan."

"Just who is laying this guilt trip on you?"

"What makes you think that?"

"Before you went to your in-laws for Christmas, you certainly didn't seem to mind a little flirting. Since you came home…"

"You've had a one-track mind!"

"Mom, that was cool! Thanks, Bryan." Her kids ran to catch up to them.

"Sure, any time."

Laura glared at Bryan and moved on, unwilling to argue with him any longer. Especially when he was twisting words again.

It was just too soon after losing Todd. Wasn't it?

And what if he was only looking for a mother and house-keeper? *"Geese mate for life." He can't be serious. The man will do anything to see me blush.*

Later, at the other end of the park, the boys challenged Bryan to race them to the polar bear pool. As they ran down the ramp to the underwater window, Laura silently confessed how right they looked together. Chad and T.J. missed their father terribly. Even Carrie's struggle for independence had improved since Laura had listened to Bryan's advice. Was she making a mistake?

Her kids even loved playing with Jacob. Knowing children as she did, she figured it was the novelty of having a baby around part-time that interested them.

Laura pulled the empty stroller behind her. She and Barb walked in silence. Chuck looked at his wife, then at Laura. "You two are never this quiet. What's up?"

"Your wife thinks I'm a chicken," Laura said, clearly ignoring Barb.

Barb nudged Laura playfully. "I know it isn't easy, but I hate the thought of you turning away such a wonderful guy."

Chuck added, "I've gotten to know Bryan well, and I see no reason for you to hesitate."

Laura watched the boys and Bryan race to the giraffe house. Carrie, who had been trying to show Jacob the wolves, joined them.

Laura felt tears coming, and blinked them away. "Everyone sees the side of me that is strong and taking care of others, but no one sees the frightened child inside. How can I be sure?"

"I think you already know, Laura. Leave these imaginary expectations behind. What do you feel for Bryan?"

"T.J.'s crazy about him, Chad's ready to call him Dad, and even Carrie has warmed up to him. Why couldn't he have left things as they were?"

Barb seemed to let silence soothe Laura's emotions before responding. "It's understandable to be afraid. Losing someone you love hurts. But sometimes, not loving hurts just as much."

"Todd's only been gone a few months."

"What does that really matter? Whether it's six months or ten years. Your love for him won't ever go away. Todd would want you to be happy. And I see a man over there who looks very happy to be with you. Place it in God's hands, Laura."

Bryan walked back to Laura, then lifted his son to his shoulders. He seemed at ease with fatherhood, and Laura loved watching them together. She thought of Barb's advice. Was she brought into their lives to keep them together? To show Bryan the riches he had already been given as a child of God?

Again, Laura wondered if it was fair to let her children get so close to Bryan, only to chance losing him one day.

Despite her apprehension, it had been a perfect afternoon. The kids were slowing down by the time they got to the pizza parlor. They pulled three tables together under the brass kettle lamps and crowded the chairs close. While they waited for their meal, Bryan lifted his soda. "To a bright future."

In the dim light, Laura looked into Bryan's eyes. She could see the emotions that frightened her most. Even worse, she wasn't so sure she could do anything to stop them.

Jacob, apparently the only one left with any energy, kept them entertained throughout supper with his cheerful babbling. When they walked to the van, Laura handed Bryan the keys. "My leg is bothering me. Would you drive?"

"Sure. Overdid it, huh?"

Laura nodded.

A ballad about a love affair ending came on the radio. The words echoed through her mind…"Where do I go from here?"…and she pushed the button to another station.

Bryan turned around to check on the kids as if he hadn't noticed. "Looks like they've fallen asleep."

"As hard as they ran, I'd hope so. I don't know how they lasted this long." She squirmed, then turned to face out the side window. "Bryan, I don't know how to say this…"

"Then don't." He reached over and took hold of her hand, tentatively wrapping his fingers around hers. "I know moving on is difficult, Laura, but I think we can help each other through it. I want to continue spending time together."

"I don't want the kids to get used to it. What happens when it's over between us? It'll be confusing enough for my kids, but what about Jacob? If he sees me day and evening, he'll think…" She couldn't say it. She hated the fact that already Jacob knew her as his only mother, but she couldn't say it to Bryan.

"You're his mother? He couldn't be any luckier than to have a mom like you. And who says I'm going to let you go?"

She turned her head and looked straight at him. "No, Bryan. You can't mean that."

"Is the thought of us together so terrible?"

Laura pulled her hand away. "We need more time."

"For what? Dating? You think dating men like Kevin is going to include no strings? I'll tell you something straight out. You are probably the first woman he's spent a weekend with that he didn't at least try to take to bed. And it wasn't his choice, I'll tell you that. You may think that you can set the rules, Laura, but the men who don't want any commitment are usually the type who expect all the fringe benefits. I guess I've been there myself, but no more."

Tears continued to blur her vision, but she hoped in the dark that Bryan couldn't see.

"My marriage was nothing like yours. I can't even begin to explain it, but suffice it to say the love was gone long before Andrea died. I tried to convince myself otherwise up until the end. With your help, I faced the truth."

Her voice was ready to break. "Bryan—I'm sorry."

"Don't be. That's past, and now I see a chance to have everything I missed. I'm not giving up easily."

She took his hand. "You've been a terrific friend, Bryan. I care very much for you and Jacob, but..."

He pulled into her driveway and proceeded to help the kids into the house. Jacob stayed asleep in his arms.

"Bryan," Laura continued, "Please. We can't let this continue. I'll see you in the morning."

Small lines appeared on his forehead when he furrowed his brows. "We have a discussion to finish. You do what you need to, I'll wait."

While Laura tucked her kids into bed, Bryan rocked Jacob to sleep and carried him to the portable crib Laura kept in the guest room. When he returned, he found Laura working in the kitchen.

"Laura. There's something I want to clear up."

The last time he'd been this serious, he'd told her he was sending Jacob to live with his sister. What was he so serious about now?

"Before you try to end our relationship, I think it's time I level with you."

"It's much easier to end it before anyone gets hurt."

"You're the one who told me to let go and move on. You can't go on living as if memories of Todd are enough to see you through the coming years."

"I'm not…"

"Don't try to deny it, Laura. You and Todd had a terrific marriage, I know. Everyone has made that perfectly clear to me." Bryan stepped closer.

Laura started to back away, but he stopped her. "I'm not trying to replace him for you or your kids. I won't ask the kids to stop telling me all about their dad, and when you need to talk about Todd, I'll be here. I'm not afraid of facing your memories head-on." Bryan took another step.

"Please don't…"

"You're happy when we're together. You have fun. You can't dress like you did last night and pretend you don't care for me, at least a little."

"I simply wore what I felt was appropriate for the restaurant. Don't read any more into it than that," Laura said, trying to sound angry without blushing. She backed up and ran into the counter. He followed her, not trapping her physically, but emotionally.

"The hair, the perfume, the purple dress, were all for the restaurant?" His eyebrow lifted. His smile was as intimate as a kiss.

"I wasn't trying to impress you, if that's what you're hoping! I don't need another man in my life. I don't want…"

Bryan pulled her close and pressed his lips to hers.

Possessively.

Needingly.

Tenderly.

Laura wanted to pull away from him, but she had waited for a repeat of his inviting lips on hers for too long. The gentleness of Bryan's kiss made her forget every argument she'd prepared. Though her eyes were closed, she saw nothing but his face, strong yet vulnerable. Laura realized that she didn't want to push him away.

He didn't seem to want to stop kissing her, and when his mouth left hers, she ached from the loss. She felt his warm breath against her cheek, his whiskers scratching her skin as he whispered in her ear, "I want you to marry me, Laura."

Chapter Twenty-Two

Bryan grinned, the look in his eyes confident, always confident. He loosened his embrace, allowing her to move away if she wished.

"You're...you...you can't be serious!" she gasped.

"I wanted to wait until we'd spent a little more time together, to be honest, but you seem in a hurry to put an end to any hope of courting you."

Laura didn't move further from him, and he made no attempt to pull her close again. "Courting me? Todd hasn't even been dead a year," she said, her voice fragile and shaking.

"Would you have turned Todd away if you'd known then that he'd die twelve years later? Wouldn't you have been sorry never to have loved him, to have missed having your three wonderful children? Do you really enjoy being alone, Laura?" He stared into her eyes, analyzing her reaction.

Laura looked away. She didn't speak. She couldn't. Of course, everything Bryan had said was painfully true. Even at the young age of seventeen, she'd had the courage to follow her heart. Where had that gone?

The silence between them became more painful.

Bryan whispered, "You feel this attraction between us, Laura. Doesn't that mean anything to you?"

She shook her head. "It means I'm lonely. Nothing more."

Bryan took hold of her hand and led her to the sofa. She found herself studying his profile and thinking of the night he'd held her tenderly while she cried over memories of Todd.

"I believe you've convinced yourself of that. But haven't you ever wondered if God brought us together because we need each other?" He waited, and when she didn't speak, he added, "Just listen for a minute, Laura. I know it sounds crazy, but I really think this could work...."

Laura listened as he presented nearly a dozen reasons why he had asked her to marry him. Love was not one of them. She shouldn't have expected him to love her, but she couldn't help feeling disheartened that a marriage proposal had come without it.

And crazy as it seemed, she couldn't argue with any of his reasons.

Theoretically, the plan could work. He was an ambitious executive in need of a mother for his son. Her three heartbroken children were in need of a daddy. She had someday wanted to find a strong man capable of being both a father and husband. She just hadn't expected it to happen so soon.

Her feelings for Bryan had nothing to do with reason. They'd caught her unexpectedly. Since the day he'd walked into her home, she'd tried to reason away the implications of his actions. She'd tried to ignore the warmth she felt at the sound of his deep voice. She'd fought for independence, broken by the reality that merely knowing he was there to help brought unimaginable comfort.

If she didn't let herself love him, she'd reasoned, it wouldn't hurt when he left. Yet Bryan Beaumont brought her numbed senses alive. She'd never imagined he would ask her to marry him. With or without a proclamation of love.

Laura again wondered what had happened between him and his wife. Was it awful enough to keep him from loving another woman?

Taking hold of his hands, she sighed, shaking her head. "Bryan—"

"Don't answer yet. Think about it."

She didn't pretend to try to sleep, didn't even change to her pajamas. The first few hours after he left were spent in a state of mild shock. The next one, crying over the possibility of saying yes. And at least two more over the prospect of telling Bryan no.

Logic told her a marriage of convenience between them could actually work. Even though they'd only known each other six months, Laura knew him well enough to respect him and honor their marriage vows. He'd already developed a wonderful rapport with her children, a difficult issue with many second marriages.

She couldn't argue that she'd been attracted to him from the moment they met, and as Bryan had admitted, the feeling was mutual. Would love eventually grow between them? Or had Jacob's mother taken Bryan's love with her to the grave? Could Laura's love ever heal his wounds?

He's been so wonderful, God. Even though he doesn't love me, I feel special to him. I like the way he treats me and the kids. Is it possible that we could heal each other's broken hearts?

Throughout their business relationship communication had improved. "Even our arguments have been good. Save that first one, I've never worried that he'd leave if I confronted him. He's patient, and kind, and..."

Laura pulled her Bible from the bookshelf and opened it to the book of Corinthians. "'Love is patient, love is kind. It does not envy, it does not boast, it is not proud.'" *He was a little jealous when I went skiing with Kevin, but then, knowing Kevin's reputation, I can't find fault in that. He was just protecting me... But why? If he doesn't love me, why would he care?*

"'It is not rude, it is not self-seeking...'" *Is considering marrying for our children's welfare self-seeking?*

"'It is not easily angered, it keeps no record of wrongs.'" *His temper is no worse than mine, and he's humble enough to apologize soon afterward. A lesson I could learn.*

She quickly read the rest of the verses, and measured her relationship with Bryan against His desired qualities. So far, she had only come up with one reason not to marry Bryan. They weren't *in love.*

Is mutual attraction, respect, and a common interest in providing the children with a family enough to build a marriage on?

The next morning she called the preschool parents to take the day off. Bryan had been in the shower: she'd been relieved to leave the message with Kevin.

It crossed her mind to let the answering machine take a message when her phone rang a few minutes later, but she knew it would be Bryan, and was anxious to see if he regretted making the proposal. She hesitantly picked up the receiver. "Hello."

"Are you okay, Laura? Can I do something, get you anything? Have you called the doctor?"

She smiled, warmed by his thoughtfulness. "I'm not sick. I just didn't sleep much last night."

"That's odd. It's the first night I've slept well in months. You sound scared. Why don't I come over and we can talk. Kevin's going to be working at home today. He offered to watch Jacob."

"Before this gets any more out of hand, I think we'd better. Give me half an hour to get the kids to school and clean up?"

"See you then."

Exactly thirty minutes later, the doorbell rang, and Laura answered. Without hesitation, Bryan kissed her.

"My proposal still stands. I was not out of my mind last night, Laura. I've known this is what I want for quite some time."

"This is the 1990s, Bryan. Only two nights ago we went on our first date."

Bryan started to speak.

Laura raised her hand to stop him. "Marriages of convenience are a little outdated."

"Marriage of convenience?"

"You want a mother for your son, and if I agree, I'd be getting a father for my three children...a terrific father, I will add. I'm not saying that's bad, really. But it does raise some questions. Of course we'd need to—"

"Good grief, Laura, Kevin's seen the attraction between us since football season. It's us that have found excuses not to be together. I started asking you out months ago."

"It's all happened so fast, Bryan."

"I have no doubts, Laura. I want to marry you."

Bryan pulled her into his embrace and ran his fingers through her hair as he had longed to do since the first time their eyes met. There were so many things he needed to tell her, about his marriage, his son and his faith that God would honor this union. Later, he'd take care of all of that.

It was too soon to expect to love one another, but he was sure that, too, would come, given an opportunity to grow. Yet if she kept pushing him away, they'd never have a chance. Underneath her brave and independent facade, was a woman who wanted a man to share her life and the many responsibilities of parenting. And like any human being, she needed someone to hold and love, just as much as he did.

"It was your faith in me that kept my son and I together,

Laura. It was your encouragement that led me to rely on God.''

''I've prayed that He will show me His plans for the kids and me, but good grief, Bryan. This is just a little quick, even for God. When you first came, you didn't want anything to do with any woman. Then, suddenly, you...'' Laura blushed.

''I couldn't get you out of my mind.''

The impact of what he was saying hit her with an explosive force. It echoed her feelings exactly. Though Todd was always within her heart, she hadn't been able to extract her feelings for Bryan. Obviously unlike him, she'd allowed guilt to act as her barrier. Though she'd taken all the steps to grieve, she'd failed.

''How? I mean, you loved Andrea. I don't doubt that for a minute, or you wouldn't have been in such pain. How...?'' Unable to finish her sentence, Bryan interjected.

''What had been eating away at me for a year, finally became clear. Instead of blaming Andrea, I was grateful to her, for being my wife, for giving me a son, even for leaving. If she hadn't left, I wouldn't have met you. Within a month of our wedding, Andrea announced she never wanted children. I see now, that was the beginning of the end. It's a miracle I have Jacob. I won't take that for granted again.''

''You are a good father, Bryan, and I have no doubt you'd be a great husband....''

''Would be? Or will be?''

Laura closed her eyes, her breathing ragged. *How could you bring us this far Father, and still allow me to have doubts? Todd is dead, there's nothing more I can give him. Is my place at Bryan's side, as Jacob's mother?*

''Bryan, there are so many things to consider. I want to say yes....''

Bryan let out a cheer, then picked her up and swung her around. ''Say you'll marry me, Laura.''

His enthusiasm lifted her spirits, and the doubt that had been thick before her suddenly cleared. "Yes, Bryan. I'll marry you."

"Soon. The sooner the better," he said, then kissed her.

"Soon is good."

There was a depth to her smile that had been missing too long. In a thousand lifetimes, he'd never tire of seeing her blush.

Powerful relief filled him.

"I need to run an errand, but I'll be back to take you to lunch."

"Bryan, I didn't get any sleep last night. It's bad enough that you have to see me like this, though I guess you may as well know what your future… Oh, Bryan. This is crazy."

"I've seen you crying and hurt, sick and mad, Laura. If I didn't like any of it, I wouldn't be here now. It's fine if you don't want to go to a restaurant, but the way I'm feeling, it would be best if we weren't alone here much longer. I'll bring a picnic. You try to rest."

When Bryan returned, they walked to a nearby park, pulling Jacob in a wagon behind them.

Laura spread a blanket beside the pond while Bryan emptied the picnic basket, then sat down beside her and took Jacob into his lap. He placed a long-stemmed rose in her hand.

"Look inside."

Laura felt her heartbeat racing. Tears stung her eyes as she saw the diamond ring inside the silky petals. "I don't know what to say, Bryan."

"I hope your tears mean you like it."

She nodded, droplets still streaming down her cheeks. He handed her a handkerchief.

"My grandmother wore it for nearly forty years. I'm praying we're as blessed as my grandparents were."

The surprised look on her face seemed to please him.

Faithfulness and fidelity were as important to him as they were to her.

"As unconventional as our courtship has been, Laura, you need to know that I promise to do everything within my power to make you and your children happy for the rest of our lives."

"You and Jacob deserve so much more than I have to offer, but if you still want me, I'll give you all I can, Bryan."

Ready to place the ring on her finger, he held her delicate hand in his. "You took Todd's ring off."

"It was hardly appropriate to cling to that after your proposal. I had hoped it would keep men at a distance for a while. Then you came along, and ignored it completely."

He smiled lazily. "I used to consider myself a patient man, until I met you. Then I realized how precious life is, and how short our time together. I don't want to waste any of it. How does Saturday strike you?"

"For what? A wedding?"

"And a honeymoon."

Laura turned to hide her pale face.

Bryan lifted her chin. "What's wrong?"

"I didn't think it would be so soon. I couldn't..."

"Is there any particular reason you want to wait? I didn't think you would want a big showy wedding this time. Do you?"

"No. The smaller the better I think." *And under the circumstances, the sooner the better, before I chicken out. Don't be a fool, Laura, you didn't really expect him to wait for love to strike, did you?*

"There's more. What is it?"

"Nothing, Saturday's fine."

Chapter Twenty-Three

Bryan loaded her suitcase into the trunk.

"Laura?"

"I'm fine, Bryan. Let's go."

"You're sure you don't want to tell the kids or your family—to have them at the wedding?"

Her hand halted on the door handle. "It's less complicated this way."

"Hmm. Less complicated, huh?"

She nodded, then got into the car.

The last time he'd made the trip to the altar, there had been months of grueling preparation. This time, it had taken a matter of hours. Yet the burning in his stomach hadn't stopped in two days.

The last time, he'd let emotions make his decision, and it had cost him a whole lot more than a pricey settlement. It was time for logic. Laura was exactly what he wanted in a wife and mother. And one day, he'd have her love. One day, he'd be able to give his to her.

She'd said yes, but why?

Money? Fear of being alone? Her children?

Whatever the answer, he knew it couldn't be love.

Which, he tried to convince himself, was fine. There would be time for that later. *Until then, we'll enjoy getting to know one another better. We'll help each other raise our children. We'll offer each other support on a bad day, share each other's joys. Love will come in its own time.*

Laura rolled her head to one side, then the other. Bryan reached over and massaged her neck with one hand, keeping his eyes on the highway. She needed him, and he needed her. Sharing her life wouldn't be a burden at all.

"How was work?"

"It was the longest day I've had in months. Let's just say this weekend comes at just the right time."

He chuckled. "You make it sound like just any ordinary weekend getaway."

She smiled cautiously. "I'm essentially a mother of nine, Bryan. What few weekends I get away, are never taken lightly. And there's no question that this one will always stick in my mind as far from ordinary."

"I'll do my best to make it memorable."

He grinned, lifting an eyebrow suggestively.

"I have no doubt you will."

His attempts to lighten the mood failed to bring even a mild blush to her cheeks. She turned and smiled as if she had read his disappointment.

"I'm getting a little nervous is all. I wish the judge could have married us tonight instead of tomorrow morning."

"Having second thoughts?"

"No! I just…"

"Want it over with?" he said, annoyed.

"Yes, but not the way you're implying."

"What am I implying?" he said, unable to keep his frustration from showing.

"You're thinking I want out of this. I don't. I said I want to marry you, and I do."

"You hardly have the look of a blushing bride."

"I'm a little old for that."

"Never stopped you before."

"If that's what you want, maybe you'd better head home and keep looking."

"I'm through looking."

"Me, too. So why are we fighting?"

"Beats me. You're just what Jacob and I need."

"I hope so." Her voice was whisper-soft, either seductive or scared to death. His vote was for the latter.

"I don't want another broken marriage, Laura. I promise to do whatever it takes to make this one last a lifetime."

A soft and loving curve touched her lips. "I promise too, Bryan." She offered her hand, and his flesh met hers in a warm clasp.

"Thank you."

This time, the silence wasn't as ominous. The promised commitment seemed to have soothed her nerves as much as it did his. Color returned to her cheeks.

They stopped for dinner at a quiet French restaurant. Afterward, they headed farther into the mountains. When Bryan turned off the highway onto a gravel road, Laura frowned. "What hotel are we staying at?"

"Beau's Château," Bryan said, grinning.

"Oh. I've never heard of it."

"It's privately owned, so I doubt you would. We'll be there in a few minutes."

"You gave Barb the phone number?"

"It's all taken care of. Relax."

"Maybe I should call Marc and Kayla and give it to them, too. I hate for them to worry."

"Then you'd have some explaining to do. I thought you wanted to wait until it was 'over with.'"

Laura playfully hit his arm. "Don't start that again."

It was good to feel her touch. Too good.

Bryan glanced at his watch. Twelve hours until the wedding. It was going to be a long night. He was beginning to share Laura's wish that the ceremony had been tonight. At the time, his plan to spend the evening before they said their vows relaxing and planning their future without distraction seemed a considerate thing to do. With work schedules, hectic evenings with the children, and taking care of the details of eloping, there hadn't been enough time for them to get better acquainted. There were things he longed to know about his wife-to-be, and things he wanted to tell her.

He pushed away the thought that he felt anything resembling love yet, merely comforted that they shared the desire to provide their children with the benefits of a family, and the commitment to make this relationship last a lifetime. The rest would come, in time.

"Do you come here a lot?"

"Not as much as I plan to, but I've been here often enough."

Laura grinned as she imagined the finely tuned engine groaning at the slow speed necessary on the washboard road. It was too dark to see much, except that they were surrounded by trees. She longed to open the window and smell the fresh pine scent.

He stopped in front of a gate and got out to open it, asking her to slide over and pull the car through while he closed it behind the car. She watched as Bryan unlocked, then opened the barrier, his strength making the job look simple.

Anticipation sent a new rush of adrenaline through her body as they approached a dark cabin. Doubt had come and gone several times in the past week. It again showed its ugly face, sending shivers up her spine. *Dear God, I'm doing the right thing, aren't I? Since the day he walked into my house, I felt something for him. If this isn't love, what is it?*

Bryan opened her door and held out a hand. "Welcome to Beau's Château."

"But no one's here." She turned, met by a sensuous kiss.

"No one else was invited."

"Beau's Château is yours? Oh. Beau, as in Beaumont. I thought it was a real château, I mean like a…"

"It's ours, Laura, if you like it. Of course, we'll need to add on to it if we want to bring the family, but for this weekend, I think it'll be just the right size."

She felt the heat rush to her cheeks, grateful that he couldn't see her face.

"Don't try to kid me, Laura. At this very minute, you're blushing like a schoolgirl. I hope you don't ever outgrow that. I love it."

The cool breeze seemed to melt as it crossed her heated cheeks. "Why don't we get unloaded?"

"In a minute." He ran up the steps and unlocked the door, then turned around. "First things first." He picked her up and carried her through the doorway, then kissed her.

"I think that's supposed to come after the wedding."

He loosened his hold, but didn't set her down. "Don't you ever stop arguing?" There was no question that he was teasing, and she refused to take the bait.

"You're full of surprises. What's next, dare I ask?"

"That's it for tonight. I hoped we could get to know each other better. After all, we are getting married tomorrow. Why don't you look around and make yourself comfortable while I unload the car?"

"I'll be glad to help."

He refused her offer.

She turned, feeling at peace with her decision to marry Bryan. It certainly was an odd situation, one that most of her friends would never understand. How could she explain to nonbelievers that for the second time in her life, God had led the right man to her? His timing was, as usual, a bit unconventional, but who was she to question Him?

She ran her hand along the smooth log frame of the sofa.

Its massive size and ruggedness had been softened with layers of plump pillows and a quilted throw.

The fireplace was clearly the center attraction in the living room, as the furniture was arranged around it. She looked at the oil painting depicting Colorado's Maroon Belles, hanging above the mantel. The fireplace tools and copper boiler set on the hearth showed hard use from another era.

Large picture windows were abundant, and she couldn't wait for the morning light to see everything. The kitchen had been updated with modern appliances, however the dining room had obviously stayed the same for generations.

Laura stepped out the back door onto a wide veranda and took a deep breath. The crisp pine air washed her lungs with its soothing aroma. Bryan's strong arms encircled her waist, pulling her back close to his chest.

"What are you thinking about?"

"How much you surprise me."

"I hope that's good."

She leaned her head back onto his shoulder. "Very good. I'm almost afraid to feel so happy again."

"I know how you feel."

Could he really understand her fears? She knew it was time to tell him all the details of Todd's death. Details that she'd never shared with anyone. Details that could only fade with time.

"You're shivering. Let's go start a fire."

"I'll be right in. You go ahead."

Bryan nodded.

This is your plan, isn't it, God? I can't deny that I want to spend my life with him, but it's happening so quickly. So soon after losing Todd. I hope that I can give him my heart and love him the way you want me to. He deserves that.

Laura closed the door, determined to tell Bryan everything. Even if mutual love wasn't the basis of this marriage, honesty had to be.

Before she reached the living room, she could tell the only light was from the fire. *I'm in trouble. Big trouble.*

In the firelight, his eyes seemed coal black. The shadow of his beard more pronounced than she'd remembered an hour ago over the safety of a dinner table. His suit jacket and tie were gone. Italian loafers were left by the fire.

"Come sit down."

Laura's feet were lead. Fear replaced determination.

Fear...

Of her own weakness...

Of loving...

Of not loving...

Of needing Bryan...

Of losing him...

I cannot be in love with him. Todd hasn't even been gone a year. She tried to regain the peace she'd felt minutes ago—confidence that she was doing the right thing.

Laura sat tentatively on the sofa, farther away from Bryan than she had intended.

"You comfortable?"

She nodded. Her body was tense, and she knew he was aware of it. He was already rubbing a knot out of her shoulder.

"Relax, Laura. I want us to get to know more about one another."

She turned quickly to hide her surprise.

"You're wrong, Laura. That's not why we came early."

Being the gentleman he was, his chivalrous denial wasn't surprising, but she doubted she was misreading the look in his eyes.

If she lost him, would she ever find another man as gentle and loving? *Never in a million years, Laura. Don't give him a reason to go.* "I guess old habits are going to be hard to break. When I saw your jacket and tie off, and your shoes by the fire, I came to the wrong conclusion. Sorry.''

''That's not your fault. You wouldn't have been jumping to conclusions, even with me, not too many years ago. I was definitely under the wrong influence. If you'd feel more comfortable, I'll put it all back on.''

Laura laughed. ''I don't get the impression you've ever minded your effect on women, or that you ever will.''

''Does what I wear or not wear have an effect on you?'' he teased.

''None whatsoever,'' she lied, rolling her head to one side.

''A lie I'll accept, tonight,'' he said, chuckling. ''So, on to twenty questions. The fire's getting a little hot. Ask away, beautiful.''

She again shied away. ''You start.''

''Fine, if you want to play that way. One warning. I start with big guns. What were you thinking about outside?''

''Okay, I'll start. What's your middle name?''

He looked at her with disbelief.

''Well, I'm marrying you, and I don't even know your full name, exactly how tall you are, what you weigh. What if my mom asks me those questions? What am I supposed to say? 'Well, Mom, I don't know his name, but he's just the right height for kissing, and has great shoulders and an irresistible smile. And his eyes are the color of fudge—made from scratch.'''

Bryan's laughter roared. ''There's a difference? I mean between the store bought and homemade fudge?''

''Of course. Someday I'll prove it to you.''

Bryan reached into his back pocket. He opened his wallet and tossed her his driver's license. ''Somehow, I think your first description would mean a whole lot more to your mom than the facts. Nice shoulders, huh?''

''Your question. And work your way up to the big guns, would you?''

"Chicken. If you could do anything you wanted for one weekend, what would it be, and who would you want to do it with? Excluding any dreams for this weekend."

"Thanks for clarifying that." She thought for a few minutes, shifting away from Bryan. "This sounds stupid, but I don't know. Thinking of what needs to be done, and who needs what comes as second nature to me."

"Then let's rediscover Laura. Thinking only of yourself, what would you do first?"

"Clean the house."

"You're kidding! That's something that has to be done."

"Believe it or not, I hate clutter. I live with it, but I hate it. If I'm alone for the weekend, I don't want any reminders of responsibility. Then after I cleaned house, I'd take a bubble bath with candlelight and soft music."

"It's getting hot in here," he teased.

"I'd read a novel all the way through without interruption. Go on a bike ride. Ski." She glanced at him, wondering if the next question would be about Kevin. "I like challenging myself. What about you?"

"Not so fast. Next question. Why did you really go skiing with Kevin?"

She laughed. "Why do you think?"

"To avoid me."

She smiled a confirmation. "You're the only man I've even noticed since Todd died. I hoped I could force you from my mind. But I couldn't, and that unnerved me, because I didn't ever want to need anyone again."

She avoided his gaze. As if her answer made him as uncomfortable as it did her, Bryan didn't respond.

"Now to answer your question. As long as we're dreaming, I'd like to play professional football, just once. Realistically, I'd enjoy spending the entire day holding the woman I love, cruise the Caribbean, and watch a game without a one-year-old climbing the T.V. screen."

Laura laughed. "Interesting combination."

"In order of priority, even."

Oddly, Laura didn't feel pressured by his admission. He was simply being honest. *If only I could do the same.*

"What hobbies do you enjoy?"

She stared at the massive elk head on the wall by the front door. "After nearly ten years of being a mother, priorities change. I used to do a lot of crafts, baking, refinishing furniture. It was enjoyable then, but now it's a matter of money, either making money from it, or saving money. I enjoy everything I do now, but someday, I want it to be different."

"What about motherhood?"

"What about it?" she snapped.

"Well, you've chosen it as a career. Do you want that to change? I mean it's okay if you do. I'll support you if you don't want to work at all."

"Don't be ridiculous. I take motherhood very seriously, to the point that even Todd couldn't understand sometimes. I can make myself feel guilty if one of the kids catches a cold."

Bryan laughed.

"I'm serious. Give me a situation, and I can rationalize why it could be my fault."

"I won't argue with you." Bryan leaned back into the corner of the sofa.

Laura stretched out at the opposite end, casually leaning her head back. Bryan reached for her foot and removed her shoe. He slowly massaged one foot, then the other.

"God's given me a desire to love and nurture children. There have been days that have been enough to quit, but everyone has days when they don't like their job. Once in a while, someone will make a comment about a successful career, and all I have to do is think of the kids. What can be more rewarding than feeling their love, and giving it in return?"

The conversation continued, but never returned to the

topics Laura dreaded sharing with him. Everything felt so wonderful, that when he told her to take the only bed, insisting on sleeping on the sofa, she kissed him good-night and snuggled into his warm embrace. *I'm going to like being married to you, Bryan.*

Bryan held her as she fell asleep in his arms. The fire had died down an hour ago, and even then, he couldn't tear himself from her. Her admission to needing him had created an unexplainable stab of anguish throughout his body. There was more to her need than simply help parenting her children, or even a supportive companion. She hadn't said it, but what she needed was his love.

The thought both thrilled him and scared him. He'd felt that need before, and he, like Laura, had tried to denounce the emotion. Both of them could be stubborn, he knew, but there was promise in her admission. Problem was, what was he going to do about it?

He carried her up the stairs to the bedroom loft and covered her with a heavy cotton quilt, then returned to the sofa with a pillow and blankets. The warmth of the fire was gone and even after he covered himself on the sofa, a chill surrounded him. He'd turned on the electric baseboard heat in the bedroom, but that option wasn't available down here. He considered rebuilding the fire....

"No!"

The scream from the loft had barely reached him before he was on his way up the stairs to defend his fiancée. She had pushed the covers away and curled into a tight ball.

"Laura," he knelt next to the bed, and held her while she whimpered.

"Laura, sweetheart. I'm here."

"No, don't take him." Her face tightened to a terrifying grimace.

Bryan touched her face. "You're having a nightmare. It's okay. I'm right here." He shook her, but the terror in her wasn't loosened. With a jolt, she lunged to her knees and began pounding on the bed with clenched fists.

"Don't go! Please. No."

He stood motionless for what seemed like forever, unable to believe the force with which she reacted. When his attempts to hold her still were futile, he was forced to watch until the episode concluded.

The pain and emptiness in her eyes assured him that it wasn't an act of violence she was reliving. It was her husband's death.

Chapter Twenty-Four

Laura awoke, startled to find herself lying in bed surrounded by heavy quilts and soft pillows. Through the window, bright blue skies brought a feeling of hope. Another night had passed.

Rolling over, she was surprised to see Bryan stretched out awkwardly on the armchair next to the bed, asleep. She stared at his mussed hair and unshaven cheeks, finding him even more endearing than usual. "I love you, Bryan. Just a few more hours, and I'll be your wife," she whispered.

Noting the wrinkled silk blouse and pants clinging to her body, she grabbed fresh clothes, and ran down the stairs to shower. She put on blue jeans and a blouse, then pulled the bulky sweater over her head to fend off the morning chill. After starting a fire, Laura brewed a pot of tea and put two large homemade cinnamon rolls in the oven to warm. As she waited for Bryan to wake, she finished her hair then straightened the cabin.

An hour later, Laura heard the shower. Shortly after the water stopped, Bryan appeared in the kitchen and sat down at the table. The silence was thick, like clouds hovering below the mountain peaks. She took the eggs and bacon from the pan and turned off the stove. After adding the cinnamon rolls, she set both plates on the table and poured each of them a cup of orange spice tea.

Laura finally raised her eyes to meet his. "I'm sorry I fell asleep so early last night. I guess the hectic week took its toll on me. The warmth from the fire must have knocked me out." She pushed the food around her plate, waiting for him to respond.

"You seem upset. Is everything okay?"

"I guess so. Isn't it?"

Maybe she didn't remember the nightmare. Was this the first time it'd happened? How could he just ignore the display of terror that he had witnessed the night before?

She placed her crumpled napkin on the table. "Maybe you'd better tell me what happened last night."

Bryan took a couple more bites, then set down his fork. "You fell asleep while we were talking. When you didn't wake up, I carried you to bed. After I moved to the couch, I heard you yelling, so I went back upstairs to make sure you were okay. You must have had a nightmare." Bryan looked directly at her. He left the rest unsaid. That her screams had called him from a sound sleep. That he'd been afraid to leave her alone. That he was deeply bothered by what he'd seen. "Are you okay?"

Laura shrugged. "I'm fine. It was just a dream."

"You aren't upset that I stayed upstairs, are you? I promised I'd sleep on the sofa, but I was concerned about you."

"Heavens no. That's nothing to get upset about."

"Good." He swallowed the rest of his tea and set the cup on the table. "It's about time to leave. It takes almost half an hour to get to town."

"I'll be just a few minutes."

"Looks like it's clouding over, I'll bring in some wood before I change. You go ahead."

* * *

She wore a white denim skirt and matching blouse, both accented with white Battenburg lace. The lace-up boots with spiked heels brought her eye to eye with Bryan. Bryan's approval had been obvious, and his steady gaze again made her blush.

"Do you, Laura Bates, take this man to be your lawfully wedded husband?"

Laura glanced at the judge, then to Bryan. His eyes seemed to reflect her feelings. *What about to love, honor, and cherish until death do…forever and ever? Someday, we'll be ready to love one another, and then, we'll say our vows in a church with our children there.*

"Yes. I do."

"And do you, Bryan Beaumont, take this woman to be your lawfully wedded wife?"

Bryan's dark gaze searched hers, his expression one of not only pain, but regret.

"You deserve more than this, Laura."

Laura choked back the urge to cry. She leaned close, so that only Bryan could hear. "It's enough for now, Bryan. The rest will come with time."

"Mr. Beaumont? Do you take…?"

"No. Not like this."

The judge seemed flustered. "Excuse me, but were you not the one who called to make the arrangements, Mr. Beaumont?"

Bryan handed the man a bill without answering, and turned, taking Laura's hand to lead her from the tiny office. She followed, not sure whether to feel relieved or hurt. Why had he backed out now? He'd had plenty of opportunity at the cabin last night to change his mind, to give her some clue that he had doubts. There had been none.

"I'm sorry, Laura."

Tears streamed down her cheeks under their own power, as Laura was still unsure of their source. Relief. Or sorrow.

Bryan reached for her, but she pushed him away.

Anger. It wasn't relief, or sorrow. She was furious that he had let it go until they were practically pronounced husband and wife. "Just take me home, Bryan."

"Let me explain."

Her finger landed in the middle of his chest. "Oh, you'll explain all right, but not here in the middle of town!" Laura took off down the street toward the car, mindless of the beautiful mountainous surroundings, of the abandoned tourist attractions, of Bryan's damp eyes.

He took a firm hold of her upper arm and turned her to face him. "I did it for your own good, Laura. You should never have said yes."

If the blow of his refusal had hit her hard, this was more than she could withstand. Her sobs were ragged at first, then came in a steady rhythm as she realized how wrong she had been. Not wrong to have said yes. Wrong to have ignored her feelings for Bryan until it was too late.

"I've lost you before I even had a chance...."

"I want you to marry me because you're—" he said at the same time. "What did you say?"

"I'm cold. Let's just go." Tears continued to fall.

He opened her car door and helped her in, then ran around to the other side. "Laura, give me a chance to explain."

"I think 'no' pretty much explains everything."

"I didn't say I don't want to marry you, I said not like this. Not yet. We're cheating ourselves, and our children."

"Thank goodness they weren't here to see you back off! It's bad enough that the judge knows what a fool I am."

The drive to the cabin was made in silence. Each time Bryan tried to talk to her, she turned away, and he stopped trying. When he parked in front of the cabin, she nearly slipped on the fresh layer of snow that had fallen since they'd left. Once inside, she ran across the room to the stairs.

He caught her. "We need to talk, Laura. This isn't some little misunderstanding to sweep under the rug."

"A little late, isn't it?" Laura turned and continued up the stairs.

Chapter Twenty-Five

Bryan watched her stomp up the stairs into the bedroom and close the door behind her. He'd never been one to enjoy fighting. Not that he hadn't had plenty of practice in his first marriage, but he wanted this time to be different.

She had every right to be mad. But so did he. Laura was the one who was obviously not ready to get married again. She should have said something earlier.

Neither ate lunch, and the afternoon faded away in silence.

Bryan stared at the snow accumulating on the handrail. He hadn't heard anything from the loft in hours. Had she cried herself to sleep? Was she waiting for him to come to her?

"What do I do now?" he grumbled. "I won't beg. Never again. Andrea taught me that much."

"Beg me for what, Bryan?"

He jumped to his feet and turned around. The delicate white denim had been replaced with blue jeans and a pink sweater. Fighting with his fiancée was the furthest thing from his mind right now. He wanted to mend the damage, not add to it.

"You look beautiful."

"My eyes are puffy and my head hurts."

Bryan stepped behind the sofa and wrapped her in his arms. He gave her a quick hug, then began massaging her shoulders. He felt her hesitate, and almost unwillingly, she pushed away from him.

He jerked back. "Did I hurt you?"

"Hurt me?" Then as she realized what he was thinking, she added. "No, you didn't hurt me physically, Bryan. You'd never do that. But what happened this morning hurts very much."

"You were right…we should have taken more time. You're not ready."

She stepped back, shocked at his accusation. "You're the one who said no. Not me."

"I said no for your sake. When we met, involvement was the last thing I wanted." Bryan pulled her into his arms and held her firmly. "Of all the women I've known, I chose you."

Bryan waited as the silence lengthened.

"Then why did you say no?"

"From what I saw last night, I'd say you missed telling me a few things about what happened when Todd died. When did you plan to tell me? Did you think I couldn't handle it?"

She placed her hands on his chest to push herself away, but Bryan turned her back to him. "You have to face Todd's death first. I thought you already had."

From his view, there was nothing more to say; Laura was convinced of that. She watched as Bryan turned away and walked up the stairs. His wool slacks and tailored shirt were a bitter reminder of the trip to the courthouse.

Laura opened the door and ran down the driveway, ignoring the eight inches of wet spring snowflakes at her feet. When she finally stopped, she noticed the heavy blanket of clouds. The forecast hadn't said anything about snow, but it was springtime in Colorado. Anything could happen. The last thing she'd expected was to be stranded in a snowstorm, alone in a cabin with Bryan, required to endure two long nights of temptation.

Even in the midst of his rejection, she discovered the attraction was as strong as ever. Laura thought of the night right after Todd's death when Chad had offered to ask God to send them a new daddy. She'd wondered then if there would ever be a man brave enough to accept her and three children. And if so, would he be man enough to dim the awful memories? Would he have courage enough to dare her to love again? Yes. Bryan was every bit that man.

She'd done a lot of thinking and praying that afternoon, fighting the tendency to lick her wounds and feel sorry for herself again, a trap she'd found herself in after Todd's death. That had tested her faith, and here she was being tested again.

She may have said yes, she discovered, out of fear. Not only of the fear of losing Bryan, but fear of never loving again, of never being loved. Fear of being alone.

Was he right? Was she not ready to get married again? Laura longed to tell him he was wrong, that she'd put that night behind her. Yet after witnessing her nightmare, she knew Bryan wouldn't believe that it was him she was afraid of losing; him that she'd been trying to save in her dream last night. How could she ever convince Bryan that she was in love with him, when her subconscious kept replaying the night Todd died next to her?

The wind began howling, and Laura turned back. Hoping to find a shortcut to the cabin, she cut through the forest. Snow blew off of the trees and through her clothes.

Laura heard a cabin door close, but could see no lights. Then Bryan called her name from somewhere in the distance. She wrapped her arms across her chest and closed her eyes, hoping to follow the sound of his voice.

"Bryan! Keep calling."

He repeated her name every few minutes, until she found her way to the driveway, where Bryan was waiting.

"What do you think you're doing out in the middle of nowhere in a blizzard?" When she couldn't answer, he continued, his voice reflecting little emotion. She'd seen him mad, but this was worse. At least anger would show he still cared.

Bryan wrapped his coat around her wet shoulders and muttered into her ear. "You have more sense than this." In the face of his disappointment, she could almost convince herself it was for the best. Bryan deserved more than a cowardly wife.

"I tried to tell you, Bryan. I wanted to."

"So, what's stopping you?"

Laura shrugged, feeling Bryan pull her closer, as if to share his warmth with her. But that was impossible, all he wanted was a mother for Jacob, and someone to bring order to his life. He didn't want a wife at all.

Snowflakes caked to them as the wind grew stronger. The unanswered question balanced between them like a growing wedge. She shivered as he guided her up the steps to the cabin.

"I haven't told anyone everything that happened that night. Not even Barb. Please don't ask me to relive that night again."

"Looks like you're reliving it as it is. When you're ready, we'll talk, but right now I want you to go upstairs and get out of those wet clothes while I start you a warm bath. You're freezing."

Laura nodded, then climbed the stairs. She paused at the top and turned to look at him, but he was out of sight.

A few minutes later, she closed the bathroom door behind her, and noticed he'd done more than just start the bath water. The glow from nearly a dozen candles danced to the rhythm of the soft romantic music that filtered in from the living room.

Laura took off the terry robe she'd borrowed from Bryan's closet and stepped into the giant antique tub. She closed her eyes, sinking deep into fragrant bubbles, wishing the warmth could melt the shield of ice around her heart.

Blanketed under the thick layer of bubbles, she wondered what had happened to the levelheaded woman she'd once been. That woman never would have accepted such a proposal in the first place. She wouldn't have fallen in love with a man just a few months after her husband's death. But more than that, she wouldn't let a few romantic gestures sway her logic.

Maybe it was a good thing she wasn't that woman any more, she thought with a smile. Inhaling the moist ocean scent, Laura rested her head against the back of the tub. Her toes barely reached the other end without causing her to slip deeper into the water.

Logic. Her thoughts reverted back to the events of the day.

She'd placed her faith in Bryan; trusted him to do the same with her. Did he? He'd trusted her to raise his son, told her about Andrea's keeping Jacob a secret from him, had even sought her approval in his decision to send Jacob to Cassandra. Laura closed her eyes and felt the pain of those early discussions with Bryan.

At the time, it had felt as if he'd revealed his darkest wounds. Yet, they all had to do with Jacob, she realized. None of them had anything to do with Bryan, or the pain he must have felt when his wife left him. How could he be so blind as to think she was the only one who hadn't been totally open?

Bryan knocked, then called through the door. "Can I get you anything else?"

"Yeah, the truth," Laura muttered, wishing she weren't so softhearted.

"What?"

"Bryan," Laura called, her voice husky from crying into the cold air. "You expect more than I have to give you."

She heard him lean against the door, and wondered momentarily if he was going to come in. "I can't hear you," he taunted.

"You're not playing fair," she yelled, knowing his confident one-sided smile was just on the other side of the door.

"Pure agony, isn't it? I can't believe I put myself through this when I could've been in there with you tonight."

Laura stepped from the tub and dried off, not sure if it was the temperature of the water, or his admission that had made her light-headed. She wrapped herself in the huge black terry robe and secured the tie at the waist.

She opened the door, and his smile disappeared. "Do I frighten you that much?"

Truth be known, falling in love again scared her to death. This whole situation did. "I married Todd when I was seventeen." Laura watched Bryan intently, waiting for his reaction. He didn't flinch. "Before Todd, I only dated two other guys. Yet I knew immediately that Todd was the man I wanted to spend my life with. I couldn't be so lucky twice." If she was right, Bryan would be more than happy to address her fears, her needs, yet change the subject when it came to his own.

"Nothing you say will change my feelings for you, Laura."

"Don't go painting your picture of sainthood on me," she warned. "Our hormones were…in control. We told ourselves that God would understand, because we planned to get married one day. Even though we had a wonderful marriage, and loved each other passionately, it took years to accept God's grace, to forgive myself for my weakness."

"Is that why you said yes, because you didn't think I'd wait? You think that little of me?"

"Maybe I don't trust myself. I've never been alone." She shook her head, "I'm afraid…"

Bryan dried his wet hair and flung the towel over his shoulder. "Of what? Me?"

Was he ready to learn that she did love him? That she had trusted him enough to commit her life to him? That what she needed was to know that he would one day share her feelings?

Laura took a deep breath and fixed her gaze on him. "That I'd miss this chance to love again."

Bryan ran his fingers through his damp hair. Even before she moved, he spoke. "Go get dressed, then we'll talk." He left the room and closed the cabin door behind him.

She'd taken the risk and lost. Bryan had given her everything but himself. He wasn't any more ready for her love than he was marriage, yet denied any of his own reasons for saying no.

Maybe it was for the better that they hadn't married. Yes, their children did deserve more, and so did they. She realized that now. She wanted them to know their parents were completely and totally, *in love*. After her marriage to Todd, she knew nothing short of a love centered in Christ would carry them through the ups and downs of life.

God, I was so sure this was your plan. I believed both of us were listening to you. Now, I don't know. From the beginning, you've led me to Bryan, told me not to give up on him. How much more pain do I have to endure?

An even more terrifying realization came over her. What if he never learned to trust her?

Laura refused to believe that. He needed time. Just as she had. Was she strong enough to give him that time, even though it would surely mean more tears and pain, for her and the children?

When she came down the stairs, he was waiting at the

bottom. She placed her finger on his lips, quieting his unspoken plea. She knew the time had come. If she was ever going to gain his trust, she would have to tell him all of her fears. She had to be painfully honest, if for no other reason, but to protect her children from paying for her own mistake. She would not be the one to blame for destroying their love.

Her voice was shaky. "I'll tell you everything, Bryan, but I want you to realize something first. I will not take sole responsibility for holding back. Just as you know Todd's death still upsets me, I know Andrea hurt you, but I don't know everything that happened to break up your marriage."

"I told you—"

"What you wanted me to know. You told me enough to understand why you couldn't adjust to being a father. There's more, and when you are ready to tell me the rest, I'll listen."

The pain she'd seen in the depths of his eyes that first time they'd met was back. And until he dealt with it, there would be no hope for their relationship.

Her voice was barely a whisper as she continued. "Todd hadn't been feeling well, but he insisted it was just a virus. When we made love, something was different. He was different."

She walked to the fireplace and gazed into the flames. Finally the words she'd never spoken aloud fought to be heard. "It was almost like he knew it would be our last time. A few hours later I woke up in a panic." Her voice broke. "Todd was holding me...I tried to move...he died holding me. I couldn't help."

"You aren't to blame."

"But I was right there. I screamed for help. The kids saw everything. Me yelling at him. Me pounding on their father. Me holding them back while the paramedics took their daddy away."

Cupping her chin, he searched her upturned face. "None of it was your fault, sweetheart. You did all that you could." He pulled her close, rocking her back and forth as she wept.

"They think I should have been able to save him. I tried CPR. They don't understand. I let Todd down, the kids...." Laura cried, secure in Bryan's arms. It felt so good to be held. His strength comforted her as it had so many times in the past few months. "I don't want to let them down again."

He brushed a tear from her face. She opened her eyes and looked into his, and felt Bryan's mouth cover hers.

His kiss was deep, gently filling every inch of her soul with his love. She was sure he loved her, and could no longer deny that she was falling in love with him more each moment they were together. But would it be enough? Would his love ever be enough to erase these awful memories?

Was her love strong enough to heal the wounds that had etched themselves into the darkest part of his soul?

Bryan held Laura, more than willing to soothe her and care for her for the rest of their lives. Yet, inside, he knew that wasn't enough. He had to trust her. He had to love her.

He needed to give her all that he expected from her. She was right, he was as much the reason he'd backed out of their vows as Laura. And then there were the children.

They would look to him for guidance, in addition to emotional support and advice. How could he, in good conscience, give them advice he couldn't follow himself?

How could he be the spiritual leader in a home where trust and love didn't abound? How could he ask more of Laura than he was willing to give?

Laura eased away from him. She looked at him quickly. Hopefully.

The look in her eyes was full of trust, as if their hearts spoke without the need of words.

I want to say what you need to hear, his heart told hers.

Not so, her heart echoed back.

As if she'd completely vanished from his presence, he felt the door to her heart slowly creep closed.

Chapter Twenty-Six

Bryan's chest tightened. It was sickeningly familiar. The secrets. The emptiness. The betrayal. The shadows had returned.

Laura had placed herself in his hands, and he'd sliced open a newly healed wound. She'd told him she trusted him, loved him and he'd said nothing. Glimpses of his past clouded his vision.

"I think it would be best if we take some time to think this through again, Bryan." She removed the engagement ring from her finger and placed it in his hand, folding his fingers around it. "When you're ready to leave tomorrow, let me know. I'm going to bed. May I borrow one of the shirts hanging in the closet to sleep in? What I brought isn't going to be warm enough."

He couldn't help but wonder what kind of lingerie his shirt would be replacing. "Sure, be my guest." Bryan watched as Laura walked up the stairs, to change into his shirt, to crawl into his bed. The bed he had hoped they would share tonight.

There were no nightmares to interrupt his sleepless night. There was no fire to chase away the chill that had seeped into his soul. There was no sleep to ease the pain.

The sun came out and melted the late-spring snow. Somewhere in the kitchen, a teakettle whistled with warmth and the promise of comfort. And upstairs, his ex-fiancée waited for a ride home.

Realizing that it had been twenty-four hours since she'd eaten, Bryan took her breakfast. "Laura, may I come in?"

She opened the door and smiled apologetically. His flannel shirt hung to the middle of her thighs. "Morning."

He looked down at the tray of oatmeal and juice, avoiding her gaze. Breakfast wasn't much, but considering the surprise storm and the few staples he had on hand, it was something. "Here's some oatmeal and juice. You haven't eaten since yesterday morning."

"Have you already eaten?"

"Yeah. About four this morning."

"Something tells me that's not your usual wake-up time."

He shook his head, and she laughed.

"Sleeping in shifts already, and we don't even have the baby along. You're acting like a married man already."

"Wishful thinking." His voice was thick and unsteady. How had he ever said no to her?

Her smile was sympathetic. "Remind me of this the next time you promise me a memorable weekend, will you?" She accepted the tray and set it on the bed.

He followed, unable to take his eyes from the beautiful woman he'd rejected. "How can you laugh? You know how much I regret this, don't you?"

"There's not much we can do to change it now. It's a choice of laughing or crying. May as well look for the humor."

She spoke with conviction, as if she really believed what she said.

"Besides, I can't cry any more, I just got rid of my headache. So tell me, exactly what is it you regret?"

His silent expression begged her to understand. She wanted to. More than anything. "How can we regret doing the right thing, Bryan? I know it was best, but it doesn't ease the disappointment, for either of us. I wanted to marry you. Even if at first, it may not have been for all the right reasons."

Laura brushed his chin with the back of her finger and swallowed the lump in her throat. The lump that contained the three words she never thought she'd say to another man.

Men. You only hear what's said out loud. Can't you hear what I want to say? Can't you hear the music in my heart? Each time your chocolate brown eyes gaze at me, I feel as thrilled as that first time we kissed.

With his silence, Laura felt the fear of losing him spread through her, wrapping her in a blanket of ice. She'd let him see her vulnerabilities, yet Bryan refused to do the same. He hadn't yet told her he was in love with her, and she hadn't the strength to say it again. What if she'd been wrong? What if he didn't love her at all?

Bryan had been unusually quiet, even considering what a mess the weekend had been. She looked out the car window, wondering how she'd be feeling today if things had gone as planned. Laura lowered her head, wishing she hadn't opened this Pandora's box of emotions. She was too tired, both emotionally and physically, to keep considering what had gone wrong.

"Laura? What do you want to do about the relationship now?"

"I suppose it's too late to claim I'm not interested, huh?"

He turned to her, and they both started laughing. "Way too late. I have a week of vacation left. Why don't we take a trip with the kids? Get an idea how they feel about us together."

"I don't want to rush this, Bryan. We have a lot to learn

about one another.'' She held her side, concerned by the cramps that had returned with an alarming intensity during the night. It had been months since they'd been so strong. Not wanting to worry Bryan, she leaned her seat back to stretch out and breath deep.

"The ring will be waiting, and so will I," Bryan promised.

As the stress from the weekend dissipated, so did the magnitude of the pain in her lower abdomen. Though it didn't go away altogether, most of the time, it was easy to ignore.

In the following weeks, their outings became more frequent. Weekends included flying kites, watching movies, or going on bike rides—on what Bryan called family dates.

Little by little, he revealed pieces of his marriage to her, and she began to understand why it was so difficult for him to trust her with his heart. He'd given her everything except that.

As their relationship progressed, Laura felt the need to tell both Todd's parents and hers that she was dating Bryan. Todd's mother cried, but seemed to accept the news. Her parents were thrilled that she was moving on with her life, and came for a short visit that next month to meet Bryan and Jacob.

"You look tired," her mother said a few days into their stay. "Are you feeling okay?"

"I'm fine, Mom. Really," Laura assured her. "Surely you haven't forgotten how draining children can be."

"No, I haven't. Have you and Bryan talked about marriage?"

"Mother!" Laura turned to her mother, shocked that she'd been so direct. The drastic change of subject bothered Laura.

"The children are very hard on you, your house…your health…."

Laura stood up and walked across the room. "I don't want to have this discussion. There's nothing wrong with my health, and I don't like you implying that I should marry Bryan to take care of me and my responsibilities."

"Bryan seems like the type of man who would like nothing more than to take care of you. How many times since Todd's death have you had to take time off because you were sick, Laura?"

"It was just cramps, nothing major. I've seen my doctor, and she agrees, it's probably stress." Laura recalled talking with her friend and doctor, Emily Berthoff after Sunday school. Though Emily hadn't seemed overly concerned about the pain, she clearly wanted to see her, soon. *Maybe it is something serious.*

After her parents went home that day, Laura spent the evening wondering about whether she and Bryan could fulfill each other's expectations.

Could he accept her need for independence? Would he ever be able to give her his heart? And mostly, could she give Bryan another child?

Laura awoke, immediately remembering that morning the previous year. The day that her entire life was shattered into a million pieces. The day her sheltered family was torn apart, and she was left alone to pick up the fragments.

After placing roses from Todd's garden on his grave, she and the children came home and chose family photos to make a memory album for each child. Bryan quietly watched throughout the evening, and Laura wondered if it was difficult for him to see and hear about their family memories. She had guarded her previous life up to now, as if doing so would keep her from blending the woman she had been with Todd and the woman she was now with Bryan.

She tucked her three children into bed with a renewed sense of appreciation that night. She had seen a very grown-up side of each of them during this past year. Was it losing their father, or gaining Bryan's friendship that had brought about the changes? Probably both, she decided.

Bryan waited for Laura on the porch. "How're you doing?"

"I'm okay." She paused at the door, contemplating the changes they'd all experienced in the past twelve months. "This morning Carrie told me that she wouldn't cry today because God had taken such good care of us that it felt like her Daddy was watching from heaven. They've grown up so much this year."

"Kids make life seem pretty simple, don't they?"

Laura sat on the wooden swing next to Bryan. "Is it that they make it look simple, or do adults make it complicated?" She felt him shrug his shoulders, but he remained quiet. "I noticed you disappear at the cemetery."

"It's the first time I've visited Andrea's grave."

"How did you feel?"

Bryan looked into the huge maple tree that hid the summer sky. His arm rested along the back of the swing and embraced her. "It wasn't the same for Andrea and me, Laura. The woman I thought I married, died long before the accident. She was a stranger to me the last year and a half, and I regret that." He lowered his head and took Laura's hand in his, running his fingers along hers.

"You loved her, though. That was obvious."

Laura felt his hand pause at her ring finger, but he didn't mention their broken engagement. He'd quit pushing her weeks ago.

"To a fault. She left me for another man, and I believed her when she denied it. I always believed her. Fool."

Careful not to reveal her confirmed suspicions, Laura asked, "How did you find out?"

"After the accident, I hired a private investigator. The police reports implied she took her own life, I had to know why. She chose death over facing me with the truth."

"Suicide? I'm so sorry, Bryan." Laura took his hand and held it tight.

He didn't respond.

"How could they be sure it was intentional?"

"She'd sent Jacob's birth certificate and a letter requesting her lawyer to notify me by courier an hour before the wreck."

They sat, sharing the healing balm of silence. Bryan took a deep breath, then released it.

"It helped to hear you and the kids talk about Todd tonight."

He'd given her as much information as he could handle for now, she realized. In time, the rest would come. "I hope it didn't bother you. I wasn't sure how you'd feel, seeing and hearing about our life."

"It was a relief. I've felt like Todd was an insurmountable legend that I couldn't compare to. I don't want to replace him, Laura. I want to make our own memories, to look back in twenty years and laugh at pictures of us in your album. I want to see that love on your face when you remember what we've had."

"You don't want much."

"I want the best. You."

Chapter Twenty-Seven

Bryan watched Laura as she washed the breakfast dishes. He could see that she was unaware he'd rung the doorbell and come into the house. She'd become more quiet and distant lately. Noting that the kids were at the table eating waffles and watching cartoons, Bryan placed the diaper bag along the wall and walked into the kitchen. "You're awfully deep in thought this morning."

She jumped. The lost-in-thought look was quickly replaced with a phony smile as obviously protective as if she were wearing football pads. And it killed him that he was the reason she was protecting herself. As difficult as it had been, he'd given her the space she wanted.

"Good morning, I didn't hear you come in." Laura dried her hands and invited Jacob to come to her, which he eagerly did.

Bryan touched her cheek tenderly, wishing he could take her into his arms and kiss her. "Why don't we go out this weekend?"

Laura walked into the dining room and let Jacob say hi to the kids. "I've already made plans. We're going camping. I need to get away."

Away from what. Me? He'd been the one to postpone the wedding, but this sounded more like a step away from the relationship. "Is your family going with you?"

"Family? If you mean the kids, yes, they're going."

Though he tried to avoid it, the words came out sounding harsh and clipped. "You and the kids are going to the mountains, alone?" Goose bumps spread up his arms.

She simply nodded. "We'll be fine."

"I don't think that it's a great idea to go without…" Just as he said it, he recalled her longing for independence.

"Without what?" Her eyes dared him to finish the sentence.

"Without…uh…protection."

"Such as you?" An unexpected smile brightened her face and seemed to boost her mood.

"I'd consider it if asked, but…" He studied her, wondering if he dared to believe her silent message. Did she really want him and Jacob to join them? "Jacob's awfully small."

"We took T.J. on his first camping trip when he was six months. Jacob's almost a year. It's supposed to be beautiful weather. We can go hiking or fishing or just relax. Do you like camping?"

"I haven't been in at least twenty years."

"We'd like you to come."

Bryan looked at Jacob and brushed the hair off his forehead. "You sure about Jacob?"

"Would I do anything to hurt him? If he cries all night, I'll stay up with him. Deal?"

"What if he gets cold?" Bryan lifted an eyebrow.

"He can sleep in my bag with me."

An lopsided grin spread across Bryan's face. "What if I get cold?" *Sorry God, I couldn't resist.*

"I'll tell you where you can find an extra blanket," she teased. "It would be nice to have you along, but if you don't want to, I'll understand. Fresh mountain air, campfires, bright stars... Well, they kind of bring out the best in me.''

"If I didn't know better, I'd think you were flirting with me, Laura Bates.''

"Maybe that wouldn't hurt as much as I thought it would.''

"I guarantee it. You're sure you wouldn't rather go out alone? We've spent a lot of time with the kids lately.''

"Nope, we're going camping. Besides, they'd throttle us both if we changed the plans. Are you brave enough to tame the Rockies with my kids and me? We have two tents, and plenty of gear.''

Bryan groaned just thinking of the cold hard ground. "You're going with or without me, aren't you?''

She cocked her head and smiled.

"Though I know you're perfectly capable, I'll worry about you all weekend if I don't go along. You know that, don't you?''

Her eyebrows lifted. "I'm flattered.''

"You should be.'' They smiled in unison.

When he arrived at Laura's Friday afternoon, she was wrestling with the ropes to tie down the gear on top of the van, more excited about the weekend than anyone.

After the tents were pitched and the van unloaded, T.J. and Chad climbed nearby boulders and explored the campsite while Carrie walked Jacob around the camp. They all were exhausted, and fell asleep as soon as they'd snuggled into their sleeping bags.

Bryan added another log to the fire, then grinned at Laura, who blushed and looked away.

"What's wrong, Laura?''

He could see her consider telling him or keeping it to herself. Every day, he found it more difficult to avoid trusting Laura, but his scars were deep and hadn't healed yet.

"Nothing, I'm just tired.''

He dropped the stick he'd been stirring the fire with and

walked up behind her and began rubbing her shoulders. "We have plenty of time. The fire's not going out any time soon."

She pivoted and looked into his eyes.

He pulled her close and kissed her, quickly at first, then with increasing intensity. Her hands were planted on his chest as if to push him away, but she didn't. Maybe that was all the encouragement he would get.

Bryan kissed her again, pleased that she was waiting. Her fingertips skimmed his beard-roughened cheeks. She inched closer, then pulled away.

"That must be what's worrying me. Good night Bryan."

Laura quickly disappeared into her tent and sighed. He doused the last embers of the campfire, and went to bed.

Awakened by low cries and a voice, Bryan staggered out of the sleeping bag and pulled on his jeans. The voice he heard was Laura's, but he couldn't understand what she was saying. Just when he was ready to unzip the tent, the noise stopped, and he realized she must have been dreaming again. He fell back onto the air mattress and drifted to sleep.

When he woke the next morning, Jacob was proudly unpacking their clothes, piling each item on him. "Is this a hint, Jacob?" His son laughed and crawled away even faster.

Laura was setting up the stove and mixing pancake batter when he emerged. Bryan could hear the kids in her tent arguing about who did what with the others' shoes. Bryan carried Jacob over to see Laura. "Good morning, beautiful. How'd you sleep?"

"Okay. How about you and Jacob? I didn't hear a sound."

"Jacob slept great."

"He probably liked having you next to him." She smiled, then quickly turned away. "Breakfast is ready, kids. Go wash up."

''You're still having nightmares.''

She looked at him with regret. Regret of his hearing? Or that she was still having them?

''Not as often, and they're not nearly as dramatic as the one I had…that night you were with me.''

''I wish there was something I could do to make them go away.'' His look was hopeful.

''Mom, we're hungry.''

Laura had never been so thankful for hungry kids. ''Let's eat.''

The older kids were off exploring as soon as the last bite was eaten. The cool morning air disappeared as the sun's warmth stretched between the trees. The aspen trees were leafing out and the flowers buds were opening. It was a new beginning in the forest, and Laura hoped it was a sign of a new start for her own life. She gazed through the trees to the mountain beyond as she finished putting away the dishes.

She poured a cup of coffee for herself while Bryan changed Jacob's diaper, then sat down to enjoy the sunshine.

Life seemed so simple here. The sun rose and set, all in perfect timing. God's timing. Here, no one argued that fact. It was accepted. So why was it still so difficult to accept the changes God was making in her own life?

Trying to replace her fear with faith, she pushed aside thoughts of her upcoming doctor's visit. Knowing the dangers of ignoring her symptoms hadn't been enough to keep her previous appointments. Since losing Todd it seemed everything she held dear was being tested—her faith, her health, her relationship with Bryan. Again, she began to question God's mercy.

Her thoughts were interrupted by Bryan's deep voice. ''Jacob took a step! Did you see him?''

"Yeah! Good job, Jacob." Laura set down her coffee and joined him. "I can't believe he's already walking."

"Great job, Jacob!" Carrie cheered. Chad stepped in front of his sister and reached for Jacob, who was delighted with the attention. The toddler stood up and staggered to Carrie again, wrinkling his nose with laughter when he reached her waiting arms.

No more babies. The thought was more than she could bear. She turned and walked away before Bryan could see her fear.

"Hey kids, would you keep a close eye on Jacob while I talk with your mom?"

"Sure. Jacob, come here." Chad carried the toddler to a grassier area. Once the three of them were preoccupied with helping Jacob walk, Bryan slipped his hand around Laura's waist.

Bryan's kiss was deliciously sweet. Her hands wrapped around his neck, momentarily easing her pain. Stifled giggles shocked her back to reality, and she freed herself from his embrace.

As usual, Bryan seemed to know when to push and when to let go. He read her emotions with an almost disturbing accuracy. Somehow, the thought both comforted and unnerved her.

"I'll take the kids fishing and give you a little break. Why don't you take a nap with Jacob?" The nap felt good. Jacob had fallen asleep immediately inside the warm tent.

Minutes before the rest of them returned, Chad tore into camp, boasting about the rainbow trout he'd caught. Bryan and T.J. cleaned the fish, then fried it to have in addition to the stew Laura had already prepared for supper.

While her three were washing, Laura leaned into Bryan, letting down her guard. "I think you've made a couple of boys very happy this weekend."

"Now if I could just work that magic on their mother."

He took advantage of her carelessness, and gave her a thoroughly satisfying kiss.

The kids sat down at the picnic table and started chanting. "K-I-S-S-I-N-G, first comes love, then comes marriage, then comes baby in the baby carriage."

"Kissing is merely a sign of affection." She looked to Bryan, but he just smiled. "Then you explain it to them."

"Don't think I want to argue with their logic, sorry."

Bryan tapped her nose with his finger. "I'd have lost my chance to be a father if it hadn't been for you. I can't imagine never having a family." His smile was warm and intimate.

Fear won. The knife turned again. It was becoming clear that Bryan wanted them to have a baby. While Laura loved seeing this new generation of daddies taking an active part in the daily lives of their children, she wondered if she would deprive Bryan the miracle of experiencing his baby's birth.

She couldn't deny the attraction between them, but she had to have more than that from Bryan. He was no longer the man she wanted to help raise her children. Bryan was the man she wanted to marry, wanted to give her heart to and never take it back. But, did he feel the same?

"Oh, never mind. Carrie, will you say grace, please?"

After dinner, they roasted marshmallows and told stories until eyelids began to droop and Laura declared bedtime.

When she was tucking her kids in, Chad looked into her eyes. "I hope Bryan can be my new daddy. Do you like him that much Mom?"

Laura felt the tears starting, and blinked them back. "Chad."

"Just ask him. I think he'd do it."

"I can't ask a man to marry me, Chad." *Besides, I all but begged him to go through with it, and he turned me away.*

Carrie piped up, "It's kind of weird seeing you kiss him."

"Does it bother you guys?"

"No," was the general answer. She was sure they all liked Bryan, Chad expressed love, but the other two were more reserved. Maybe because they'd had more time with Todd, maybe because they were more mature and understood love a little more.

"I like seeing you happy again," said T.J. "When you're sad I know you are thinking of how much you miss Dad, huh?" T.J. had always seen emotions others missed.

Laura thought about the many blessings her children brought to her life. Bryan's question about regretting taking the chance to love Todd came back to her clearly. *No, I wouldn't have made a different choice if I'd have known how little time I'd have with Todd. How could I have survived without these kids?* "Yes, I miss your daddy a lot. I'll try to smile more, okay?"

The three seemed content and settled down.

"I'll be right outside if you need me. I'm going to see if Bryan needs any help with Jacob." She kissed each of them and crawled out of the tent.

Before she zipped it, T.J. asked, "Mom, do you think Dad would mind too much that we like Bryan?"

Where do these difficult questions keep coming from? "I'm sure your dad would be glad you have such a good friend, don't you think so, T.J.?"

T.J. nodded, then snuggled deeper into his sleeping bag. "Night, Mom. I love you."

"I love you, T.J. I love each of you more than you can imagine possible. Go to sleep now."

When she returned to the fire, Bryan was getting ready to feed Jacob his bottle. "I'll take him. I think the kids would like to tell you good-night."

"You really think Todd would approve of me?" Bryan whispered.

Realizing that if he'd heard, the kids could hear them as well, Laura lowered her voice. "You heard that?"

He nodded roguishly. "I'll go tell them good-night, then we can discuss their ideas."

Laura closed her eyes, wishing he didn't know her so well. One look into her eyes, and he'd know something more serious was bothering her. She was determined to keep these fears to herself until she'd seen the doctor and knew for sure. It wasn't fair to worry him unless it was absolutely necessary.

After all, she'd reasoned earlier that afternoon, he doesn't even trust me enough to say he loves me, and until he does, this is my problem, not his. He has enough to handle.

When Bryan returned, they talked about how the children had adjusted to the many changes, and what others there were to watch for. Bryan's personal experience with his father's death offered them both valuable insight. His understanding of the pain was right on target. She wondered how many men she'd find who'd encourage her children to keep the memories of their father very much alive without feeling threatened by that love?

Jacob guzzled his bottle and went right to sleep. She put him over her shoulder, rocking her body in a soothing rhythm as Jacob's relaxed body swayed along. Laura tucked him into bed.

When she returned, Bryan invited her to sit next to him on a blanket by the fire. He lifted her chin and kissed her tenderly. The fire crackled. The stars were bright, and the air was brisk.

Her cheek rested on his shoulder. "Look at the sky. Isn't it beautiful?"

Bryan pulled away from her long enough to wrap the blanket around them. "You're beautiful," he whispered into her ear and ran his fingers gently through her hair.

She began to pull away, but hesitated as his lips touched

hers. This time she firmly put her hands on his chest and pushed him away.

Bryan let out a deep breath and leaned back on his elbows.

"I'd like to help with whatever's bothering you tonight."

"I just wish I could be more like you sometimes."

"I wouldn't be interested if you were like me. I love you just the way you are."

"What did you say?"

"I love you." He looked at her, astonished. "Did you think I would've asked you to marry me in the first place if I didn't?"

"You never said it before."

He chuckled. "You knew before I did. So it took me a while to admit it. It's fourth down and two yards to go. One of us has to make a decision."

She slept fitfully, unable to ease the pain. It was physical, as well as emotional. *Bryan, how can I put you through this again? How can I ever tell you?*

Laura awoke that morning to the smell of coffee perking and bacon frying over a crackling fire. She pulled on her cold jeans and sweatshirt and unzipped the tent. Bryan knelt next to the fire, his jeans stretched tight against his muscular thighs. The sleeves of his flannel shirt were rolled up past his forearms.

Laura looked at the kids, still cozy inside their sleeping bags. She stretched, running her fingers through her tangled hair.

The sun's rays reached through the trees as it peeked over the mountain. She looked at Bryan. "Please tell me you're not a morning person."

"Only for you." He laughed roughly and turned the bacon.

"I didn't think I slept very well last night, but I must have. I didn't hear you get up."

"Good. You needed a full night's sleep."

She walked over to him and ran her fingers through his hair. "Didn't anyone ever tell you it's a crime to look this wonderful in the morning? Look at me. This is normal, circles under the eyes, tangled hair, stiff joints. You're just too perfect for me."

Bryan stood and placed his fingers under her chin, lifting it slightly. "I love you, Laura. *You* are perfect for me."

He pulled her close and gave her a kiss. Bryan's arms around her were gentle yet solid. His good-morning kisses were tender and satisfying, the kind she could get used to waking to every morning.

"Let me help make those nightmares go away. Marry me."

He's expressed his love twice in the last twelve hours, but was it enough to erase all of her fears?

Chapter Twenty-Eight

It had been a week since they'd gone camping. A week since she'd agreed to set a date for their wedding. A week of contentment. It was amazing how much could change in seven days.

The anniversary of Andrea's death had passed, without any recognition, which was the way Bryan wanted it. The less said about his ex-wife the better. Laura had suspected something was bothering him, but he'd insisted it had nothing to do with Andrea. In a way it didn't, but in a way, this was all because of her.

If it hadn't been for his wife, he'd never have requested a transfer a year ago. As it turned out, it had already been too late to save their marriage. And when she'd left, his work had been all that mattered to him.

He'd worked his way up in the company. Set goals, then worked toward them. Because of his broken marriage, reaching them had been easy. He'd devoted all his time to his career. Everything was just the way he had planned it, except that he'd never considered how a family would affect his plans. But now, more than ever, succeeding was imperative. If all went well, he would have a family to support.

Before going into the house, Bryan paused to ask God for guidance. He had to believe the timing was right. It could be a fresh start, for all of them.

"Where have you been?" Laura asked without looking up from the bread she was kneading.

"I needed a run. Where are the kids?" Bryan wrapped his arms around her and kissed her cheek.

"Already asleep." She shrugged him away and finished working the dough. "You could have called so I wouldn't have to make up answers to the kid's questions. We were all worried. I don't like the feeling I have tonight, Bryan. Something's wrong."

Bryan placed one hand on the counter next to her. "Your female intuition?"

"Don't make fun of it."

He wouldn't think of it, especially when it was so darned accurate.

"Is that bread a substitute for me?" Bryan propped himself against the counter and crossed his arms over his chest.

"I guess that depends on what you needed time to think about. Doesn't it?"

"I didn't realize I'd been gone so long. Sorry I worried you. Let's sit down and talk."

Laura put the sourdough into a bowl and washed her hands. She followed as Bryan led her to the sofa, sat down next to her and took her hands in his.

"I'm not sure there's an easy way to tell you." He looked at her, struck by the look of trepidation in her eyes. For a moment, he considered backing away, turning down the offer. Then he thought of Andrea, of all the plans he'd changed for her. He couldn't do that again. "I've been promoted to a vice president. I'll be setting up the new office in Kentucky."

She blinked her eyes, then pressed them shut. Laura inhaled deeply, trying to remain composed.

"I'm not sure what date you had picked for the wedding, but..." He felt a knot forming in his stomach.

Laura didn't speak, and eventually lost the battle with her tears. They streamed silently down her cheeks and onto her faded jeans.

"I can't afford to turn down this promotion, financially or for my career, Laura." The ache in his gut zeroed in like a three-hundred pound defensive end barreling over him. Bryan took a deep breath and reached for her, "Laura?"

She choked back the tears.

"Let's get married. When everything is settled here, you and the kids can join me. I don't want to be away from any of you, but I could manage for a while."

Bryan pulled her closer to him, and kissed her tenderly. He unclasped her barrette, then ran his fingers through her silken hair. He leaned his forehead against Laura's. "Marry me, Laura."

"Don't do this again, Bryan. There's a season for everything, but obviously, this isn't ours. I've told you before, I don't want to rush this time."

"We're hardly rushing into anything. It's been over a year. I'm in love with you. What more do you want?"

She jumped to her feet and mumbled, "Men."

"This promotion means you won't have to work at all if you'd like a break. There's no need for you to work so hard."

"Selling this house, moving halfway across the country, setting up a home, settling kids in new schools, leaving all my family and friends and adjusting to a new husband who'll be preoccupied with a new job doesn't sound like my idea of taking a break." Laura lowered her head. *Why do you keep taking people I love from me, God? Was I wrong? Are you punishing me?*

Bryan took hold of her hand. ''What's really wrong, Laura?''

She pulled away from him, then continued, her voice getting more agitated as she spoke. ''Nothing's wrong,'' she said, defiantly wiping the tears from her cheeks. She'd planned to talk to Bryan about her upcoming doctor's visit tonight, before they decided on a wedding date, but now, there was no need. ''Good luck, Bryan. I wish you the best. Life goes on, right?''

She stood up, walked out the door and stood looking into the darkness. Bryan followed. ''Don't turn away. You can't deny what you feel. We're in love. We've made a promise to each other.'' Bryan blocked the steps.

''Go Bryan, I won't stop you!''

''It's not that simple and you know it!''

''Sure it is,'' Laura said stubbornly. ''It's as simple as walking out that door!''

''Stop it!'' Bryan grabbed her by the shoulders. ''This is absurd. We can work something out. Sit down so we can talk. Please.''

''What's left to say?'' She looked into his eyes, seething with anger.

He'd expected her to be surprised and maybe a little upset, but not *this* angry.

''You didn't even consider not taking the job.'' She didn't accuse him, simply stated the facts.

''No, I didn't. I'm sorry. I've wanted this all my life.''

''I'm happy for you, Bryan. I'm proud of you for reaching your goals. Don't worry. I won't come between you and your career.''

''This isn't a choice of coming between me and my career. I want you to come with me. As in for better or worse, till death do us part. I want you to share my life.''

''It's not that easy. I have a business and three children to consider, let alone friends and family nearby.''

"They're as close as the telephone. I didn't make it to the top by turning down promotions."

"And I didn't become who I am by following orders. Did you ever think of asking whether I want to quit working? Did you think about my kids leaving their school and friends? They've been through a rough year, too." She recoiled, then started again. "In my marriage, decisions like this were made together. You didn't even trust me enough to confide in me first."

"Open another child care in Kentucky if that'll make you happy. I'm not saying it won't take some adjustments for everyone, but I know we can make it work."

Bryan held her close, even though she fought him. He tried to understand what she was feeling, but all he felt was confusion. "How long, Laura? Are we talking about a few weeks, a month or won't you ever consider leaving Colorado?"

Laura pulled out of Bryan's embrace. "I can't answer that."

"Tell me what you want, honey." Bryan touched her cheek, then gently grasped her by the shoulders.

"I don't even know any more, Bryan. I'm tired of everything—the loss, the endless questions, expectations. Everything."

"I'll turn the job down and stay here, if you'll name the date, right now. Just ask me to stay."

"I won't ask you to give up something that means so much to you."

"You've asked for time, and I'd say I've given you plenty. I don't want to leave without you, Laura. You've had a lot to deal with. I want to take care of you. Why can't you see that?"

"That's just it, Bryan. You can't take away what's hurting me. You can't make everything better."

Bryan took her into his arms. Laura closed her eyes as

Bryan trailed kisses along her cheek. "Don't do that, Bryan. I don't want you…"

"Yes, you do. As much as I want you."

Her head was filled with all the reasons she loved Bryan: his gentleness, his strength, his desire to know the Lord…. The list could go on forever.

"Wanting you isn't enough anymore, Bryan."

Bryan let her go, stepping away with cold resolve. "A little while ago, you said you need time. But it's fourth and two. I want your heart. I want your trust. I want you to need me, to depend on me. It may sound old-fashioned, but I want to feel you can't survive without me. Because that's how I feel about you."

He collected his son, and left her to suffer the loss alone. What was wrong with her? Why couldn't she accept what he could offer her? He loved her. He wanted to take care of her. He wanted her, forever.

But he didn't trust her. She had to have his trust.

She went to bed, knowing there would never be another man who could capture her heart. She'd already had her second chance at love, and was turning it down.

Chapter Twenty-Nine

A week later, Bryan's sports car was neatly packed with everything he and Jacob would need on the long drive.

Laura tried to remain strong. Her pulse throbbed. A voice inside her told her to ask him to stay. She wouldn't. She wanted to go. She couldn't.

Bryan had come for dinner the night before and said goodbye to the kids then. Now they were at school. When Bryan left, she would be alone. For the first time in months, she would be truly alone. There would be no preschoolers to occupy her today, no Jacob to cuddle, no rowdy boys to referee. She'd be alone with the horrible reminder that she was turning away this wonderful man.

Laura leaned into the car and kissed Jacob. His little arms reached out for her, straining against the straps of his car seat. "Wora," Jacob screamed, as if he knew exactly what was happening.

She blinked back tears. "I love you, Jacob," she whispered.

"It doesn't have to end this way, Laura."

Laura looked at the house, at the huge tree covering the driveway, then back. "Maybe not, but it is. We both have things to sort through and put behind us. It isn't just you. I do, too.''

''We could do that just as easily together.''

She looked down, wiping away the tears, then glanced into his eyes for a split second. ''I found a passage in Isaiah last night. It says, 'Those who wait for the Lord will gain new strength.' I don't know about you, but I have a lot of strength to regain.''

Bryan wiped more tears from her cheek and held her face between his hands. His gentle kiss was interrupted by Jacob's wail. ''Come with us, please, Laura.''

''Goodbye, Bryan.'' Laura turned and ran into the house.

Laura took the kids to her parents that weekend, hoping to get away from the memories trapped within the walls of her home....

Memories of Todd. And Bryan. And babies. And dreams that had come to an end. Somehow, she'd survived the week. After Bryan had gone, she went to the doctor for her dreaded exam, figuring the day was already ruined, and couldn't have gotten much worse.

She was so wrong....

Laura crawled into the twin bed opposite Carrie in her parents' guest room, but couldn't sleep. She got up in the middle of the night and fixed herself a cup of tea.

Her mother came into the kitchen, tying her robe. ''Why don't you tell me what's wrong, Laura? You're too edgy for it to be just the argument with your father.''

''He told you?''

''You should know by now that we have no secrets. And for the record, I agree with him. Bryan and you should be together. But enough of that. That's your decision. What else is wrong?''

Laura looked into her cup of tea. She took a long drink while she thought about her answer. ''I went for a checkup last week. After looking at the ultrasound, Dr. Berthoff wants to do surgery right away. I go in on Wednesday. I tried to delay it, but she insists I shouldn't wait any longer. I'll have Barb call you when I'm out of surgery.''

"What about the preschoolers? Do you need help?"

"I can't afford to take time off since I haven't filled Jacob's position yet. All the calls I've had are for infants." She fought back the tears. "I just can't be with another baby right now. I have a friend who's offered to help me for a few weeks."

"Have you told Bryan?"

"No, and I would rather he not find out yet. The way you and Dad feel about him, I suspect he's kept in touch with you. I don't suppose I can do anything about that, but I'm not ready to tell him."

"Bryan would want to be there with you."

"If he wanted to be here, he wouldn't have accepted the promotion without talking it over with me. And if he comes back, I need to know it's because he loves me, not because he feels obligated to take care of me. I'll have a better idea of our future after the surgery."

"What does that mean?"

"Andrea left him without telling him she was pregnant. If this looks like…" Laura stumbled over the deadly word "…*cancer*…Emily will remove whatever she feels is necessary right then. If I can't give him a baby…" The tears finally came, including all the tears she had suppressed the past week. "I want time to adjust to the results before I tell him."

Her mother held her, stroking the hair off her face. "I wish that I could take the pain from your life, Laura. You've had such a tough year."

"I'm so tired of fighting, Mom. I just want to be the same woman I was before Todd died."

"You can't ever go back, sweetheart. But we're all here for you and when it is over, you'll be even stronger than before."

* * *

Three days later, Barb spent the evening with Laura, talking, praying and listening as Laura considered the possibility of never having another child. As crazy as it seemed, she couldn't bear the thought of never holding her own baby in her arms again. Bryan's baby.

Early Wednesday morning, Laura was wheeled into the operating room. The bright lights blurred above her. She prayed that everything would be all right.

When she woke up, she was reassured to see Barb beside her. Laura mumbled something, and fell back asleep. When she woke again, it was a man's face in front of her.

"How're you feeling?"

"Can I still have a baby, Bryan?" she said deliriously.

"I don't know, but we could find out." Kevin laughed.

"Kevin?" she slurred. "What are you doing here?"

"I went by the house to see you. Barb told me where you were. I expected to see Bryan here."

"Don't tell him." She grabbed his shirt sleeve. "Promise me."

"We'll talk about this later. In the meantime, why don't I see if I can find your doctor to answer your questions." He patted her hand and went out the door.

As promised, Kevin returned, having left a message with a nurse that Laura wanted to see her doctor. Kevin was his usual charming self and she enjoyed the gentle sparring.

One glance at Kevin from behind, and Emily froze in the doorway. She took a deep breath and pasted a professional smile on her face. "If you'll excuse us, sir. I need to examine Laura. I'll call you in when we're through."

Kevin looked at her intensely, then strode to the door. "Watch what you say, Laura." Emily stepped through the curtain and closed the door tight.

Laura looked at her doctor and grinned. "Is it the anesthesia, or have you two already met?"

Emily laughed. "It's the anesthesia. Darned stuff has that effect on some patients. Aren't you lucky?"

After the examination, she opened the door, pausing to let Kevin back in. She returned to Laura. "The nurse will be right in to give you something to alleviate the pain."

"Not again. I just woke up, Emily. The kids are coming soon."

Kevin watched Emily intently, his eyes telling Laura it had nothing to do with the anesthesia. It had everything to do with love…and a broken heart.

"I'll call Barb and tell her to give you a few more hours. You'll be glad they waited."

"I look that bad?"

"No worse than when you ran into that tree," Kevin teased, clearly struggling to fight unwelcome emotions.

Emily's sharp response surprised even Emily.

"Guess that's why you're the doctor. My bedside manner leaves much to be desired."

Laura, trying not to giggle, felt tears running down her cheeks.

Emily eyed them both. "Now look what you've done, Kevin. Laura, don't listen to him. It's pretty rough when a child sees Mom looking so pale and weak. Children don't understand. I'll come and help you freshen up for them before I leave."

Laura wiped the moisture away and smiled. "Thanks, Em."

Emily left, and Kevin quietly walked to the door and peeked at her one more time. "Just as bodacious as ever."

Laura grinned. "Okay, Kevin, fess up. What's between you and Emily?"

"Nothing. Nothing at all."

The medicine was beginning to have its intended affect on her. "You be nice to me, or I'll tell her everything I know about y…" Laura blinked and fell asleep.

Later on that afternoon, the doctor returned. "I need to

wait for the test results to be sure Laura, but I think you'll be fine. The cysts were the size of an orange. I can't believe you didn't come in sooner.''

Laura ignored the lecture. ''What about another baby?''

''One step at a time.''

''When can I go home?''

After sharing her concerns, Emily consented to letting her go home the next morning. ''Of course, that depends on how well you behave. You have to tell me what's really going on.''

''Ditto. And I want to hear everything about you and Kevin MacIntyre.''

Emily cleared her throat. ''That was a long, long time ago. Nothing left to talk about. Let's make you presentable, shall we?''

No sooner had Emily finished than Barb and the kids arrived. ''Hi, Mom. How do you feel?'' Carrie said, stopping halfway between the door and the bed.

''I feel better than I look. Emily said I should try to get up and take a walk, how about helping me?''

T.J. watched as Barb helped Laura sit up. ''Does it hurt?''

''A little bit. It's going to be sore for a few days, I expect.'' Laura noticed Chad standing in the doorway, looking terrified.

Laura understood his fear. First their daddy died, then Bryan left. They, like she, probably wondered who would be next.

''I'm going to be okay, honey. I missed you this morning. Give me a hug? Be gentle.'' Tentatively, Chad stepped inside and Laura gave him a kiss on the top of his head.

Kevin came back that evening, though Laura suspected he hadn't really come to see her. Her queries revealed nothing more, from either Emily or Kevin.

Finally, he asked her the question that she'd expected all day. ''Why isn't Bryan here?''

"He doesn't know about it. And if he shows up here tomorrow, I'll scalp you myself."

"You'd never catch me in your condition." His nonchalant smile came easily.

Laura laughed. "Ouch, Kevin, don't make me laugh again. After I know the test results I'll tell him."

"That's not very fair to him, is it?"

"Why is everyone so concerned with Bryan? He chose to leave. He's not obligated to us."

"You're wrong about all of this, Laura. He won't give a hoot whether you can give him another kid or not."

"It matters to me. Besides, he agreed to move on without us."

"You are one stubborn lady. Does that mean you're ready to move on, too?"

"I won't be moving on, ever. God gave me two chances at love, which is more than I deserve. Bryan took my heart with him."

"Then why are you here, alone?"

"I know you mean well, but this is something Bryan needs to take care of all by himself."

"You two are getting to be a pain." Kevin smiled. "Visiting hours are almost over, I'd better get going. You take it easy and do what the fine doctor tells you."

"From the looks of things, the feeling's mutual."

"At one time, maybe."

Laura smiled. She had him over a barrel. "Keep this surgery to yourself, and I'll talk to her."

"That sounds like blackmail to me."

Laura grinned. "You got it. I can't make any promises, though. She's just getting over someone. Men aren't at the top of her want list right now."

"Feeling's mutual."

Laura recovered quickly, and was back to her regular routine within a few weeks. The news had been good. One more answered prayer. As her worry disappeared, it became easier for Laura to accept responsibility for the misplaced resentment she'd placed on God during the past few months.

How easy it had become to depend on Bryan instead of allowing God to work at His own pace. Again, she'd fallen out of step with His plans.

Barb had invited Laura to go for lunch the next Saturday, so Laura arranged for the kids to spend the afternoon roller-skating.

When they finished ordering, Barb turned to Laura. "I don't understand why you don't call Bryan and tell him you want to work things out."

"My relationship with Bryan is out of my hands. I've come to realize that sometimes God brings a special person into our lives, if only for a short time. If that was all it was, I'll always cherish what time we had."

"He also said, 'Seek, and ye shall find.'"

Laura sighed. "I've turned it over to God. This year's been terrible and frightening, yet wonderfully exciting." Laura paused as the waitress set her plate of chicken salad on the checkered tablecloth. "It's made me realize that no matter how hard I try, I'll never be in control. Since I turned it over to Him, I've felt such peace. The timing just wasn't right."

"Don't you ever want to change the clock, though?"

"I'm really trying to let God handle this according to His own timing, Barb. Quit tempting me."

Chapter Thirty

Bryan had put in long hours hiring, making new contacts and setting up new systems. His mother and sister had come to take care of Jacob for the first two weeks while he interviewed child care providers and got settled. The women had offered to unpack, and he'd quickly accepted. Anything was fine, just so he didn't have to face those boxes alone.

When the movers had gone, he'd walked into the living room and realized that though the furnishings were his, after a year in storage, they were no longer "him." The elegant furniture from his and Andrea's elegant house immediately reminded him of failure. It would never be home. In a matter of hours, he'd donated the old and replaced it with new.

The blue plaid sofa was comfortable and practical, as well as the distressed end tables and coffee table. No matter how much Jacob banged his toys, it wouldn't matter, as the furniture already had dents and scratches. The bedroom set, an oak sleigh bed and dressers, were reproductions. The cranberry-and-green plaid bedding reminded him of the previous Christmas, and Laura. After deciding that the room looked like something she would have planned, he'd asked his mother to take over decorating. Neutral territory.

He pulled into the driveway at eleven o'clock one night after an unusually stressful day, and realized what Laura had said was more than true. He'd expected a lot of her. What he wanted was someone to take care of him, his life, his son and make a house into a home.

Yet somehow, each time he'd called to apologize, the conversation had ended the same way. That this is the decision he'd made, and he wanted her here with him. No matter how he tried, he couldn't make the problem between them go away. After a couple of months, he'd given up. Quit calling. Tried to forget.

It was a slow transformation to living alone, without anyone to help with Jacob and lighten the load of their busy evenings. He'd thrived on his career for the last six years, so why did bringing work home at night annoy him now?

Bryan turned the television on, ready for an afternoon of football. When the phone rang, he didn't question who it was. Kevin. They made the usual wagers on the games, a pair of tickets to an upcoming game. Problem was, they usually went to the games together, thus, both winning. "You coaching the boys again?"

"We started this week. And yes, T.J. is playing."

"I figured he would." The line was silent.

Kevin coughed. "She seems to be recovering."

Bryan thought Kevin's choice of words was interesting. Recovering. *Yeah, I guess that pretty well describes it. Breaking up takes a lot of recovering.* "Good. I hope she's happy. She deserves it." They visited a few more minutes, then said goodbye.

Jacob napped through the first half of the CU versus Nebraska game, then sat with Bryan, watching quietly. After a couple of minutes, his son ran into his bedroom and returned with a soft football that Chad had given him. Bryan wondered if Laura and the boys were watching games now. Would she enjoy weekend sports as much as she did her son's games?

Recovering? From our breakup? Must be nice. Just say goodbye and move on, huh? Deal with it Bryan, you blew it. Get over it.

A month later, he sat at the mahogany desk with the brass name plate boldly stating Bryan A. Beaumont, Vice President. Success. He'd made it to the top. Reached those goals. For what?

The intercom buzzed. "Bryan, Jacob's sitter is on line one."

"Thank you, Sharon." He pushed line one, and picked up the receiver. "Yes, Mabel, what's up?"

"Jacob is running a fever."

"How high is it?"

"I thought you could take it when you get him home. He needs to be picked up. I think he'd be happier at home."

"Does he have any other symptoms?"

"Mr. Beaumont, you know Jacob better than I. He's fussy."

Trying to keep the annoyance from his voice, he responded. "I'll be right there." He pulled files, placed them in his briefcase, and asked his secretary to call him at home with questions.

By the middle of the night, the fussiness had turned into croup. Unable to recall what Laura had told him to do for the virus, he called the doctor. For three days and nights they went through the same treatment: cold air, steam, snooze while Jacob was quiet. When he was better, it would be back to Mabel's.

Oh, how he missed Laura.

It had been three months since he'd arrived, and he hadn't even had time to look for a church yet. While he was home with Jacob, Bryan looked through the yellow pages under churches and made phone calls, determined to begin the search. The third week, he'd found one he liked.

The fourth week, the sermon had been on contentment. The fifth, on materialism. The next on forgiveness. Each week, Bryan returned home with questions that wouldn't leave him alone.

He continued reading his Bible and study books, looking for the missing piece to why, when he and Laura were in love, could they not work this out? Night after night, he prayed that God would show him how to bridge the gap between them.

Reviewing notes from the recent sermons, he read several scriptures that he'd jotted down. Under contentment, he had written "undermining forces" and the examples of money, riches, time and job.

The same was true of materialism, along with the verse 1 Timothy 6:17 telling him not to set his sights on uncertain riches of the world, but to set his sights on God, that He will richly furnish us with everything to enjoy.

He'd done just that, Bryan realized. He'd put his career and financial success before the riches God had given him. Salvation, as well as Laura and the family he'd always wanted.

Laura's strength had given him hope. Allowed him to move on. Yet when she'd needed him to be strong, he'd turned from her and followed his own plan. Not theirs. Not God's—for he was certain that His plan was for all of them to be a family.

When it came to the promotion, he'd never even given Laura the chance to show her trust in him. His instincts had returned to the many times when he'd given in to Andrea, and paid the price later. He'd returned to a time when he'd taken control of his own life. It was time to place his life back in the hands of the Almighty. This time, he would cling to God's promise.

Again, he surrendered his anger to Him, freeing himself from guilt that he could have done more to save his marriage to Andrea. He'd loved Andrea, mourned their broken vows, grieved her death and learned to love the son she'd given him.

And God, in His tender mercy, had given him the precious gift of Laura's love at a time when they had both needed comfort and support. Over the next weeks, Bryan waited, trusting Him to prepare his heart for Laura.

There would come a season, when they could find forgiveness and happiness, together. When he would return to Laura, able to give everything to become her husband.

Chapter Thirty-One

With the kids delivered to Marc and Kayla's for the weekend, Laura was free to finish her Christmas shopping. She'd spent Friday night in Denver with them and headed home early Saturday morning.

On the drive home, she turned off the busy interstate and onto a country road. She weaved her way through the frosted farmland, feeling the peaceful serenity that reminded her of a Currier and Ives Christmas card.

In the quiet of her van, Laura realized this was the first time in months life had slowed down enough to feel the intensity of the emptiness Bryan's absence had created.

She'd managed to fool herself for a few weeks, that she had only been infatuated with him, that circumstances had kept them together, that once he quit calling she'd be okay. Eventually, though, she admitted to herself that Bryan was the only man she'd ever love again.

Smoke swirled from chimneys in the distance, meandering through the early morning fog as it lifted from the valley. Momentarily lost in her own reveries, Laura caught sight of the white-peaked Rocky Mountains against the clear blue sky.

She realized that for the past year, her moods had been like those jagged Rockies. When Bryan had offered comfort and harmony, she'd chased it away. She had even tried to cope without God. The verse that had seen her through each stage of her grief came back to her: "'To everything there is a season...A time to weep, and a time to laugh...A time to mourn, and a time to dance...A time to love.'"

But now, she felt at peace with life, and herself. She knew that she could overcome the challenges that faced her, with the confidence that came from walking with Christ. While she'd proven that she could manage on her own, she wanted nothing more than to share her life with Bryan.

Turning into the driveway, a snowman's smile welcomed her home, reminding her of her children, and their Christmas request—to be with Bryan and Jacob. Laura sighed. "How in the world can I fulfill their wish?"

Bryan pulled up to the house, feeling like he'd just parked a bus. The shiny new vehicle was advertised to be "the Cadillac of four-wheel drives"—perfect for a growing family on the go.

To the right, was a lopsided snowman wearing an old Broncos cap and an enormous flannel shirt. He smiled at the thought of Laura and the children creating this frosty character.

Fingering the green velvet box in his coat pocket, Bryan prayed. "Dear God, please let us work everything out this time."

He took a deep breath, then stepped up to the door and knocked. And waited. It seemed forever until Laura answered.

"Bryan! What are you doing here?"

"I came to take care of some business I left behind. Thought I'd see how you are." He'd wanted to surprise her, and he'd obviously succeeded. She stood in the doorway with her lips parted in a trembling grin, as if she, too, were afraid of saying or doing the wrong thing. He longed to touch her hair, but settled on gazing into her eyes, his half smile acting as a peace offering. "Don't worry, I'm not here to turn your life upside down again."

"You're not?" she teased.

"Well, maybe I could shake it up a little." Her smile instantly erased the pain of the past five months.

"Come in before I freeze." She leaned out the door, and looked at his new vehicle. "Where's Jacob? Where's your car?"

"Jacob's at the hotel with my mom. And, I traded the sports car for this. What do you think? Holds eight, and more gear than you could dream of hauling."

She looked amused and closed the door. "You haven't traveled with four children."

"Not yet, but I'm ready to give it a try. How about you?"

Laura became silent as tears formed in her clear blue eyes. Though she held her head high and stubbornly fixed her eyes on his, her voice was whisper soft. "Before I answer, I need to ask you something, Bryan. Let's sit down." She led him to the sofa.

Neither spoke right away.

She blurted, "Do you want kids?"

This is a joke. Laugh, Bryan. Yet, when he looked into her eyes, he realized she was serious. "What are you talking about, Laura?"

"Another baby. Do you want more children?"

"Can't we discuss that when the time comes?"

"No. I need to know now, before this conversation goes any further." Laura sat, her hands clenched in her lap.

He wanted to say the right thing, but the truth was, he didn't know what to hope for. He stood up and paced. "If God's plan is that we have another child, fine. If not, I'll be the best father that I can to the four that we have." He hesitated, then sat next to Laura. "Does this have something to do with the appointments you never wanted to talk about?''

She nodded. ''I had some ovarian cysts removed. I don't know if I'll be able to conceive.''

He could see she was struggling not to cry. ''Did you know about this before I left?''

She looked at her hands in her lap and shrugged.

''Is this why you wouldn't come with me? You thought I wouldn't love you if you couldn't give me another child?''

''Well, Andrea…and you missed all of that with Jacob…I thought…'' her words faded.

''And you made me go, and leave you to face this alone?'' Bryan wrapped his arms around her and buried his face in her hair, whispering in her ear. ''Why didn't you call me?'' The minute he asked, he regretted it. He wasn't here to make her feel guilty.

''When you accepted the transfer, I was angry that you made the decision without consulting me, but that only convinced me how much you wanted the job. I couldn't ask you to stay, then tell you I may not be able to have a baby. Not after what Andrea did.''

''You are not Andrea. She and I never had what you and I share. We have so much more.''

''I know it sounds selfish, but I want to have your baby.''

He couldn't imagine anyone less selfish than this woman. ''That's not selfish. Nothing is more natural than wanting to create a life with someone you love. And nothing is more natural than wanting to be by your side when you're in the hospital.''

''Kevin…''

''Only told me you were recovering. At the time, I thought he meant from us breaking up. But the next time you need me, the whole offensive line won't keep me away.'' The tone of his voice left no room for discussion.

''I'm sorry I couldn't tell you, Bryan.''

"As long as we're together, I'll be happy."

"I was so miserable," she whispered.

"Good, because I was, too." He pulled her closer and kissed her parted lips. "I don't ever want to be without you."

"Me, either."

Bryan kissed her deeply, then pulled the small green box from his pocket. He opened it, removing the antique gold band with a marquis diamond solitaire. He knelt before her. "Will you marry me, Laura Noel Bates?"

"Yes, Bryan Alexander Beaumont. Yes, I'll marry you."

"*Je t'aime,* Laura." He slid his grandmother's ring on her finger.

Laura kissed him, first slowly, then fervently. "I love you, Bryan. No matter where we live."

"We'll decide on that later." Bryan drew her close.

Laura looked into his eyes, and he knew this was exactly what God had planned. In each other, they'd found the strength and courage to overcome their fears. In Him, grace.

"From now on, there will be no more secrets."

"No more. I promise."

He laughed, that deep, confident chuckle that always brought a blush to her cheeks. "You won't regret marrying me."

It did exactly as planned. "Never."

Peace washed over them. They were ready to be together for a day, a week, or forever—however long God had planned.

* * * * *

Dear Reader,

There Comes a Season lived in my heart long before pen met paper. I've always enjoyed writing, though I never planned to be a writer. After months of speculation, words began to flow. I felt at peace when finally accepting writing as part of God's plan for my life. He continues to affirm each step of this journey, both difficult and joyful.

I've often questioned challenges that arise in life and have come to trust that there is a purpose for each one, even though it sometimes takes years to fully understand. I find strength and comfort in knowing that in some way, each experience prepares me for the future. It is exciting to discover where, when and how we can utilize the gifts and talents He has given us.

When I wrote this book, I had no way of knowing how devastating it is to lose a spouse. Eleven months before *There Comes a Season* was accepted for publication, I learned another reason God had placed this story in my heart—to help me understand what my sister would go through when she would lose her husband to leukemia. God is indeed all-knowing. Throughout all, He is my comfort and my strength.

"For I know of the plans that I have for you," says the Lord, "plans for welfare and not for evil, to give you a future and a hope." *—Jeremiah* 29:11

I hope that you'll enjoy reading about Laura and Bryan's personal discovery of God's plans for their lives.

In His love,

Carol Steward

2 Love Inspired novels and 2 mystery gifts... Absolutely FREE!

Visit
www.LoveInspiredBooks.com
for your two FREE books, sent directly to you!

BONUS: Choose between regular print or our NEW larger print format!

There's no catch! You're under no obligation to buy anything. We charge nothing—ZERO—for your first shipment. And you don't have to make any minimum number of purchases.

You'll like the convenience of home delivery at our special discount prices, and you'll love your free subscription to Steeple Hill News, our members-only newsletter.

We hope that after receiving your free books, you'll want to remain a subscriber. But the choice is yours— to continue or cancel, anytime at all! So why not take us up on our invitation, with no risk of any kind!